D1824882

Call Off The Search

Comyenti Series, Book One

By Natasja Hellenthal

Also by Natasja Hellenthal

The Queen's Curse

Chained Freedom

Children of the Sun, Comyenti Series #2

City of Dreams

Fallen Stars

The Cursed

Sky Whisperers

Copyright©2016 Natasja Hellenthal. All rights reserved.

This book is a work of fiction. Names, characters and incidents therein are entirely the product of the author's imagination and any resemblance to actual persons, living or dead, is purely coincidental.

All rights reserved. No part of this book may be reproduced, stored in a retrieval system or transmitted in any form, or by any means, electronic, mechanical, photocopying, recording or otherwise, without prior permission of the author.

Cover design by BeyondBookCovers

Website: www.beyondbookcovers.com

Editors - Martine, Brian Jackson and Kate Johnson

Beyond Books Press

Perpignan, France

Fifth Edition - April 2016

Acknowledgements

I would like to give a heartfelt thank you to my editors: Kate Johnson, Martine and Brian Jackson. And the proofreaders: Rene Meijer and Dermot Doherty. The end result wouldn't have been the same without your helpful input and suggestions.

Thank you and my gratitude to Sir David Attenborough for all his enthusiasm, facts and insight on life on earth.

I am dedicating this book to my daughter Amelia who turned two on the day of its first publication on Kindle.

Note to readers: This is a work of fiction and as such, controversial points of view may be written to enhance the readers' experience. The author's goal has been, aside from providing an enjoyable story, to make the reader think critically about the abuse man heaps on our planet. Not all the views expressed necessarily reflect those of the author.

She would like, however, to help readers realise what harmful effects we are having on our own world and on all the creatures, big and small, we share it with.

Table of Contents

Prologue

'Run! Run like you've never run before, boy!' the man shouted, catching up to his son, half dragging him by the elbow. Kaleis could hear the dogs barking nearby, they sounded frantic. He obeyed his father, trusting him, taking up his quick pace but they still weren't fast enough. Not nearly as fast as they could be…

As they made their way up the mountain pass, climbing over one ridge, and then another, the boy tried to ease his breathing whilst chanting softly. Adrenaline poured through his body and his heart was like a mad bird trying to break free. Anger and fear tugged at him.

'It's no use! It doesn't work now! Don't you think I've tried?' Damaz exclaimed, helping the boy up over a large boulder. His father's handsome face was pale and half covered in blood. There was a big slash on one side, even though he tried to hide it with one hand stained red, his son noticed when he looked over his shoulder. His father was bleeding profusely.

'Dad, your ear!' Kaleis called out with a startled face. 'And where are mum and Cohel?'

'They've got them.' Silent tears were welling up in Damaz's eyes, fighting off the thought of not being able to save them. They had been so careful, to no avail. 'We'll have to come back for them later.'

Kaleis sensed his father's defeat and it angered him.

'No, we have to help them!' he screamed incredulously and made an attempt to jump off the boulder but his father caught him by the waist.

'We can't turn back now! They'll kill us. Against their dogs and weapons we are defenceless, son.'

'No!' Kaleis screamed and struggled to free himself.

His father's face looked grim and his eyes gleamed as he turned his teenage son to face him. He held Kaleis by the shoulders in an attempt to stop him resisting so.

'Listen! They won't kill them straight away. They'll try to get the magic out of them first as they did with... We've...we've got time.'

Kaleis could tell his father didn't really believe it himself and this made him more alarmed.

Both father and son knew very well that there were times the hunters didn't take prisoners and instead just killed their catch straight away. Especially now after decades of hunting and experimenting, trying to decipher the magic, humans were beginning to loose faith in ever knowing the powers Kaleis's and Damaz's people had and instead had called out for global genocide to get rid of them.

The barking of the dogs was interspersed with the loud shouts of the men, and father and son grew more anguished. They looked up at the mountain. Perhaps they could take off from there.

'Come on! Remember what your mother said. If something ever happened to her she wanted us to be safe!' And he urged his son to continue their escape. The summit was hidden behind grey clouds. His instinct, as any animal hunted, was to run, to hide and regain the courage needed to help his family; what was left of it...

'They won't be able to get their powers,' Kaleis said angrily. 'They'll kill them! That's what they do when they can't get what they want. We can't let them do that!' The boy jumped away skilfully.

'No!!!' Damaz screamed after him, grabbing air and falling down to the ground.

Kaleis ran straight into the dogs coming around the ridge, but they were too busy fighting amongst themselves to pay much attention to him. Just then an arrow sent the boy staggering. He hit the ground, and landed close to the edge of the ridge. More arrows hit their target and he flinched from pain. The dogs were called back, accompanied by cheers. Grunting in pain the boy scrambled half up on his hands and looked his father in the eye. Damaz sat frozen on his knees looking down at the boy horrified.

Before he could do anything his son gasped for air and rolled over the ridge and disappeared out of sight.

'Attack!' the men yelled, getting closer with their weapons and nets. When they spotted the man arrows and spears went flying.

Damaz reached out for the edge of the ridge where his son had just been, but a spear was faster hitting him in the side and an arrow his arm. Lying flat on his stomach he looked down to see the lifeless body of his son causing another pain to hit him hard; a sharp pain from within his heart.

Feeling the life ebbing out of him, tears out of his eyes and blood seeping out of his mouth, Damaz glanced back at his attackers to sense their fear and hatred for his species.

'Yes! Get that you freak of nature!' one man shouted in triumph.

'Let the dogs have him!' another man roared and the hungry pack was set loose.

No, neither beast nor men will ever have me! And with his last ounce of strength Damaz pushed himself away from the hunters and off the edge…towards his son.

Side by side they were left to the elements and as the sounds of men and dogs grew fainter, peace once again was restored.

Rain began to fall; a persistent drizzle on the forest floor hitting the father and son's opened eyes at the mountain's foot. Rain soaked through their bloodstained clothes, over their now marble skin and on into the soil, as if to wash away the crime.

PART I Winter Heart

The storms and snow may kill the flowers,
but cannot deaden the seeds,
for the snow keeps them warm from the killing frost.

Kahlil Gibran

Chapter 1 Frozen

In wintertime everything seems to stand still, all frozen and hidden beneath the snow and ice; unseen by the eye. Everything and everyone hidden away, asleep in burrows and caves, between roots and in holes dreaming about summers past and summers yet to come. All waiting patiently for the sun to bring back its warmth.

Only a few know that that's not completely true. Some things just don't rest, don't linger or stand still. They're always moving; even in winter.

A bitter sharp wind rushed along Sula's bare face. For a moment she closed her eyes against the pain, concentrating on her Mindskill. Tears falling, slowly turning to frost on her eyelashes, hindered her view. Losing contact with the goose, Sula's cheeks and chin hurt all of a sudden and her skin was getting numb from the cold. She wore a hood over her head while the rest of her body was well wrapped within a few layers of cloth underneath her dark green woollen cloak, just in case. Clothes as warm as feathers, next to wool, the best insulating material.

She was the snow goose now, not physically, but in her mind and she was flying high up in the thick winter sky. She controlled the bird's ability to fly so fully that she tricked her body to *think* it to *be* a goose. Luckily she didn't actually have to use her arms like wings to fly by flapping. Instead she held her arms spread out wide to balance it; the way her mother had taught her, years ago.

By late afternoon, she had been flying the entire day since sunrise, and she was beginning to feel worn-out; slowly losing contact with the goose's abilities and that side of her mind; her Mindskill tricking her body. The high level of concentration and her aching limbs began to exhaust her and take its toll. Her body commanded her to take rest and recharge. And she had to obey her body's natural instinct in order to survive, goose or not. She couldn't keep demanding more from her body than it was able to give, otherwise it would simply stop serving her.

The frozen landscape, almost completely white, apart from some specks of dark green or grey; the hint of treetops, beneath her became almost monotonous. Pine woods lay buried underneath mounds of snow. The snow, almost creamlike, covered the rolling hills, numerous ice lakes, and a single frozen river covered in snow she had been following since dawn. So much of the scenery was white and her panoramic view so dreary it became more and more of a blur beneath her. She blinked a couple of times to try and regain some focus. At least she was in Northland now and it wouldn't be far to her final destination.

Sula tried to get to the uninhabited lime caves of the Balla mountain range; a mystical old volcanic landscape, showing itself already as a blue-grey white peaked wall in the distance.

She felt free and content in spite of her physical weariness and the elements. The flying almost became as easy and natural as walking. She loved seeing a clear view over everything and that feeling of being weightless. As close to freedom a humanoid would ever feel. Defying gravity; free of the heavy weight of one's body and the world pulling it down. Sula imagined only death could be any closer to that feeling; being just spirit.

Snowflakes began to whirl from the dense clouds just above her and they were more rapid and painful than she had expected. Snow this high up combined with wind meant ice. Snow swirled into her face, stinging her eyes like small knives, which she couldn't do anything about, for even geese had eyes and they weren't immune to pain. Sula had to fly lower.

The snow had found its way up her nose; blocking her breathing, nearly choking her. She was human enough to be affected by the elements and *that* side of her was too weary now not to feel it, above the goose's abilities. Moreover she flew too low by now and she was paying the price for her misjudgement.

The thick grey clouds blurred her sight altogether and the icy flakes remained on her eyelashes, almost freezing her eyes shut and melting in the slits of her eyes which were hard to keep open. It was time to go down.

She was late this year. Last year she had already settled in the cave by the time the snowstorms began.

With mixed feelings she thought about the group of travelling gypsies she had followed earlier during the autumn in the East; the reason why she was late. People, whom she had believed, held some useful information. It had been a mistake and now she had put herself in danger.

"Your duty is to survive" she heard her mother's voice say in her head. All of a sudden she saw smoke rising above the treetops. Sula sharpened her weary eyes. On flying closer it revealed itself to be several plumes of smoke coming from…rooftops. Panic overcame her. A human village!

Instantly she lost contact with the goose inside her and began to fall to the ground with incredible speed. With a lot of effort she managed to regain control of her mind and reached the goose that was controlling her body, in order to stop herself from falling further. She flew lower; almost level with the trees. Branches and needles nearly hit her in the face, and with the snowflakes still hindering her sight, making her virtually blind. She held her hands out to protect herself whilst gasping for air…

It went all terribly wrong.

She couldn't risk anyone seeing her, but at the same time she had to avoid being hit by the branches and trees. Whilst trying to fly as low to the tree line as possible, back to the river, she lost her balance and like a young bird just learning to fly, she tumbled more rapidly than she would have wanted, towards the river she had been following.

As she fell she spotted someone or something through the branches; a dark shape on the icy river and she headed straight toward it!

Luckily she could still steer to some degree, and managed to miss the figure narrowly. This figure appeared to be a well wrapped up person, standing with his or her back towards her, with a strand of fair hair coming from underneath their hood. *That* was the only thing that caught Sula's eye though: that fair strand of hair amongst the whirling snowflakes, wind, branches, and chaos.

As she flew past she quickly glanced back in case she had been seen, but it seemed that the snow and wind had saved her. The dark hooded person still looked down at the frozen river and appeared to be deep in thought. Somehow Sula regretted she had not been seen. She didn't know why; perhaps because she had been travelling alone now for so long. Even wild animals gathered with their own kind for the winter seeking warmth and comfort in dens and caves. Never before had she felt this lonely. She usually followed their pattern and even embraced being alone in the natural world with all the elements, the smells, the sounds, her friends the animals and the trees. It was only when she started to think about who she really was that she felt mournful and lonely amongst others not of her kind.

Her kind…where were they? Was she truly all alone then? It certainly looked that way after all those years of searching in vain. The Search had taken her around the globe; everywhere and nowhere. Always on the move. Never staying anywhere long enough to make friends. In fact Sula had not even been in one place long enough to be able to see the same scenery in *all* seasons.

The wind was her only true friend; it held whispers, echoes from another world, like those of long lost generations before her. She could sometimes hear the wind talking to her; helping her, as before.

Sula glimpsed back at the person on the ice, while still flying low above the river against the wind and snow, recovering and regaining her balance. She tried to remember what it was like to be human.

A dull pain struck her hard on the shoulder and before she realised it, she fell and landed face down on the hard snow covered ice.

Turning herself over; she rubbed her aching right shoulder and looked at the obstacle above her that she had flown into. It was a wooden bridge.

***

'I'm lucky to only have a sore shoulder!' she grunted and still shaken she stumbled to her knees, checking herself; making a valiant effort to control her emotions. She removed the heavy pack from her back. It had been a long time since she had fallen like this, losing the Mindmode. Way back when she'd first learnt to fly, as a child, she had had trouble concentrating and maintaining the Mindmode the first couple of times after her first MindMerge with a snow goose. But since then she had not fallen and the ability had become mastered.

I must be getting old, she thought ruefully and quickly glanced at the dark shape who walked towards her.

Large thick snowflakes whirled towards her as well so she couldn't see much, but enough to know it was a man that had discovered her. He headed in her direction, faster than she liked.

As he got closer, she noticed he had an axe in one of his hands and she started panicking and made sure her hood covered her head. Her heart thumped in her throat and her body broke out in a cold sweat. She concentrated on the wolf, jamming her eyes shut; thinking only about its sharp teeth, fast feet and claws at the ready.

Ignoring the throngs of pain radiating from her shoulder she started to chant softly, 'Your heart, my heart, your beat, my beat,' and she felt the heart of the wolf drumming in her chest; thump-thump, thump-thump. 'Your breath, my breath, your spirit, my spirit, your mind, my mind…' But her fear, that old feeling of raw panic so deep, so real, tugged at her so strongly, confusing her mind… broke her Mindmode.

'I have to run now, Spirits protect me!' she mumbled. It was all she could do.

Why Sula, why? A little voice answered and confused her so much that she couldn't move. Frozen…

Chapter 2 Fish

There is nothing in the world as quiet and pure as snow, swirling slowly through the air like a silent dance, silencing steps, gently hushing voices speaking too loudly. There is nothing in the world as soothing as snow.

Sula looked up from her thoughts to find that amid the falling snowflakes a brown-cloaked man with bright blue curious eyes observed her.

'Hello there,' he said in a low, but youthful voice. The young man freed his face from his hood using his woollen mittens. Unlike her hood, covering only the top of her head, forehead and ears, his had almost hid his complete face apart from his sparkling blue eyes. She could never have worn something like that, for she needed *all* her senses to maintain control of the goose inside of her when she flew.

The hood no doubt aimed to cover his delicate flawless skin and to keep him warm. Snowflakes immediately melted on his rosy cheeks and nose.

'Are you alright?' he asked, concerned, holding out his hand to her.

Ignoring him her eyes flashed to the axe in his other hand.

'Where did you come from all of a sudden, the sky?' He jerked his head up jokingly and chuckled. His laughter sounded warm and friendly and although Sula felt a little frightened at first, she realised she needn't fear this young human.

Sula, still on her knees, looked from his face down to his axe and wondered *why* he carried it in the first place. But she remembered humans always carried weapons, because they had no claws or teeth with which to defend themselves. Not like her. Nevertheless, she hated weapons, although she had always known it was not the weapon she had to fear; that didn't hurt or kill anyone, but the *person* using it.

She ignored his extended hand, and rose to her feet, whilst not losing eye contact with the armed stranger.

'I saw the smoke and…fell,' and she pointed up at the snow covered bridge. 'From there.' Her voice sounded deep and rough through not using it. It had been months since she last spoke to anyone.

The young man raised one eyebrow. 'From the bridge?' He looked briefly at the wooden construction a few feet away. It didn't show any tracks from what he could see, although they could have been covered up by fresh snow by now. Gazing back at her his expression showed concern.

'I'm sorry about that. We usually try to keep the bridge clear but it's no use in this weather. Not many people use it anyway. Did you slip, was it icy? Were you on your way to Rosinhill?'

Sula started to brush the snow from her heavy cloak and trousers, without much luck; being wool, it only stuck more.

'Sort of,' she grunted at her valiant attempt and only then noticed the frozen waterfall at the other side of the frozen river. It was quite beautiful.

He watched her with concern, tilting his head, like a cat.

'Did you hurt yourself?' he asked worriedly.

'I'm all right,' she murmured quickly, sounding annoyed at all his overwhelming questioning, trying to avoid his examining but compassionate eyes. She couldn't help but notice them, although she tried to avoid looking at him by continuing to brush the snow off.

He sniffed through his elegant nose and narrowed his eyes against the cold wind offering a gloved hand to her again.

'My name is Felix, I live in the village nearby.' He waited patiently for her to respond, with his hand still outstretched to her, but she didn't. She also ignored his gesture completely and looked around for a place to take off from again, hauling her rucksack onto her back, fastening the straps.

'So…what about you, Miss?' he started shyly. 'I have never seen you around here before.' He had a funny lilt to his voice; an accent she had never heard before, she noticed herself thinking.

She made him feel a little uncomfortable. He had lowered his hand by now and embraced himself against the cold wind, waiting.

'It would have been better if you hadn't seen me at all,' she retorted quickly and started to walk away towards the bridge adding 'Farewell!'

'No, wait, please!' He trotted after her with snow crunching underneath his feet. She stopped and her glare darted thoughtfully towards his axe. He followed her eyes and smiled sheepishly, 'You are afraid of me because I'm carrying an axe, huh?'

She sighed and for a fleeting moment their eyes met.

It wasn't fear he saw in her moss coloured narrowed eyes, but something else; distrust and annoyance. But also something Felix could not fully grasp. Loathing? But if so, why?

'Well, you are probably wondering what I am doing with it anyway,' he tried to lighten her mood, ignoring her rude attitude.

'*Not really,*' she felt like saying, but refrained.

'No, I haven't chopped down a tree, just the ice.' He looked at her for a reaction. 'Sounds silly, huh?'

'What was the plan; make an ice sculpture?' she remarked sarcastically.

His eyes shone even brighter now; an inner light as bright as a star.

'You are very funny Miss, but I'm not that skilful.'

'Well, whatever you are doing, I wish you luck,' she mumbled and continued to walk away. Felix just stared at her perplexed.

Sula only walked about ten steps when she started to feel slightly guilty. He wasn't any threat to her and he had treated her with respect and kindness so far; something she wasn't normally accustomed to. Most people were not to be trusted; she had learnt her lesson well over the years.

When she glanced back, she saw him standing where she had left him; staring disappointedly at her. He had a sad look about him. It made her feel mournful and culpable. Her other curse, besides the search:

compassion.

'Oh, all right!' she cursed under her breath and after a short moment walked back. *Just a brief introduction and I will be on my way again. I don't want to attract unwanted attention. Act normal, act human,*

'My name is Sula,' she said briskly while she briefly looked at him in the eye. 'I am just a passing traveller. Hello and fare thee well.' Her tone of voice still wasn't exactly pleasant, but at least she had said *something*.

So she is a traveller. Felix was always interested in news from other parts of the world not to mention new tales. His sister was the true adventurer in their family and she always came back with some amazing stories.

He smiled gratefully at her.

'In this kind of weather? Well, pleased to meet you, Miss Sula the traveller. But do be more careful crossing bridges next time, especially in wintertime.'

His genuine concern came across as heart warming but she tried to ignore it. She did her best to smile, tugging uneasily at the straps of her rucksack, but it wasn't a friendly smile as it never reached her eyes. It made him feel miserable. What had happened to this woman to cause her to act like this? And what had *he* ever done to *her* to deserve this attitude? Not that it was his business but still...

She saw him thinking and opening his mouth so she quickly tried to distract his thoughts and prevent him asking any more questions. This boy was full of curiosity!

'So, what *were* you doing with that axe?' He on the other hand had made her curious enough to ask. Felix tried to hide his gratitude and moved closer to the river and gestured.

'I was trying to make a hole in the ice... to fish,' Felix tried to sound casual. More strands of blond hair blew from underneath his hood in the growing blizzard. Sula got distracted by the simple beauty of this, but she regained her firm composure in an instant.

'Show me your effort.' It sounded more like a demand, but Felix seemed not to care. He captured her attention; something she would not give to everyone, he guessed. She was probably a loner, like him.

***

Carefully they crossed the ice for it snowed heavily now with thicker flakes whirling around them, making it harder to see. Sula followed Felix a few paces behind. He halted at almost the exact spot where he had been standing when she had nearly flown into him and knelt down to remove the fresh snow.

'You won't find any fish *here*,' she announced with only one quick look at the white cracks, like scars, on the black ice.

Felix looked a little shocked at her. 'Why not?' he asked.

A cold breeze blew past them. Sula stared to the South and Felix could hardly hear her voice when she said, 'They've gone…to the warmer waters.'

He looked surprised at her and arched one eyebrow.

'How do you know that?'

'I just do. Besides, I can't hear them,' she stated matter-of-factly and looked rather plainly at him, having forgotten for a moment he wouldn't– being human.

'You can't…what?' His voice died in the next cold breeze and he shivered. Whether that was from a sudden thrill of excitement, or the cold or perhaps both, was unclear.

'I mean…just listen. There's nothing there,' she said annoyed at him. He was only human and she had to forgive him for his lower senses but somehow she couldn't. A little voice inside of her did warn her not to talk about these things for it might endanger her. She had, in fact, already said too much.

Felix looked in astonishment at her and then down at the ice. She knew something he didn't, even though he had been living here all of his life? True, he wasn't a fisherman and didn't know a thing about fish or their migration pattern, but still. He chewed on his bottom lip.

After a short while he grinned uncomfortably at her, just when she was beginning to look around cautiously.

'Well, it's getting dark and I still haven't caught any fish and now you're telling me that there are none, huh?' he exclaimed.

'Are you *that* desperate?'

He grinned at her choice of words. 'Yeah, I am actually. I have almost run out of food. The whole village has the same problem,' and he rubbed his shoulders and arms; they hurt from his fruitless attempt.

'*This* early in wintertime?'

Sula's lips were red and warm, unlike her eyes. Felix stared at her mouth. The winter solstice had just passed, so the sun was slowly on his way up in the skies again, making the days slightly longer with every sunrise. However, winter was far from over and the worst of the snowstorms had yet to come.

'I'm afraid so, Miss Sula. To be honest, I don't think we'll make it with the supply we have left.' He sounded sad but not because he wanted her sympathy, but just because he was being honest. He turned himself completely towards her and cocked his head again. Yes, a cat with bright keen blue eyes. One that whirled around your legs and wanted to be stroked. In need of attention, not wanting her to stop stroking him or for her to leave.

Sula even wondered a little bemused when he would start to purr. She would have laughed at that under different circumstances; if it hadn't been for their conversation about hunger in his village.

A hungry cat, then, she concluded.

'Do you have a place to stay the night, Miss?'

She wished he would stop calling her that.

'Not really,' she heard herself responding, a little too quickly for her own liking. He shrugged his shoulders, blinking his eyes against the snow.

'We don't have an inn but you're more than welcome to stay at my place. I have plenty of wood to keep the fire going, fresh water and some potato soup. Enough for a traveller such as yourself.'

'I don't know—' she started to say.

'It is perfectly alright you know. I can see that you are used to travelling but even *you* will freeze to death in this kind of weather,' Felix interrupted her.

You'd be surprised, boy.

Sula looked uncertain towards the North in the direction of the Balla mountain range and the prospect of a cold damp cave. She found herself doubting her strength. She was sure she was going to make it tonight; *if* she hurried. But haste was dangerous in wintertime and when already exhausted. Upon arrival she would make a fire in the cave with the pile of wood she had gathered last year. The cave would be warm and comfortable enough with her thick cloak as a blanket and it was going to be even better if she used her Mindskills. She could easily go in Polar bear-mode to save herself from hypothermia.

But did she really have to lie on a hard damp surface again? It would be much better to relax and restore her humanoid body right now and top up her energy levels without using any animal skills.

How she longed for a soft warm clean bed and maybe some company would do her good after all. Sula started to feel confused, for she hardly ever stayed in human villages. Only when she really needed to look for clue's and information, and *always* in disguise. It was risky and the chance of discovery high and perilous. Ultimately, this man and his people were humans; her sworn enemy.

She felt like the wolf, always hunted and driven away like her kind: the comyenti with their shifting eyes, pointy ears, unusual traits, and unique abilities.

"Follow your heart," her mother would have said but had she not also told her to avoid large groups of people, in fact any people, so what was she to do?

Looking into the young man's sapphire eyes, the choice was quickly made and she decided to go with her mother's favourite sentence. She finally nodded at Felix who patted her gently on her painful shoulder. Sula flinched and recoiled, both from pain and the sudden touch.

'Are you hurt?'

'I'll live,' she replied sharply.

'You're a tough lass, Miss Sula.' His tone of voice had sounded genuine. She had trouble believing it still. 'Come. It's this way.'

She followed him across the river, through the dense woodland until they reached a clearing. That's when the first houses came in sight and Sula held her breath.

***

'You don't have much luggage, huh?' Felix noticed pointing at her small rucksack.

Sula replied nonchalantly, 'This is all I need. If you travelled like me, you would learn how little one can make do with and be satisfied.'

She noticed him pause a little as if he was thinking about her words. He turned round to look at her.

'Are you...?'

She met his bright curious eyes, 'What?' she asked a little annoyed.

'Satisfied,' he repeated a little louder, thinking she hadn't heard him above the growing wind. But of course she had, her hearing was excellent; even when not making use of her special abilities.

Sula made a tight face and carried on walking.

'Sorry, I had no right to ask, forgive me, Miss Sula,' he spoke walking beside her with his axe over one shoulder, sensing her annoyance.

'My name is Sula, not *Miss* Sula!' she snarled back.

'We always regard young women as 'Miss' in these parts. I apologise if I've offended you in any way. Where do you come from, if I may ask?'

'How many people are there here anyway?' She ignored his last question and made light conversation in order to distract him from any more unwanted questions.

'In my village? Not many. It's quite modest; you'll see.'

Soon enough they came across a low slope of a valley scattered with birch trees. About twenty round houses with thatched roofs were spread here and there. It looked cosy, especially with the smoke plumes rising from the chimneys and the orange lights behind the small glass windows. It gave Sula a sudden warm feeling around her heart; a feeling she had not felt in ages. It surprised her but then the sounds that she heard somehow made this village feel a little sad as well.

From one of the houses she heard a baby crying and from behind her, in the surrounding woods, a tree scraping heavily against another, moaning.

Symbols, all symbols! she thought wearily.

Chapter 3 Hunger

They ambled past most of the brown-grey round houses with the sound of their feet crunching in the snow until he apologised for the slightly steep hill they had to climb. Felix went a little ahead and glanced back, reaching out his hand for her but she refused his help. She didn't seem to be struggling much, so he went on. It seemed that his house was on the top.

Felix stopped when they reached the brow of the hill and announced, 'This is where I live,' as he pointed to a small cottage. It looked dark inside, but Sula felt relieved it was on the outskirts of the village, overlooking it. 'We don't have an inn because there's hardly ever a traveller in these parts and if any ever pass through then we offer them our hospitality. You met me!'

'I don't have much choice do I?' she replied half-heartedly.

He grinned widely at her showing his white teeth, 'Nope.' It was the grin of a boy; fresh and honest and it made her feel regretful. Intuitively she felt she could trust him and if not she always had the wolf inside of her.

'A blizzard is coming, we must hurry,' she stated confidently when she looked at the heavy dark sky while narrowing her eyes against the whirling snowflakes. Her warm breath circled like smoke from her mouth. Felix had his back turned to her for a moment. The thought crossed her mind to use this opportunity to go into a Mindmode. She concentrated on the giant-winged albatross that could glide in windy conditions perfectly for hundreds of miles with scarcely a wing-beat. Visualising its large wings, the biggest wings of any bird, she knew she had to make use of a steep cliff to take off to simply tumble into the air and then use the wind to glide on. The albatross wouldn't do in this moment of time. The goose might, but it could prove to be dangerous to fly right into a storm and *then* change into the albatross. Before she had the strength to do anything and risk exposure, Felix glanced back at her for a brief moment as if he felt her hesitation.

He fiddled with the door handle and glanced at the sky with piercing eyes. He, being a farmer and herdsman, knew a lot about weather predictions by looking at the behaviour of animals and even plants. In the summer it was a lot easier though, when there were swallows that would fly high when it was going to be clear skies and sunny and fly low when it was going to rain. Bees would be returning to their hives when a thunderstorm was on its way and most flowers would close their petals and some even their leaves when rain was due.

Now, with many of the animals in hibernation and flowers absent, he just had the clouds and the sky to look at. For Felix, and most farmers like him, it was almost impossible to predict the weather in wintertime. Although Felix's mother would claim that she could feel a tingling up her spine when it was going to snow. She was usually right. Perhaps Sula had something similar. He'd always known women were more sensitive to these things anyway.

'Maybe you're right.'

She opened her mouth to say that she *was* right, but snapped it shut again just in time. He just stared into her jade eyes for a moment and was startled by the life and depth in them. She looked away quickly but he thought he had seen them change shades from jade to emerald with orange specks!

He decided it must have been his imagination. His parents always told him he had too much of that.

Felix opened the door and out of respect let her in first. She cautiously stepped inside. She hoped he lived alone for she was not up to facing yet another curious talkative human.

Then he closed the door behind them, hung his coat and scarf on a hook on the wall and put his axe in one corner next to the door. He walked straight to the fireplace opposite the entrance to build the fire up from the smouldering coals. His blond locks came almost down to his shoulders.

It was then that she saw two cats lying curled up on a couple of pillows before the fire. One was grey and the other a black and brown striped one.

*Of course…*Sula thought.

They greeted Felix enthusiastically by rubbing their furry bodies against his legs. She heard him talking softly to them with warmth in his voice.

He used a lit stick to light some candles that were spread along the walls. It grew warmer and light in the house within no time.

When Felix turned to face her he found her standing at the very place he'd left her, with her cloak still dripping wet.

'Oh, I'm so sorry, where are my manners?' he said uneasily taking her heavy leather bag from her. As he turned and placed it near the warm fire to dry it out she noticed he was indeed young. In his early or mid twenties at least with a slim and toned gracious body, perhaps a bit on the skinny side. He wore a dark blue woollen jumper and brown breeches. His blond hair was longer than she had ever seen on a man. It suited him very well though.

'Small as it is, you must be a lumberjack to have carried this rucksack. Are you carrying stones in there?!' Felix grunted when he dropped the bag, glancing from her bag to her.

She only stared at him and when she did not respond he bit his lip and added softly, '*That* was a joke.'

Sula noticed how neatly and cosily he had decorated his small house. There was only one big round window with blue curtains by the bed with a dark brown cover. Next to his bed sat the fireplace with a comfy big orange woollen cushion and some smaller red ones. Left of the fireplace stood a large wooden chest with tiny carved wooden figurines. In the middle of his house was a small round chestnut table with two chairs. Right of the entrance, where Sula stood, appeared to be a book case filled with many books. Her eyes grew bigger, for she'd always loved stories. Maybe because of the history of her people and her search. Regardless, she had always been intrigued to hear tales of long ago; even as a small child.

Several sheep skins covered most of floor. Sula looked in disgust at them. Felix who had stared at her while she was studying his house interpreted it right away. She had had the same look on her face when he told her he tried to catch a fish. He seemed to be able to read her facial expressions and could understand them at once.

'Don't worry,' he said. 'The sheep died but not at my hands, or the hands of the villagers.'

She was stunned he knew what she was thinking but managed to respond, 'How then?'

He sighed, 'A wolf mauled three of them about a year ago. The sheep were part of my parent's flock,' he assured her with sadness in his eyes. 'The last sheep they had kept in fact. It's just goats now. My dad is too old to go up with them into the mountains, so I took over last year. We've got twelve goats and I'm protecting them with my life.'

Sula nodded sombrely, wondering what had happened to the wolf. She too only used fur and leather from animals that had died from natural causes for her clothes and gear. And only *then* because there were not many alternative materials suitable for her rough lifestyle. She went through too many clothes in a short space of time and had tried many materials, but unfortunately found that leather and fur were still the best. Sadly for her, as she loved animals, she hated the fact she had to wear their dead skins. But she supposed it was also a way to make use of something that would have gone to waste otherwise. Wearing their shells also made her feel less lonely.

How pathetic am I? she thought at that.

Sula looked at the loam walls painted in a soft yellow pastel, like a warm autumn day. She immediately loved the smell in this house; sweet and earthy with the burning of pine and birch wood.

'Very tasteful.' She nodded approvingly.

'Why, thank you,' Felix beamed proudly at the compliment, which he knew didn't come easily. He spread his arms wide. 'It might not be a castle, but it's what I call home,' and he walked over to her and their eyes met when he added, 'For what is a home if you can't relax in it?'

Sula avoided his stare, instead fiddled with the broach on her cloak.

I wish I had something like this, she thought but just nodded. *Then I would stay a while.*

'Now, try to relax and warm yourself by the fire. May I take your cloak?'

Sula suddenly felt very vulnerable and tired as she unbuttoned her heavy wet cloak with numb fingers, shaking her head. He went on with tidying his house at her refusal which he took for granted. There were several books and carpenter tools spread about all over the house. She slowly took off her gloves and hood making sure her long brown wavy hair covered her pointed ears; unmistakably unhuman.

The cats had discovered her and the grey one came to examine her first. Sula held out a hand to stroke its back and the cat whirled around her legs, purring and rubbing its head flirtatiously against her.

When Felix finished tidying and turned around to glance at Sula again, her remarkable beauty stunned him. As if struck by lightning he stood in awe. Never in his life had he seen anyone like her. He could not guess her age for some reason. She could have been in her early twenties, but something in her eyes and the way she acted told him she *had* to be older. Her wavy long hair was a blending of dark brown and almost black and fell around her face and shoulders like waves. Her skin was like a bronze pearl, her mouth a rose and her eyes…mysteriously sometimes dark jade and the next moment emerald.

Yes, they had again changed colour and it wasn't his imagination or the light shining in them. No, it were her eyes themselves or rather her mood it seemed.

He walked over as in a trance, took her cloak from her and couldn't help but stare at the rest of her. She wore dark-brown tight suede leggings with black knee high boots and a long moss green woollen tight fitting tunic, with a leather purple sleeveless vest lined with scarlet.

Men's clothes but very suitable for travelling in weather like today.

They did suit her very well; matching her eyes and hair. He noticed with his observing eyes that she was slender, athletically built, but unmistakably feminine. It made him feel drunk. She was *so* stunning that he almost dropped her weighty wet cloak on the floor in wonder.

Sula didn't notice him staring because she had fallen in love with the two cats both whirling about her.

'I see they like you,' Felix said with an astonished voice.

'They're probably like that to everyone,' she responded with the kindest voice he had heard from her so far.

'Actually no! Usually they are a bit shy at first but this is quite rare. They really do like you.'

Sula knelt to touch their soft fur.

'That one is Wave,' he pointed to the grey female cat. 'And this one is called Tiger, no explanation needed.'

'I know,' she said without thinking, for she could communicate easily with most animals almost instantly; especially mammals and birds. More so after a full Mindmerge, and the two cats had just told her their given human names.

'What?' Felix said confused.

'I said…,' she remarked quickly, a little flushed, 'Hello.'

He looked suspiciously at her, cocking his head, while she sat on the floor, trying in vain to remove her boots. Her hurt shoulder ached and her body was too weak.

'Here, let me help you.' He leaned towards her, held her foot, and pulled her first boot off with a little effort. Whilst trying to remove the second Felix fell backwards and laughed while lying stretched out on his floor. His laughter was contagious so much that Sula had to turn her face to hide her smile behind her hair.

She still felt cold but had thawed a little whilst she sat near the hissing and popping fire. At last she could start to feel the blood returning to her face, so that her cheeks turned hot and red. She touched the side of her head and felt her ears getting warmer too, underneath her hair which she made sure she covered them.

***

Felix warmed up some soup for both of them. It had been a long time since Sula had stayed in a house.

"We are not born to live our lives in houses," her mother had always said and Sula understood that very well. The immense sense of freedom and space she felt when she travelled could never be beaten by staying between four walls in one single place for every season; let alone several years. To feel at home outside, almost everywhere she went; be it mountains, woods or plains being a part of her. The adventure of it all and thrill of not always knowing where she would lay down her head for the night would always pull her back. But somehow it was nice and familiar to be here and she would try to enjoy it while it lasted. Looking into the dancing flames, she suddenly saw the beautiful face of her mother who died from a serious fever twenty years before. She still missed her terribly.

'I myself have travelled some,' Felix interrupted her thoughts as they moved to the table to eat their hot soup while the cats were running around the room after a little ball of wool. 'But at this time of year I prefer to stay close to home unlike my twin sister.'

'Of course.'

When she didn't comment further, Felix left it at that; assuming she was too weary to listen to his or his sister's adventures. He had wanted to impress her with his tales, not tire her.

'What about you? And what are you doing in Northland at this time of year?'

'Like I said, just passing through,' she answered plainly and he nodded politely, taking the hint.

Sula savoured the soup and ate it with delight whilst glaring at Felix for eating his so fast. She suddenly remembered he had talked about hunger in this village and she ceased eating.

'I don't want to be any trouble to you,' she began staring at her bowl, avoiding his eyes.

'You are not,' he responded questioningly.

'But you already have so little to spare and–'

'Look,' he sighed. 'I don't know how they treat visitors where you come from but here we share *everything*, even if we have little. I only think it is fair and besides...' he glanced shyly at her and bit his lower lip. 'I love the company. I don't get that many visitors you know, and certainly not from travellers!'

She took another spoonful of her potato soup and watched the cats play.

'I can pay you for the bed and board. I... have some coins.'

'Now you've offended me!' he remarked shooting her a look of disdain through narrowed blue eyes with his lips tightly pressed together. She heard him breathing fast while he clenched the bowl of soup firmly in his hands.

People can do it to...Sula thought, slightly confused, but then she remembered that all animals showed their personalities through their eyes; like mirrors to the soul.

She stayed calm, for she could really see the hurt in his eyes; not blind anger, and she shot Felix an apologetic glance.

'We will just pretend we didn't hear that,' he added softly, looking at the cats, and placed the bowl again to his lips.

They sat in silence for a while staring at the licking flames like dragons with long tongues spewing fire. What was she doing anyway? She was perfectly able to look after herself, even in a storm, and now she was eating the last of this man's food!

'I am sorry,' Sula whispered sadly, at which Felix turned to face her. 'I realise I've not been that kind to you. It's just...I'm not that used to having company.'

His eyes grew warmer and he accepted the apology.

'How come?' But immediately Felix lowered his head in regret. 'Now *I'm* sorry,' he added. 'Everyone always tell me I ask too much.' He sighed.

She smiled at him, a warm soothing broad smile this time, showing her teeth. Her canine teeth were pointy like his, cat-like. Sula accompanied the smile with tender bright eyes; the warmest he had seen so far. Felix felt his heart melting like the ice on his doorstep.

He made her some herbal tea and gave it to her in a homemade ceramic cup.

'I'm just a little tired. I have come a long way,' she explained to him.

'You have?' But then he bit his lip angry with himself again, drawing in a sharp breath and slapping his own head. It made Sula laugh again and forget her troubles for the moment. She was also starting to feel better with a full stomach and warm body.

'How much food have you got left?'

He let go of his breath.

'Me personally a few onions, apples, and carrots. Some potatoes, a small piece of cheese, and half a loaf of bread. My goats still give a little milk, although during the cold season it's always less, it's not a lot. It's for the children.'

'Didn't you all build up enough supplies to see you through the winter?'

'We did, all of us. We have a system here; we share the profits of the land. I grow fruit and my goats produce milk and I make cheese. Others grow barley, corn, onions, and potatoes. At harvest time, because most people lack the storage space, the majority of the harvest goes into one big stock barn. We normally have enough left to feed the whole village during wintertime. We rely on that barn so much that we build little in terms of supplies in our own homes. And if something happens to that one barn, well… All my apples and cheeses were in there!' he added upset.

'What happened, a fire?'

He shook his head slowly and waited a moment before answering; taking a deep breath, 'A mountain giant took it from us. We're basically slowly starving. There are about fifty mouths to feed, including children and old people. The villagers even speak of killing some of their stock for their meat! Animals who hardly have enough to eat themselves and have always given us wool, milk, eggs, and their help on the land.'

That thought disturbed her and soothed her at the same time. This man felt sympathy for animals? Most people didn't even consider them to have feelings or a soul for that matter. How very unhuman! She even found herself looking at his ears. But no, his eyes had already told her he was human alright. However, one could always hope. He certainly was very handsome.

She stopped that thought immediately and turned to their conversation again, making sure again her ears were well covered when he looked into the fire for a moment.

'Your barn has been raided by a giant?' Sula asked moments later when gathering her thoughts, puzzled. They were seated in front of the fire now, on the comfy cushions with their teas.

'Yeah,' he looked sadly at his slender hands on his legs. 'Springtime will have to come soon or we won't survive on a couple of onions, carrots, some cheese, and a few loaves. Even the chutneys and jellies have been taken,' and he glanced at her. 'We've already put everything together and the children and weak are getting most of course, but it's hard. There's nothing much to find in the woods either, everything is covered with a layer of snow. I'd have to dig deep to find some acorns or roots, but there must be some left from the autumn, so that's my next plan for tomorrow!'

Sula raised one eyebrow and Felix saw the orange flames reflected in her eyes.

'I cannot believe it!' She'd never heard of giants thieving before. Giants usually kept to themselves in the mountains and didn't bother a soul and she told this to Felix.

'Well, this one is different.' He shrugged his shoulders.

'He stole your barn because he was hungry!' she stated the obvious.

'Yeah and now so are we!' Felix replied almost angrily.

'When did this happen?' She still looked disbelieving.

'About a month ago, in the dead of night. He was clumsy, but quick! Almost as if he knew his way around. We could do nothing to stop him, for he was gone when we found out.'

'He lives in the Balla Mountains?'

Felix glanced suspiciously at her.

'How did you know?'

'I guessed, for those mountains are nearest,' she answered stolidly.

'Do you know where he has his home?' Sula asked, emptying her bowl.

'Probably in one of those large caves. I don't know. I have travelled there but I never discovered any cave large enough to hold a giant or our barn,' Felix replied shrugging his shoulders.

'Then you haven't looked well enough for there is one such cave. Last winter it had still been uninhabited though.'

'You have been in those mountains? Last winter?'

Sula avoided his curious big eyes and answered in a plain voice, 'I was on my way to it again this time when we met.'

'You were?' He looked at her unbelieving. He knew how harsh those mountains were, especially in winter time. What would a young woman like her be doing there? It didn't make much sense. But he decided to keep the conversation light.

'Why have you never visited our village before now? It is the nearest one to the Balla Mountains,' and he added with a sneer, 'and closest to my house!'

Felix put a new log on the fire while Sula kept quiet, appearing deep in thought. She didn't actually hibernate in the cave, but did take a short rest and reflected on the year that had passed and made plans for the next.

She closed her eyes against the sudden smoke; they still hurt from the snow and she had little energy left to do anything about it. She needed to recharge her energy levels to be able to call upon any Mindskill.

When she didn't respond Felix proudly grinned, 'Well, luckily this time you met me. The giant in that cave surely would have attacked and eaten you!'

Sula began to laugh, 'I am not so sure about that.'

Felix laughed as well, but then he suddenly stopped and she could see him thinking.

'Why do you say that? Everyone knows giants attack people and are always hungry! Where *are* you from anyway?' he couldn't help but ask.

She ignored the question which had sounded kind enough.

'So, have you claimed your barn back yet?'

'What, are you mad?' His behaviour changed again, but it didn't frighten Sula. She remained calm.

'No, bu-'

'Have you ever *met* a giant?' he asked accusingly.

'Well, as a matter of f-'

'Then you don't know what you're talking about, do you?' Felix almost spat at her, assuming of course she had never met a giant and just pretended to be tough again. Most people would probably get to see one or two in their life times by chance, but mostly giants tried very hard to remain hidden from humans, for very good reasons, and lived in remote places. That's why Sula did not understand why a giant would have risked his life to plunder a village.

Sula sighed and decided not to argue any more. She saw Felix chew his inner cheek in frustration and regret. He flushed a little.

'He trampled two of my family's goats,' Felix explained softly, a little sorry for his temper. 'and left a trail of destruction in the woods.'

'That is indeed very sad, but he was most likely just being clumsy.'

Felix looked disappointedly at her. He on the other hand didn't understand why she defended the giant the way she did. The goats were his life.

'We're afraid, Sula. Can you blame us?' his voice shook a little.

No, I can't, Sula thought grimly. *Humans are weaker, I forgot. And frightened, always frightened.*

But it did surprise her he admitted his fear, for humans hardly ever did that; especially not young males.

He is afraid for his goats and his family…

'I just don't fully understand why you or your people haven't done anything yet.' She shook her head in disbelief. Her hair fell a little over her face, blocking her eyes. With a slender hand she rubbed her forehead, brushing a few locks away.

'Perhaps we are not as brave as you,' he said in ingratiating tones and he gazed at her with admiring eyes and marvelled again at hers. She reminded him of a fairy he used to see in picture books back at school. Uncannily charismatic and beautiful and he couldn't stop staring.

'Aren't you curious?' she asked him. For a moment he forgot what they had been talking about, but then he remembered painfully enough. He glanced back at the flames for comfort, knotting his brows and poked absently at the fire.

'Curious? Yes, but curiosity can be dangerous,' he paused, looking uneasy. 'We also try to be wise and save our skins. For who has ever heard of anyone coming back alive from an encounter with a giant?'

'I see.' Sula sighed disappointedly.

'We are not aggressive people who go looking for trouble, Sula. This is a village of simple farmers protecting our animals. We are not going after the ones that kill them or take away our food. I feel you think differently, don't you?'

Not all that much, 'I just think… things will never change if you think and act ignorantly and frightened. You people have already made up your minds about the giant without knowing the complete truth. He stole your *only* food supply. He might come *back* for more or again next year as this was *easy* pickings!' She emphasised her words with effect.

Felix found her whole attitude a little accusing, but it was also compelling. He liked strong women. She reminded him of his twin sister, Feline. 'You sound as if you know him, do you?' he asked.

'*You* don't know him either, Felix. Don't you want to know if there's any food left?'

Felix sighed and raised his hands in surrender. They finished their meal in silence and after that Sula helped him clean the dishes.

It looked like she had found herself another adventure.

***

'At dawn I will head for the mountain cave,' she announced boldly. Felix turned and looked with big eyes at her, for he knew she was making sense.

'Why? What can *you* do?'

She narrowed her eyes a little at that, her pride hurt, but then her eyes grew soft again. She hesitated, thinking before she answered, 'Something... more.'

'You can't be serious, surely? What can you do, other than be his dessert?'

'Look. Felix, I appreciate your concern and your hospitality, but this is something I *have* to do. I wouldn't even have to tell you that I am leaving, it is of no concern to you.'

He opened his mouth and shook his head.

'Oh, but it is, can't you see? *I* was the one who told you about the giant. If you get yourself killed then *I'm* the one responsible for that.'

She turned around so she didn't have to see his frightened eyes.

Suddenly he grabbed her by the shoulders; turned her around and looked helplessly at her. 'Please, don't go. The food is probably all eaten anyway. There is no point in going!' And he added laughing nervously, 'If you want to do something you can help me by digging up some of those acorns I told you about so we can turn it into flour to make bread.'

Sula looked at him incredulously and wriggled her way skilfully out of his hands with her hands sweeping his slowly aside, not loosing eye contact. She had goose bumps when his hands brushed against her skin. Felix had an urge to hold her close and caress her long dark manes and smooth skin. He caught her sweet warm scent like honeysuckle and wanted to nuzzle his face in her neck.

'I... just want to find out where your barn is and if there is anything left,' she reasoned, relenting a little, looking away now. 'But don't you worry. I can look after myself pretty well, thank you.'

He turned around and rubbed his chin in anger while he said through clenched teeth, 'I wish I'd never told you about it!'

'Too late now.' She tried to smile at him, for she did indeed appreciate his concern. It had been a long time since someone really cared about her or even that she had wanted them to.

He paced the room trying to think of a way to stop her.

'When are you planning to go?' he asked hurriedly.

She returned his gaze, sighing, 'At first light.'

He stepped in front of her showing her his broad chest, taking a deep breath, placing his fists on his hips.

'I won't let you go, Miss Sula!'

Angrily at those words, she faced him and he could almost feel the energy radiating from her.

'I am *not* your prisoner!' But more composed and calmer she added, 'You have invited me here, remember?'

It softened him and he made his voice gentle again when he steadily said, 'I will come with you. You'll be needing my help to carry back the food *if* we find it. And you will need someone to look out for you.'

Now she was the one surprised. She agreed and once she had drunk her tea, she pulled her cloak off the hook and away from the fire. Felix watched her lie down on the comfortable cushions and cover herself with the still damp cloak in front of the fireplace.

'Sula, you are my guest! I will not let you sleep on the floor! At least sleep in my bed.'

She glanced over at his even more comfortable big bed and all of a sudden she had a vision of Felix's naked slim body bending over hers, kissing her sensuously all over and holding her tenderly...

Sula felt her face heat up and immediately blocked her embarrassing thoughts, brushing her hair in front of her face so he wouldn't see. However, she didn't have the energy left to refuse his polite and innocent offer. He knew how to treat a guest, she gave him that.

Distracted, she opened her bag and put on a long dry flannel nightdress that reached just below her knees and shyly slipped underneath his blankets which still smelled of him; like wood. Felix didn't look at her once out of respect.

She closed her weary eyes and heard him wash his face and hands quickly and make his bed on the sheepskins on the floor.

The mattress Sula laid on was stuffed with a combination of straw and wool and therefore quite soft. She could smell this too. It was pleasant. She wasn't used to anything so luxurious. The thick woollen blanket covered her completely and soon was warm. Sula felt her body relax as she grew more comfortable and the welcome sleep approach.

One last time she looked at the figure on the floor and her sleepy thoughts were of her strangely pleasant evening. It had felt so familiar. To talk to someone, to argue and even laugh a little. She realised that she had really missed that.

Felix on the other hand couldn't sleep at all. He listened to her soft breathing. He had a few female friends yet no one like her; so mature, so strong and self-confident. His only sister came close but he hardly ever saw her as she stayed away for most of the year. He hoped she was treated with the same kindness he was giving his guest wherever she was.

It was as if a whirlwind had blown through his house, leaving him shaking and full of questions. During the night he heard the storm raging outside just as Sula had predicted.

Chapter 4 The Giant

Felix opened his eyes slowly. His door appeared closer than normal; was he hallucinating? Remembering that he'd slept on the floor, he pushed the blanket away stretching out his stiff muscles. He quickly turned around to look at his bed with his sleeping guest, but found it to empty. It was still dark outside, yet Sula had already left.

Cursing to himself he jumped up; quickly pulling on his trousers, a tight fitting shirt, and the blue woollen jumper he had worn the day before.

When he tried to pull open the door he found out that he couldn't. Something was jammed against the handle from the outside.

'Fool!' Felix shouted after her but she was of course too far away to hear him.

Her heavy cloak was gone, but her rucksack with all her belongings, was still there next to the bed. That was a little hopeful; although deep down he knew where she had gone to and was almost certain she would not come back alive once she had found the mountain giant.

Felix had a worried look on his face. The thought of her body crushed between the giant's strong arms made him feel terrified.

He grabbed his coat and scarf hastily hurrying to the window, and tried to open it. It was covered in thick ice and the window wouldn't budge. With his knife he slowly hacked away at the ice formed on the latch until he was able to give it a little push to open it wide enough for him to squeeze through.

He fell out of the window and landed face down in the snow. A cold breeze welcomed him and the sharpness of it hurt his face. Wrapping his scarf tightly around his neck, he scrambled up. An almost full moon was rising and this would give him just enough light to search for her.

Felix hoped she had not got that far yet, but had an uncomfortable feeling.

Glimpsing at his shovel wedged against the lock of his door and her footprints leading away he grumbled. As fast as he could he ran through the small village. Everyone was still asleep, save for one single old man removing snow from the path in front of his house.

'Oldevar,' Felix noticed the man leaning with distracted eyes on his work tool. 'You're up early?'

The older man looked up but just stared at Felix in silence.

'What is it, my friend?' Felix asked.

The grey haired man opened his mouth slowly in response, 'I... I just saw a wolf.'

'A wolf in our village?'

Felix knew there were wolves in the woods, sometimes killing a few sheep or chickens wandering off too far. It was hard to avoid; living side by side, but he had never heard of a wolf coming *that* close to humans. They were too afraid of people to come near unless they were very hungry and came looking for scraps or weak or young livestock.

'Are you sure?' Felix asked. Oldevar glanced with wide-open grey eyes at him.

'As sure as I see you, son.'

'What about a woman?' Felix pointed at Sula's footprints in the snow close to the old man. No wolf prints were to be seen. 'Surely you must have seen her?'

Violently he shook his head and replied, 'A she-wolf.'

Felix sighed and laid a comforting hand on the man's shoulder. He didn't know what to think. Oldevar was known for his well-developed senses and some said he had the Sight. He saw different things; things behind the visible world. But for now, Felix didn't have time to think about his words.

Sula walked into the cave's mouth covered with bright green moss on the inside; almost the same colour as her woolly hat. She had decided to wear a hat to hide her unusual ears instead of her hood. The cave could easily fit a giant. This was a large high chamber; damp and humid.

She knew it was not her business, but she wanted to help Felix and his people despite her thoughts about humans in general. She wanted to learn more about this giant and perhaps set something straight. There were already too many conflicts between people and other species including hers. She saw it as her task to help her fellow beings. Even her mother would have agreed with her on that. She also had loved all creatures, big and small.

Sula also understood humans by now; they were useless and acted out of egotism, greed and ignorance, sometimes even indifference. Worse than hatred. For people not to do anything about acts of evil carried out towards animals and innocent people, and just let it happen over and over again– knowing full well it causes great pain and death– Sula considered just as bad. Sula was more than all that.

The inner chamber of the cave in which she stood in was dark, but she used the navigation senses of the bat.

'Your breath, my breath, your spirit, my spirit, your mind, my mind...'

As her vision failed her, the deeper into the cave she went, she became one with the bat; producing high-pitched signals to determine the distance to the nearby objects and find her way.

'Your heart, my heart, your-' She could smell life...hear breathing...

Carefully she walked towards the sound, not losing contact with the bat. It got closer with every step she took. She swallowed away her fear. Oh yes, she too knew fear. She was of course mortal and could feel pain and die as much as any living creature. Despite her courage and strength; despite any animal ability she so far made her own.

A loud snoring filled the space. The giant lay stretched out on his back. Sula had to admit she was curious and what was wrong with that? Most of her adventures started out of curiosity.

Sula now used the heightened eye vision of the cat, allowing her to see more clearly in the near total darkness to observe him.

And she could see him. He looked enormous and covered the whole floor. She had forgotten how big a giant could actually be…

Concentrating on the bat again, to use its flying ability mainly, she landed on the giant's huge swollen belly. It seemed obvious he wasn't hungry, at least not anymore.

Now, observing this sleeping giant with ease, she shifted to the cat again, studying him with feline eyes. He lay very still with his huge hands, as big as her, across his chest. Whilst sleeping, even the most horrible of creatures appeared innocent. This one seemed like a big baby with his bald head and podgy body wrapped in fur. He was young, incredibly young. It was clear he was still an adolescent.

Sula pondered what she should do: look for the barn and food, and carry it, with the strength of an elephant, back to the village or…wake the giant and talk to him? Give him a warning, for he might come to the village again and steal their barn next winter? Even if the giant was just hungry and Felix's people non-violent, accidents did happen; like the goats who got trampled. If next time a human got trampled the villagers would want vengeance all the more. And that hatred would be the start of negative stories and make all giants look bad. It could even start a riot. Sula was sure there weren't that many giants left. For generations they had been, like her kind, hunted and killed for what they were, not for *who* they were. And true enough, like Felix had already said before; no one had ever truly met a giant, not even Sula…

Now I am surely losing my mind, Sula thought. *Reason with a giant? How? Maybe Felix was right; it is insane*, but then she thought: *What is the worst that can happen?* And it was her inquisitiveness that finally won her over.

'Hello?' she asked in a loud voice but not loud enough to wake a giant. So Sula concentrated on the call of the bear, began her chanting covering her sensitive ears with both her hands while she roared,

'WAKE UP!'

It echoed through the entire cave. Anything alive in that cave would surely be awake now…

The giant sat up at once and asked in a dull low voice: 'MAMMY?' and Sula flew backwards by the sheer force of his voice and thumped with an agonizing thud against the wall.

***

Felix almost jumped out of his skin when he heard the roaring, 'WAKE UP' coming from deep within the cave. He had followed Sula's footprints in the light of the moon and the rising sun.

Luckily it stopped snowing and he finally found the cave's mouth. His stomach was protesting loudly and he felt exhausted from ploughing through the deep snow. He lent one arm against a rock and rested a while catching his breath.

Sula's footprints had stopped right there; she had gone inside. His concern for her made him overcome his fears so he followed.

It was cool in the cave but not as cold as it was outside. Here there was no wind like in the rest of the Windy Mountains as the Balla mountain range was also known. He cursed himself for not having brought a torch, for it was pitch black.

But what about Miss Sula, he thought. *How will* she *find her way?*

Once again he was amazed whilst still considering her perseverance and courage. Why had she wanted to help his people anyway? Why did he have the uncomfortable feeling she was on the giant's side? And why did she act like she wasn't afraid to be hurt? Surely she was mortal just as he was; although Felix began to think he had dreamt her up. The woman had been the fairy from his childhood dreams coming to life. But the footprints outside the cave were evidence of her existence; together with the footprints she had left in his heart…

'Maybe I wished for her to come to rescue us all. Great Bhan, let her be safe! That is all I care about for the moment!'

Lightly he touched the grey stone wall with his cold stiff fingers to help guide him deeper into the cave. Normally he would never have gone into a cave at all, especially if he knew it housed a giant, but now…the lady needed his help. No matter how strong she appeared to be. He grinned at that; he loved stories about heroes saving damsels in distress. How he would love to rescue that strong willed Sula from the beast! That would surely soften and win her heart!

Suddenly he heard drumming from deep in the cave followed by falling rocks, cascading and echoing. More closely he heard a soft moan which sounded somewhat familiar.

'Miss Sula, are you there?' Felix stumbled his way over to the dark shape on the floor. He fell once before finally reaching her. He could hardly see her at all; only her silhouette, but he reached out with his hands in front of him feeling for her in the dark. He found her leg first.

'Are you hurt?'

'Why did you follow me?' she replied in a quiet but annoyed voice.

She heard him sigh with relief. He knelt next to her and managed to touch her head. He noticed she didn't have her hood on, but a woollen hat. She slapped his hand away.

'You shouldn't have!' she snapped at him.

'You didn't wait for me. Now, can you stand? We have to get out of here in case the giant finds out we're here,' and he helped her up. 'I heard an awfully loud noise, didn't you?'

Sula leant on him and found nothing to be broken, except maybe a few bruised ribs from when she landed hard. She could feel a mild headache coming on.

'Uh,' she replied. 'I think he is awake now.'

Felix still couldn't see her, but had heard the sudden change in her voice and she heard him gasp.

Pounding footsteps were coming towards them, the cave shook, more small rocks fell and Sula sought Felix's hand in the dark and grabbed it quickly. Felix felt electricity run up and down his spine upon her touch.

'Come on, hurry.' She made him follow her.

Chapter 5 Listen

Together they ran, with Sula leading, holding his hand tightly. Felix's hand felt a little rough and calloused and she was intrigued by it, for she had imagined his hands somehow to be soft and yielding. He stumbled behind her, struggling to keep up with her, wondering how she could make her way in the dark so easily.

Sula didn't know if she would be able to hide Felix from the giant in time. Even if giants couldn't see in the dark; she knew they could certainly *smell* well enough.

It was a little gloomy in the large chamber so in that light when Sula looked back in alarm, Felix thought that she might be afraid and he noticed a large bloody cut above her dark eyebrow underneath her green hat; all the way down her right cheek. Blood ran freely, smearing one side of her face shiny red. But before he could worry about that, they heard the giant's feet stamping closely behind them.

In one sudden movement Sula pulled Felix towards her and spun him around. Before he realised what she was up to she pushed him quickly and firmly with both hands on his back, and with great strength out of the cave.

Well-aimed, Felix landed on a pile of soft fresh snow, in front of the cave's mouth quickly rolling onto his back to see what Sula had seen: an enormous giant well over twenty feet tall with long, powerful arms that reached down to his knees. He even had to bend his head to fit in the cave. The giant looked down upon Sula who looked miniscule in comparison.

It was the first time in Felix's life he'd ever seen a mountain giant so he held his breath in utmost tension.

The giant's fur clothes were old and shaggy with many holes and were frayed at the edges. He couldn't be that old yet, maybe between a hundred and hundred and fifty years; a teenager in Giant years and quite young to be living on his own. She just hoped she wouldn't meet his parents.

His big brown eyes grew wide as he stared right at her and bellowed:

'GO AWAY! GROBO LOOK FOR MAMMY.'

Sula realised that he must have mistaken her earlier shouts for his mother. The giant seemed confused when she responded calmly, 'I haven't seen your mammy, that wasn't her calling you.'

'THAT'S BECAUSE YOU'RE HERE. MAMMY HATES TINY PEOPLES.'

Sula had to cover her over-sensitive ears with her hands protecting her hearing from his loud rumbling voice. Which was actually pretty normal for a giant but deafening to other species. It felt like her brain was going to explode out of her skull, it was so painful.

'I guess I woke you up, sorry!'

He scratched his huge head and asked dully, bending his head her way, 'YOU WOMAN PEOPLE WOKE GROBO, NOT MAMMY?' A few stones fell down from the ceiling. Felix, who got himself up and looked in from outside, ready to help Sula, stared in concern at her.

'WHY?'

Sula relaxed a little, for she knew, from her mother's stories, that young giants were easily frightened and could cause a landslide with their voices alone. She had to be careful for this cave mouth could collapse and she didn't want to be imprisoned for ever.

'Please try to keep your voice down, try to whisper! I have come to ask you something.' Sula attempted to calm him.

'GROBO SLEEP, NOT TALK.' And he moved to turn around, disappointed his mother had not come to pay him a visit. A few more rocks, each the size of a fist, fell in front of Sula. Dust rose up and she had to cover her eyes and take a step backwards. Felix already stood close behind her and she could feel the heat of his body, but she wasn't finished yet.

'Grobo, please listen and wait just one minute before you go back to sleep.'

He looked at her and yawned indifferently.

'Yeah, Grobo,' Felix added suddenly, thinking the giant was harmless and stupid. He was trying to show Sula he could be brave as well. 'We have just one question.' He stepped in front of Sula, shielding her with his body.

When Grobo noticed Felix for the first time his eyes grew even bigger and his attitude changed instantly. He stepped forward with one big step and leant towards Felix in order to pick him up between his thick fingers in one quick motion.

'GROBO, NO LIKEY YOU!!!' His voice filled with anger.

Felix struggled to get himself free, using his arms to try to pull himself out, but failed. Sula watched on with an annoyed expression. Why did Felix have to ruin it?

'Grobo, release him right away!'

The giant sniffed disdainfully at Felix as if he was not really worth the effort and then dropped him. Felix fell a few feet before hitting the hard floor, breaking his fall with his supple legs and rolling himself on his back. When Sula saw he was all right she angrily said, 'This is not the way to treat us, Grobo!'

His look changed and became a little friendlier.

'WHY TINY PEOPLE COME TO GROBO?'

Cursing, Felix got up, brushing down his clothes before coming to stand next to Sula again.

'Please try to whisper, the cave will collapse otherwise, Grobo,' Sula warned and noticed he was actually listening to her. Felix was amazed.

'Well now, we thought you must have been a bit *lonely* and *hungry* since you've taken all our food. Do you remember that?' Sula decided to talk to him like she was one of the villagers. She could see him pondering.

'Food?' he asked in a lower voice; low for his standards.

'A wooded barn, a box to you, full of food you took about one month ago from a village, do you remember?'

'Grobo take box with food, yes.'

Sula smiled at Felix who appeared to be a little frustrated, scratching his chin.

'Yes and that food did not belong to you,' Felix answered him, grimly.

'Belong not? Food is for all, Mammy told Grobo.'

'Not really, this was ours, we worked hard for it!' Felix announced impatiently.

Grobo scowled as he looked at Felix and with big watery eyes at Sula.

'Hasn't your Mammy told you that you must make a food supply yourself?' she asked quickly to distract Grobo from the human man. Sula would never be able to resolve the ancient feud between giants and humans with a couple of words, even if she tried.

He nodded in response to her question. 'Grobo gather food; found lots in box, now eat every day, not hungry.'

Sula had to repress a snigger because he was right about that, she simply smiled at him.

'Well, winters are long. Is it your first winter alone then?'

Gobo's lower lip went down and his eyes became even more watery. He heavily slumped down on his bottom and started crying his eyes out with heavy sobs. It cut Sula like a knife through butter. As tough as she sometimes appeared to be, her heart was an open door, always; especially with pain felt by other creatures. A pain, which she could simply not ignore.

'Mammy gone to other cave east, left Grobo here,' he cried with a red face, 'said Grobo big boy now.'

Feeling sorry for him and with little fear Sula stepped a little closer, quickly followed by Felix. 'You've still a lot of things to learn, but that's all right. I guess one of those things is to be frugal.'

'Fru...gal?'

'Yes, in this case it means you must not eat too much all at once. If you eat a little everyday, you will have enough for the whole cold season and you won't have to steal other people's food.' she elaborated.

'I have enough now,' he responded bluntly, not understanding. 'Plenty for Grobo, eat everyday.'

'You do, but... it wasn't yours to take,' she explained patiently whilst rubbing her forehead, thinking.

'A better way would be to gather food and not through stealing; wouldn't it?'

'Grobo not steal, Grobo *take*.'

Sula felt Felix's hand on her shoulder.

'Look, this is not going to work,' he whispered in her ear. 'He doesn't understand. He is...not very bright obviously. Maybe if we just *ask* for whatever food is left? He seems a little hot tempered.'

She didn't look at him or answer, but just stood rigid.

After a little while looking at Grobo, who still sat staring dumbly at her, wiping his nose on the back of his hand, she opened her mouth to speak again but then closed it. It was true; mountain giants were stubborn and hard to convince especially by other beings and it took a long time for them to grow up. And this one wasn't too bright to say the least, but she was not going to give up that easily. Nor was she just going to take back what he had stolen (which she could have done very easily); not without exposing herself to Felix though.

'Grobo, do you have something that you really like in your cave?' she asked after a brief moment. 'Something you wouldn't want to lose in the world?'

He glanced around uninterestingly and seemed to search his mind, while his hairy thick brows went up and down questioning.

'Blanket,' he answered after a little while.

'Alright,' she retorted hopefully. 'And why is this blanket so important to you?'

'Mammy gave Grobo blanket when he was small. It's comfy, nice

51

and it's all mine.'

Sula nodded approvingly and said in a calm way, 'So, in a way you *need* your blanket. If I took your blanket away, how would that make *you* feel?'

Grobo's expression changed from upset to anger and then back to upset again, his features eventually growing milder. She could already see by his face that he understood. He nodded and said with a steady low voice, 'Sad. It would make me cry!'

Sula nodded but kept quiet.

'Grobo has something Tinypeoples don't want to miss.'

Felix sighed in relief. The giant wasn't that dumb after all. Sula did it, Sula actually reasoned with a giant!

'Yes, the barn with food. You see, that's *our* blanket for the winter; our supply which we cannot do without. We gathered the food with a lot of care and effort throughout the summer and fall. It's *all* we have. We are not only *sad* but *hungry*. If we don't get our food back, we will surely die,' Sula explained.

His eyes grew wide.

'GROBO, DON'T WANT TINYWOMAN TO DIE,' and he lowered his voice in embarrassment. 'Grobo likes.' and his face flushed deep red. It was a funny picture. She smiled happily at him.

'My name is Sula, Grobo, not 'Tinywoman', but I guess I am to you,' she laughed and dared to shake one of his big fingers with both of her hands. Felix looked still in awe at the scene, open-mouthed.

'Sula nice.'

'Why, thank you. And this here is Felix, he is nice too. A little stupid, but nice,' she chuckled.

But Grobo didn't look at Felix, he had his eyes fixed only on her, with drooping eyelids.

'Sula hungry, Sula eat.' He got up and walked deeper into the cave.

She met Felix' gaze and gave him a proud glowing look. He bowed knightly for her and although he looked a little defeated, he gave her a most grateful warm smile.

She didn't need me after all…

When Grobo came back he carried a huge wooden barn which he could barely carry. He rummaged in it and pulled out a round cheese.

'Sula eat.'

She gladly took it, although she didn't eat dairy products, she would give it to Felix.

'Thank you, Grobo,' Sula said. 'May I have the whole barn back? I am not the only one who is hungry, you know. There are children and babies…'

Grobo slowly looked at the barn and showed her some cheeses, apples, carrots, potatoes and two sacks; one with flour and the other with red beans.

'I keep a little and give barn back, *if* Tinypeoples not hurt me.'

Sula looked questioningly at Felix who shrugged his shoulders in response, raising his eyebrows.

'Did humans hurt you, Grobo?'

'Tinypeoples *always* hurt giants, mammy told Grobo. That's why we hide.'

Sula nodded at that statement, thinking about her own mother who had pretty much said the same thing to warn her!

She turned to Felix.

'You have to promise him, Felix.'

'Yeah, of course,' he gazed up at Grobo. 'I promise on behalf of the village people you can keep some of our food and we will not hurt you, if…you do not steal our barn again,' Sula stepped on his foot. 'Ouch, why did y–'

'Grobo agree. Sula and Felix friend of Grobo?'

'Yes, friends,' Sula said smiling up at him. They all nodded, relieved.

Chapter 6 Understandings

Sula and Felix went back to the village to inform the villagers about the return of their barn with enough food remaining for the rest of the winter.

'I don't know how you did it Sula,' Felix mused a little quietly rubbing his hands together while they walked through the mountains back to the village. The snow crunched beneath their feet and the day promised to be another grey and snowy one.

'Well, you were there. What did you see me doing?' Sula pulled her hat tight over her ears. She knew now why they called these mountains 'The Windy Mountains'.

Felix stopped walking and stared at her, then smiled.

'You listened, didn't you?' he replied rhetorically and was rewarded with a big grin from her, as they made their way over the last mountaintop and headed down into the sheltered valley away from the wind.

'But I still don't feel I could have done what you did. It simply wouldn't have crossed my mind,' he added in all honesty. Sula stopped in front of him and stared at him intently.

'But would you...if there was a next time?'

Felix timidly stared at his boots and answered gingerly, 'With this knowledge I have gained, I would surely try!'

She touched his broad shoulder lightly.

'Well, that's a start. Although I believe trying isn't the same. You shouldn't think too much. You either do or don't. But of course I didn't even know if I would succeed.'

Felix shook his head at that, grinning, 'But at least you did it *and* succeeded. It must be that you are brave and I'm so...foolish.'

A smile flickered across her face, her eyes shining. Again it touched his heart how beautiful she was, how divine. Her mouth twitched and her words when she spoke did not conceal her laughter, 'You

Tinypeoples all are!'

***

All the villagers had gathered on the main plaza that was bordered by beech trees, when news spread. Happiness and relief filled the winter air. Felix explained that the mountain giant was not as malicious as they had thought. That Sula had talked with him making him promise to bring their barn back. No villager had ever even considered doing that.

Many questions were fired at Felix, while Sula hid herself behind one of the trees to watch him deal with the confused men and women. He promised to tell them the whole story after the giant returned the barn. He simply asked them to stay on the plaza and wait.

They were talking and laughing quietly amongst themselves when suddenly all they could hear was the loud thud of the giant's feet as he made his way down from the mountains.

I wonder why they didn't hear him last time? Sula thought.

All the villagers were standing frozen in anticipation. When they eventually saw the big clumsy giant carrying their barn, Sula could feel the tension rise in them.

They always feared him, or were told to fear him.

Sula tried to forget about them and started walking to greet Grobo and the people of the village followed her from a safe distant in amazement. Felix only smiled when he broke free of his people and walked proudly beside her.

'Thank you, Grobo,' she said when he put the barn back where it had stood before.

The child giant looked at the villagers with big frightened eyes. Sula understood the reason why perfectly well.

'Grobo go now,' he announced.

'We will always be grateful, Grobo,' Felix said to him stepping forward from beside Sula. 'Please remember that.'

'And never forget your friends live here and should you ever be hungry again, please ask if the villagers have anything to spare,' Sula added and smiled. 'I'm sure they will share some with you. But remember they did work hard for it, so maybe you could help them in return?'

Grobo simply nodded and yawned.

'Grobo sleep now. Wait for summer.' He turned around.

Sula couldn't help but still feel a bit sorry for him. He was all alone, an outsider. It was as if she watched herself going back to that cave.

In her heart she promised herself that she would check up on him after his hibernation period teaching him how to find food without having to steal. She had to make sure he was alright and self-sufficient.

The villagers never bothered to come any closer and actually meet with the giant. Fear still held them back, and Sula even saw a couple of the men firmly holding rocks in their hands; ready for an attack. They greedily examined the barn when Grobo had left and divided the food amongst each other.

Sula watched sadly as they carried away the sacks, even though she knew it was *their* food and they were hungry. Something just didn't feel right…

Before she knew it she felt two strong arms around her shoulders, Felix hugged her closely from behind. It made her jump, but the simple gesture felt very good. It gave her butterflies in her stomach. Suddenly he let go as she turned to him and he saw her face more closely.

'I… forgot that you're wounded,' he remarked and pointed at the large cut on the side of her face. She touched it and felt the dried blood.

'It's nothing.'

'Better let me take care of that, it must be cleaned or you'll be sick and die with a full stomach!' he called out with a hidden smile and then chuckled.

Sula thought about why she didn't seek human company before, for she had missed this side of it. She in fact found herself wondering about things she normally never questioned and that worried and confused her.

I never ran away voluntarily; it's the destiny of my kind to stay hidden, our duty, but should it therefore be mine as well?

***

After dividing the food Felix talked to the villagers from a small stage that they normally used for performances and announcements back on the village plaza.

Sula tried to blend in with the thin crowd, whilst Felix explained how it all began. She made sure she was right at the back, near the trees; ready to run in case of danger.

'It was all Miss Sula's idea. If it wasn't for her we never would have got our barn back. Her courage is an example to all of us.'

The audience started searching amongst themselves for her. Felix's eyes found her just in time before she crept away entirely.

'Come on, Sula… please.' He beckoned at her to join him.

She narrowed her eyes briefly at him in annoyance and they seemed to flash emerald! Then the villagers were already approaching her, offering her their friendly handshakes, nudging her gently towards the stage. Sula noticed each and every reaction of the people around her. Nature had cursed her with the gift of observation and the intention behind a look. It was almost impossible for her to ignore. Sula tried to control her fear, overcome quickly by emotions; theirs and hers; barely able to move…She felt a cold sweat coming on and her hand went to her hat, making sure it covered her ears. Felix extended his hand to her and she took it. His hand already felt familiar to her.

He grinned when he pulled her up on to the stage, fighting off the urge to hug her.

'Now, please give a warm hand for our saviour.' Felix had not even finished speaking before everyone started clapping their hands. They even cheered and whistled, embarrassingly for Sula.

It made her feel uncomfortable. She had always felt ill at ease in crowds. She didn't even know where this part of her personality came from; was it inherited, or nurtured into her system? Or maybe just genetically part of who she truly was. For the first time in a long time she wondered about these things.

Felix tried to calm the crowd when he saw the discomfort on her face and wanted to protect her from them and from herself. But he couldn't do anything for she was already surrounded by them. They were so grateful and relieved. She closed her eyes so as not to see all those people; blocking them out and she was thankful for standing next to Felix who radiated serenity.

'People! Calm down and listen,' Felix started. 'Sula talked in reason with the giant whose name is Grobo!' The noise subsided and the crowd calmed down. 'Something we were afraid to do. I even tried to stop her, foolish me,' and he grinned at her with that fresh boyish grin of his. 'But she taught us all a very valuable lesson that I hope we will never forget.'

Briefly she glanced at him and noticed him swallowing a knot in his throat.

The sun suddenly came out and the lavender clouds disappeared. Golden rays shone upon his now golden hair and made him look like an angel. Felix glanced back at Sula, who couldn't take her eyes off him, holding her gaze as he finished his speech, 'Things are not always what they seem and only if we care to listen; truly listen to the other side of the story, will we forget our fears. You see,' he licked his lips. 'We only care for what we think we know, but what do we really know? We protect what we love; our families and our animals, but we only love what we *understand*. We only understand what we've been *taught* to. I say it's about time we start to listen to our hearts instead of our brains and extend our love.'

The men and women were silent at first, thinking, but then nodded in agreement at each other and Felix. Thankfully they all smiled at the two of them.

'You'll have to say something.' Felix leaned nearer to Sula and whispered closely in her ear. The crowd waited patiently for the mysterious woman to open her mouth.

They stared at her in wonder and Sula tried not to look at their faces, or their eyes, but she had to. They were so small and pathetic; yet in a group they seemed so very fearsome. She felt they could turn on her in the blink of an eye and even found herself looking at their hands for rocks or other weapons, like they had before when Grobo the giant came to their village. Mankind; the conqueror of Bhan, destroyer of species. The taker, the hunter, the builder, the oppressor. Powerful in their greed and arrogance. Strong with their weapons and in their unity. She didn't feel she could trust these village people; today they loved her but what about tomorrow? They might very well turn their backs on her and might even try to kill her if they found out what she truly was. Humans could never be trusted completely, she had always been told by her mother. It had been drilled into her effectively over the years and many times she had experienced it for herself, so why would she change her attitude now? But then she remembered Felix's words: *"It's about time we start to listen to our hearts instead of our brains and extend our love,"* and grew softer.

'Well,' she started in a small voice touching her forehead and her hat slightly. 'Felix already told you part of the story. Grobo the giant isn't fully grown yet; he's just a teenager really and not the brightest of giants. I believe he had been left by his mother to fend for himself far too early. He never meant any harm to you people. He was just hungry and took the food that was the easiest for him to obtain. He knows better now, he showed you that to you by returning your barn and its contents,' she paused for a moment, quickly looking over the audience, feeling suddenly out of place. Her heartbeat slowed as she studied their faces, realising they were looking up at her, not down on her. They were like children in need of guidance.

'I just hope that you can learn to live in peace with *all* the creatures you don't know or understand so well and try to love them', she said smiling at Felix, using his words. 'What might seem like an evil act to you could actually turn out to be an innocent deed. Please try to look closer with open hearts and just see things for what they truly are. And listen, really *listen* to *understand* and *feel* for the behaviour of other creatures who are not that dissimilar from us. So that we can all live in harmony and no one has to hide away in caves, now wouldn't that be something?'

For a moment there was a deep silence, like the villagers were weighing her words on a pair of scales. But then another applause burst out for her, louder than before. She could feel Felix's warm comforting hand on her lower back. It felt very sensual and a warm feeling grew inside her; a feeling she didn't know she was capable of feeling.

One other vital lesson the villagers learnt after having their one and only barn stolen was to have *several* barns to store their food in and not to rely on just one, however big. It was what they talked about for the remainder of the day. Sula would help them build those extra barns of course. That she had already decided, even though her instinct told her to leave as soon as possible.

She had really done more than enough for Felix and his people; but it would be the final thing she could do. She just needed to ensure she kept her secret safe by not using any animal ability and simply limit herself to just being human, but could she?

***

The villagers arranged a party to be held that evening especially for Sula and several dishes would be prepared using the returned supplies. After the speech, they all thanked her in person, although Oldevar, the man who had seen the wolf, looked rather suspiciously at her; not in an unkind way, but questioningly. It made her feel very uneasy and so she politely declined the invitation to the party for fear of exposure. Felix was disappointed, but he tried to shrug it off.

They both carried a sack full of various kinds of food to Felix's home. He was surprised at her strength, even though she tried to pretend to struggle with the load.

'You really taught me a good lesson today, Sula. I will never settle for anything less than the truth again.'

'You were pretty amazing yourself,' she replied lightly.

Back in his house Felix lit the fire and poured some fresh water in to the pot to make some tea. Sula took off her hat and went to wash her face and hands. While doing so she glanced in the small round mirror that hung on the wall to check if her hair covered her ears. She also examined the wound. It throbbed a little now but it wasn't as bad as it looked. It would heal well. Besides, it wasn't the first time she had had a cut or a bruise and comyentis tended to heal quickly and without scars, even if she was only a halfling.

Sula suddenly shrank back and a shiver went down her spine as Felix lightly touched her hair. She hadn't seen it coming and it took her off guard, but she soon relaxed when she saw the bowl and a piece of cloth in his hands.

'I'm sorry to startle you,' he said apologetically. 'I could clean the wound for you, if you'll let me.'

Quickly she tried to grab the bowl and cloth from him.

'It's ok, I'll do it myself,' she said with her hands outstretched. But Felix kept the bowl held tightly to his chest.

'Please, Sula, let me do something for you after all you've done for me.'

Absentmindedly she stared in the fire, which popped and hissed, afraid the moment had come where he would discover her true identity by seeing her unusually pointy ears. Maybe he'd already seen them? She knew questions would then come, which always happened when people found out, but somehow she wasn't afraid of Felix's reaction. Until now, he had seemed fair and kind towards her and to animals as well, but still...you never knew. People's reactions and attitude could be so awkward sometimes. That was something she was always wary of, especially when they were in a group. People could be so utterly mean. And the only species that drove her to despair, more times than she cared to remember, was humankind.

'You've done more than enough already,' she said thinking quickly.

'You gave me shelter. I probably would have frozen if you hadn't done so,' and she regretfully smiled at him when she saw the hurt in his eyes. Felix wanted so much to do something in return for her. He felt inadequate after their meeting with Grobo.

'So as a matter a fact *you're* the one who saved my life,' she continued. 'Let's say we're even now.' Sula reached for the bowl again but he held on to it. He suddenly looked at her with a wise mournful look; she had not seen in him before.

'There is more than just life and death. Suffering is worse than death,' Felix exclaimed.

Sula was surprised, wondering what made him say that. She felt she couldn't do other than allow him to clean her wound, whatever the consequence might be. She was already like wax in his hands anyway, worryingly so. Never should she have let a human get so close to her. But somehow, it didn't feel wrong…

Sula stood before the mirror and looked into her own frightened eyes. The wound started above her right eyebrow and ended high on her cheekbone, close to the ear. Felix dipped the cloth in the boiled warm water, standing beside her. Her hair got a little in the way so he had to place a couple of strands behind her ear. She closed her eyes, pressed her lips tightly holding her breath.

'It's not that deep, don't worry. It probably won't even leave a scar if we treat it properly with the right herbs and ointments. So your beauty will remain, Sula.' His voice sounded so close and he pronounced her name in such a lovely way.

That's the least of my worries, really!

She could hear him drawing in a sharp breath and holding it. He didn't say a word.

Well, it doesn't necessarily mean I'm not human, she thought. *Throughout my travels I've seen humans with the oddest big pointed ears and I mistook them more than once for being like me!*

Tenderly Felix cleaned the wound until it started bleeding a little again. He got up and came back with a tiny jar containing a green substance.

'This will stop the bleeding and help it heal.'

While he was busy applying the cream, she looked around a bit and studied the wooden sculptures on the chest to her right side, left of the fireplace. She forgot all about her worries when she picked up the tiny figurines one by one. There was so much life and energy in them.

'May I?' she asked timidly, trying not to move too much.
'Sure, it's a little hobby of mine but hold your head still, please.'

She examined the wooden sculptures gently touching them with her slender hands. Lots of them were of cats, tiny children climbing a tree, a young man with a walking stick and a cat standing in front of him like they were talking. Also an old man sitting with his back towards a tree with an owl in one of its branches, an elegant woman with a ball in her hand with waves at her feet, and a man and a woman beautifully entangled in each other. Sula was particularly fond of a woman with a fine bird; either a robin or wren, on her shoulder and a big wolf by her side.

Creatures big and small…

She caressed the pieces in her hands one by one while Felix bandaged her head. He was moved by her delicate touch on the wood that he had somehow not expected from her.

'Do you like them?'

She blinked her eyes at him in wonder for a moment before glancing back at the sculptures.

'Like them? Why, I love them! You have a gift, Felix, you truly do.' To Felix's surprise, she gently picked up his free hand with both of her hands and looked meaningfully at it. 'That human hands can make beautiful art such as this is a miracle. A *miracle*.'

He crimsoned at her touch and her sudden kind words; he was not used to her being this kind. A pleasant shudder went through him.

'Did someone teach you how to make them?' She stared into his eyes now with an examining look.

'Nah, I taught myself.' He shrugged, avoiding her eyes, gone shy.

'How?'

Sheepishly he laughed at her, whilst tidying away the things he had used to tend to her wound; quickly adapting to her questions.

'Friends of mine asked me the same and I always answer; the wood guides me,' and he lifted his hands. 'These are just vessels.' He lay a hand on his heart. 'My inner self links to the wood and the Great Bhan who created the tree... why, the creator of everything. We're all linked together. That's why I can do this.' His eyes locked on to hers and seemed to make contact with her soul before saying, 'Actually...all I do is listen... to my heart.'

Her mouth opened slightly, she was really moved and her eyes darted from Felix to the little sculptures.

'So...you don't ever have an idea before you start working on a piece?'

'Sometimes I do roughly but it's not as if I think a lot about it. The images just come to me, like dreams,' he walked off and threw away the dirty water outside, closing the door and looking at her again and at one of the pieces she now held in her hands.

'That's the last one I made, only last week.' He gestured to the one of the woman and the wolf. 'I want you to have it, somehow it feels right. If... you want it of course.'

Sula stared at the polished wooden gracious woman and touched the head of the wolf carefully, like a caress.

I wonder...how is this possible?

The figure looked very much like her own mother who had lived among wolves and was friends with every animal, big and small. A tear came to her eye.

'I can't, it's too lovely,' *Dreams? More like visions. He must be one of those people who can see glimpses of the past and future. My past, how?*

Her thoughts were interrupted when he approached her and folded her hands calmly around the warm smooth wood and looked at her straight into her wonderful jade eyes.

'Not nearly as lovely as you are, Sula. I can never equal nature. Consider it my gift to you.'

She had to look away from his clear blue eyes at that moment and his intense stare. Touched as she was by this simple gesture of sincere kindness, she felt hot tears well up in her eyes and her throat closed up. She said in a broken soft voice, 'Thank you... Felix.'

That was more than enough for him. He had noticed her sudden emotion and found it irresistible in such a strong woman.

Chapter 7 Revelations

They prepared a meal together from some of the many vegetables, bread, and cheese they had retrieved from the giant and ate it with delight while they sat at Felix's small table.

After the meal Felix stared at Sula with a serious look and finally dared to ask, 'I noticed you have unusual ears, Sula,' *and how hard you try to hide them...*'I have never seen someone like you before. I mean…it's not just your beauty or the way you talk and act. And it's more than simply the fact you don't come from these parts. You're…different. I feel–' He weighed his words very carefully she noticed with warmth in her heart. 'If you don't mind me asking...are you… from the fairy world?'

Swallowing away her initial fear, she avoided his stare and answered with a half smile, 'Not a fairy, but flesh and blood, like you.'

'Of course, I never doubted *that*,' he said, remembering the warmth he felt coming from her when he hugged her, smelling her sweet scent, whilst tending the wound.

'Well, to be honest, at first I thought you were an angel.' He gave a sudden wheeze for a laugh, showing his white teeth and a cute dimple in his cheek. It was the most beautiful smile. Then a look of sudden insight washed over him, thinking about the accident with the bridge. When she did not respond he added, 'A 'fallen' angel! You must be!'

No, you are, Felix,

'I am part human, part comyenti, Felix. A Mindmerger,' she said it so quickly not allowing herself time to think or back track.

His mouth fell open and he frowned.

'Mindmerger…com…yenti… Are you saying that they really do exist?'

She glanced at him with a sad look, surprised he had even heard of her species as most hadn't.

'*Existed*, I'm probably the last, a distant memory...'

He needed a moment to think, she could tell, licking his dry lips. He looked excited that she was something rare.

'Great Bhan! I thought your kind only lived in myths!'
'And what do those myths tell you about us?'
'Let me see, if I can recall, comyentis were human-like creatures with the powers of... animals?'

Sula nodded silently. A real brightness came to his eyes then. Felix was gifted with a great memory and could recall a great number of stories by heart. Sula was impressed what he told her next. For decades her species were luckily thought to be extinct so people had stopped searching and hunting for them, but they had lived on in stories.

'They're also different and beautiful, unnaturally beautiful.' He slowly moved his hand to touch her, but watched her face closely to see if she approved. When she did not flinch or move, he stroked her delicate cheek lightly up to her ear and she closed her eyes against the intimacy. 'But despite this unnatural beauty, comyentis looked very similar to the most alluring of humans and would be able to live undetected amongst them, as long as they never showed their powers.' He cocked his head in thought when he withdrew his hand. 'But aren't they all supposed to have identical features in common?' He examined Sula's face closer. 'Pointed ear tips, slanted bright coloured almond shaped eyes, but more importantly very intelligent and immensely strong. If I remember correctly, it was because of all these characteristics that your kind was hunted and eventually driven away. Brought to extinction by mankind a long time ago and not seen for so long that people doubted they ever existed in the first place and not listed in any records, just fairytales.

'Hmm, 'driven away' is mild to say the least, 'wiped out' would be more accurate. Sadly it is not a myth or a fairytale, but actual history,' she responded grimly and sat down at the fireplace on one of the comfy cushions.

'A comyenti,' Felix said with his mouth still slightly open. 'You're the first one I've ever met!'

'Well, obviously... And also the last,' she added a bit cynically.

He bit his lip at that. 'So, it is true? Are you... nearly all wiped out to the brink of extinction?'

He came to sit next to her with sympathy in his aura. His response had been heartfelt and emphatic and Sula was touched by it.

'I have dedicated my whole life to searching for others of my kind, as my mother did before me...without any success yet. The Search is my life.'

Astonishment faded from his face as he placed his hand upon hers.

'I am sorry, I didn't know.'

'Your kind knows so little.' She flinched and retracted her hand from under his.

He tilted his head at that, pursing his lips.

'Hold on, Sula. I may be human, but it was not me who did this to your kind, you know.'

'It's not the fault of an individual, if it only was,' she ruefully reflected. *It would be much easier to deal with if it were only one who captured us; enslaved us, tortured us in trying to get us to 'expose' our secret abilities, killed us... Yes, if it were only 'one' who was ignorant and evil, but no; an entire species. And no one to stand up for us. We encountered fear, greed, ignorance and hate from the hunters and indifference from the rest of mankind. Small wonder my mother had been so full of wrath towards them. And I? What am I doing here? In one of their villages, sitting by their fire as if we're friends? The same fire that killed many of my people.*

She found herself drawing back from Felix; as the old familiar feeling of loathing humans, re-emerged.

'Will you tell me your side of the story?' Felix asked softly, understanding her character a bit more now and her sympathy for animals, even giants.

Solemnly and with dark narrow eyes she had already withdrawn from him, both physically and mentally. He saw before him the same person she had been yesterday when they first met. Sula however noticed the honest sympathetic look in his eyes; the look of a child and how could she not answer a child?

Or a cat, she thought with a small smile painting her mouth. She sighed and warmed to him again.

'There is little to tell, and what I have learned through the years is not very pleasant.'

But she started to elaborate, about the hunt. How they came with their dogs, nets and weapons. The brutal global torture of the comyentis in order to extract the secret of their powers from them. And when all their efforts failed and humans got desperate and envious and dangerous in their hatred, the slaughter of every comyenti left alive followed; near total annihilation. And how there had been a price on their heads for the ones left alive. That had only been decades ago, in the time of Sula's grandparents. Sula told him. It had always been risky for Sula to enquire about similar stories when amongst humans and she and her mother had always known to be careful. For to be exposed could mean the end of everything. But Felix needed to know her story, she felt deeply and instead of asking like she was much used to, she was now the one who did all the talking.

'In your village it may be a myth but I have learned from many people that it's not. Humans did exterminate us; they despised us. To hate is easier than to understand. The same reason why they hate each other, or more precisely...because of a lack of reason. I'm the living proof because as far as I know it all ends with me.'

She stared at the shadows formed by the opened door suddenly wanting to escape, to leave this village while she still could. Her eyes were darting back and forth and Felix felt her discomfort. Comyentis were very sensitive beings he remembered from the books and from seeing Sula in the crowd before. How she resembled a caged animal...

'Your mother, you mentioned her before, she...died a natural death?' Felix asked gingerly. She nodded, staring in the flames again, but not really seeing the fire. Briefly she told him about her mother's life.

'My mother's parents were both full comyentis, not mixed with human blood. She had two younger brothers. The whole family were discovered whilst on their travels and captured by four brutal men who were going to sell them to a circus. The circus people wanted to use them in their shows; to perform super powers on command to make these people rich and famous. The family managed to escape whilst the men were slept, using their powers, but…accidentally killed one of their captors. They travelled freely for a few days, staying low, thinking they would be safe on the open plains but didn't know that the locals had put a price on their heads and that all that time they were being followed by their dogs and horses. They were soon traced and completely surrounded by numerous local huntsmen and murdered when they attempted to escape, except for my mother who managed to flee…using her ability to fly.'

'Fff…fly?' he stammered.

She nodded, painfully aware of his curiosity but she also saw how visibly shocked he was by the horrors of her story.

'Of course she would, stupid me, huh?' he added. 'Using abilities of animals, but it sounds wonderful to me. To fly…' He looked at her suddenly, like he had just remembered what they where talking about. He cleared his throat, feeling embarrassed.

'How old was your mother when this happened?'

She sighed and stretched her legs a little.

'She was still a child, only eight.'

'Orphaned and alone. Great Bhan, that must have been hard for her! How did she survive?'

'She flew to the mountains in the East, far away from humans and was accepted by a pack of wolves. She often told me how content she had been considering the circumstances. She had great respect and love for her wolf friends. My mother loved all creatures, big and small. When she was in her twenties, she dreamt of her parents calling her to search for other comyentis. She was afraid to at first, but then remembered the promise she had made them and said her goodbyes and left. That was the start of The Search passed on to me.'

Sula told him about her mother's promise to her own mother and how she had to continue the line whilst continuing the search.

'Your mother used a human man to conceive you and then left him?'

She nodded and frowned. Shrugging her shoulders she replied, 'Of course, she had no choice. She had tried to find others of her kind; she searched Bhan in vain for years. She knew reproducing with a human was the only chance of our survival as we do match. However, she couldn't have stayed with them for it would have been a great risk for me to grow up amongst or even close to humans.'

Felix was silent for a moment, but then shyly remarked, 'I guess so, but this promise...will you...?'

'What? How do you know my mother made me promise the same thing?' she asked bewildered and confused.

'Well, it's only logical. It might all end with you, now that your mother is gone. It's what you do with a dying species, I understand that much. I'm not judging you or your mother. I'm just asking, if I may?'

He kept surprising her. Sula stared at her hands in silence and answered a little sternly, 'Yes, my mother made me promise the same thing before she died, knowing it to be our only chance for survival.' *and it's a binding promise,* Sula thought grimly. *If I break it, I will lose all my abilities and will be...human.* But Sula wouldn't tell him that!

He nodded looking thoughtfully. 'So, you er–'
'So, what?' Sula shot him an angry glance.
It's none of his business! 'A child doesn't really fit in to my lifestyle! My mother fulfilled her promise and because of that I never had a *real* home. I couldn't do that to a child!' She responded upset. *Nor will staying somewhere be any better...*

'If you find yourself a home, it will.'

'How can I? I *have* to continue my search, haven't you been listening at all?!' Her face tightened with frustration.

He acted like he wasn't moved and remained calm.

'But why? I mean, of course I understand, but after all those years...What if you really *are* the last one?'

Sula stared at the wooden figurine he had given her. She moved it in her hands. A hot silent tear fell into her lap, as she remembered her mother. She missed her so much.

'I have to know for sure. I have to know that… I am not alone.'

Felix didn't respond, he wanted to but thought, *You're not alone, Sula. Not anymore.*

It was awfully silent for a few moments.

She had turned towards the door, so that he could only see her back and tensed shoulders. He had treated her too much like a human. She was very sensitive, her comyenti side was so overpowering.

'I could never begin to imagine what a heavy weight they have put on your shoulders Sula. Of course you wouldn't want the burden. You must hate The Search, don't you?' His voice was tender.

She turned around briefly to find herself looking at his chest, for he was a head taller than her. Glancing back at the flames, she thought to herself with a shudder, *I never did until now.*

'I love travelling and to have my freedom; the vastness of it. To be able to sleep under the stars, and be surrounded by open spaces. To hear the song of birds all around me and have the scent of flowers and trees in my nostrils. To feel the softness of the clouds and the wind in my hair. To wake up with dew on my face and feel the sunlight on my skin.' She seemed to glow with an inner light on saying all that and Felix bathed in that light almost feeling the warmth of it. He closed his eyes against the intensity.

'No, you don't know me.' And she shook her head.

I'd like to, Felix thought to himself, but instead he said, 'I'm not saying you don't need all that, I myself love to travel too, for the same reasons, but I have all those things everyday right here on the farm and in the mountains, where I take my goats to each day. But to wake up every morning somewhere new, after all those years, your search-'

'Will you please stop talking about it?' she interrupted annoyed. She could feel her body temperature rise. Wearily she flopped down on the cushions. Felix stared at her considerately.

'I'm sorry,' he whispered moments later, gingerly perching beside her. 'I had no right.'

The hours passed by quickly as they talked about more general things and got to know each other a little better. After a while, Sula started to feel relaxed again in his company, as the tension eased off with Felix talking about his life in the village; about being raised to be a herder and a farmer, his travels abroad, his parents and his twin sister. All the while she listened quietly and only interjected when she needed to. Wave slept on Felix's bed and Tiger lay between them, washing himself all over. Sula blinked at the cat and when she looked up at Felix she saw the love in his eyes.

'I am ashamed on behalf of my species, Sula, I truly am, if it helps at all. It's a harsh unforgiving world.'

Touched by his words, tired and warmed by the fire she almost smiled, 'A little, Felix. Be proud of the person you are; you seem different. Forget that you're human,' *I know I did,* Sula thought.

He laughed wryly, brushing it off.

'This gift of yours, to merge your mind with animals, sorry to ask, but did you have to learn it?'

'No, it comes naturally to us, just like walking and talking.' She hesitated, wondering if she should tell him more or not, but decided it might help him understand. 'We never 'take' an ability from an animal without asking first. A Mindmerge is established only on a mutual agreement. Once we have 'been given' the ability we never lose it and we don't physically have to be close to that animal any more. I only have to control my newly acquired abilities to master it, for only then we can call it a Mindskill. At first it was hard and took me some time,' she glanced at Felix. 'That's where it went wrong you see. People thought it was a trick we could teach them. They treated us like witches even though it was just a trait of our species; like our ears and colour shifting eyes,' she swallowed hard. 'They killed us because they feared us. Comyentis were not the only victims of human ignorance and their bloodlust you know.' She stared at Tiger.

Sula's dark brown hair caught Felix's eye, it shone auburn in the light of the fire and again he was mesmerised by how beautiful she was, comyenti or not; he couldn't care less. He had set his mind on her. Trying to focus on their conversation he tried to remember what they were talking about.

'I know,' he said, 'In most parts of the world, people take animals for granted and treat them very badly and I loath it, but times do change. I think people are slowly learning from their mistakes.'

Sula leaned a little towards him, like she wanted to reach into his soul.

'But do they? If I look around I don't see a lot of changes and I have seen my fair share of human settlements and animal abuse, more than my mother ever did. I had to take my chances, to see whether there were any comyentis; something my mother never did. It was however all in vain. I have always done what I could for the caged animals and tried to keep hidden from your kind,' she sighed and remembered what they were talking about. Change. 'Are you *willing* enough to change?'

Felix stared into her hurt eyes and tried once again to place himself in her situation. Yes, he could understand her bitterness, to a point. Her species had been treated with hatred and violence, but wasn't she, herself, doing the same thing towards her enemy, the whole human race? Felix thought about what she had said though.

'To some people change might be hard, having to change yourself; your habits or your attitudes,' Felix started saying. 'Do we listen if we get lectured by someone else or if we get told off? I think we might even rebel more. I know I would!'

'At first, yes, but wouldn't you take it in your stride and listen out of respect to someone else's point of view? I mean; to accept the truth is often the hardest. I know *you* did.'

He smiled at that. *Ah, but I'm different!* 'You have to look at it this way,' Felix tried to comfort her and licked his lips. 'People are stubborn and not always ready to listen and accept the truth. But I know one thing for sure: the people who did all those horrible things to your kind have paid their price by living and dying a lonely unloved life. A person who hurts and kills cannot truly love, and therefore will never *be* loved. Now how lonely and sad is that? That to me is the greatest punishment.'

'Hmm, if it were true,' Sula responded dryly. 'There are so many who live unpunished, even respected in community life, because violence and ignorance is tolerated in your barbaric society. I have seen it with my own eyes! Violence towards animals, children, people; anyone different basically!' Her mouth trembled a little while her eyes flashed orange like the fire and filled with tears. She thought about how people domesticated and caged animals to kill them for their meat; sometimes slowly to preserve their skins or flesh or just for the taste of it...taste, people would kill to satisfy their taste alone. So unlike wolves and other predators, who only killed because they *had* to eat and only took what they needed, never more. And if they do kill more it's usually out of self defence or by accident.

Sula told Felix she more than once witnessed a fox enter a chicken coop at night and anyone by hearing the screeching would think the chickens were being murdered one by one, but actually when Sula went in there to have a look for herself, she noticed that the chickens were all defending themselves and their eggs for dear life and *attacking* the fox with their claws and beaks! Sometimes the fox would flee but usually he would kill his attackers and take what he came for, so that in the morning the farmer, upon seeing the slaughter would blame the fox for being a ruthless murderer, having killed all the chicken and left them mutilated. No wonder foxes had such a bad reputation.

'The farmer wouldn't realise the truth until seen by his own eyes,' she said. 'and what or who is worse; the farmer for keeping live animals in captivity and killing one or two of them every so often, or the fox, driven by the same hunger, killing them all at once?' She shrugged and Felix nodded thoughtfully.

Sula was also horrified to have witnessed premeditated animal cruelty with her own eyes; their death screams and the nauseating smell of burnt flesh and skin would always stay with her. She had rescued and set free as many animals as she could, however it did sometimes mean she was being hunted herself if the trail led to her. Luckily she usually managed to stay safe and keep the animals safe and even taught them how to survive in the wild by restoring to animals such as pigs, cows and chickens who were born in a cage or pen, their natural survival instincts, with her ability. The very abilities she had 'borrowed' in the first place from their kind. But to know that these people would only start breeding and caging animals all over again and never change, de-motivated her. She did as much as she could, but would have liked to have done more.

Felix had to think about her words. He had travelled some, not much, and only near Rosinhill, due to his commitments on his farm. It was true that compared to his village these people she spoke about seemed barbaric.

'Hmm, true, I regret that some people still seem to live as cavemen. Not in these parts though! Nevertheless, did you also see love?'

She shook her head feeling uncomfortable.

'What do you mean?' She had the feeling he was again trying to stick his head in the sand, not wanting to see and hear what was going on in the world around him and continue to live on in oblivion or worse; ignorance.

'Well, did you see the helping hand when someone was in need, the look friends give each other, the arm around someone who needs comfort in bad times, the shoulder to cry on, the kiss lovers share?'

Sula gave him a long glance and bit her lower lip, tucking a strand of her hair behind an ear, now that she didn't need to worry about that anymore. Felix could finally see her face a bit better.

'I did see that part of humanity too, but rarely and almost solely between people; hardly ever to other beings. Children still have it, though, but soon start to copy their elders only to be caught in this dark web of adult life with its traditions and practices. Yes, I have seen people care for the animals they use to work the land, and maybe for their livestock and pets, but only because they depend on them for their own survival. It's a selfish kind of love. They wouldn't think twice about eating them if they were hungry whereas they could be farming more vegetables, fruits and nuts. And what about general wildlife?' She gestured wildly with her hands now, getting herself all worked up. 'They disturb them; they hunt and track them down for their meat and bones; sometimes stupidly and without skill so that the animal suffers unnecessary pain, whilst there are so many other things people could eat. Do you also call *that* love?' Her mouth was set in a grim line. 'Some humans even believe animals don't experience pain, feel, think or have a soul! Remember what you said earlier in front of your people, that we only love what we know?'

Felix nodded.

'I really believed you understood what you were saying even if it was about the giant,' Sula said. 'To me it meant other beings as well. We love what we *know* and *understand*; what we have been *taught* to understand. Anything else is wrong and can be either used, abused, ignored, or destroyed however we see fit!'

Felix lowered his shoulders. He felt really bad, for she was right.

'I can only say that doesn't count for these parts. There are exceptions you know, perhaps hard to find but it's true. We're not hunters, but simple farmers and know we don't need to eat flesh to stay alive and so we don't. It's always been like this here. We only have animals for their milk, but only for our children and we make cheese but just enough. We do keep hens for the eggs and sheep for the wool for our clothes, but we all treat them really well,' and he grinned. 'Maybe we are a bit ignorant or superstitious at times, but at least we're no longer cavemen. We keep small flocks and give them good clean shelter in the winter and we know all of the animals by their faces. And how can we kill and eat something with a face? That's been our tradition for generations. And why should we change it with all the fruits and nuts around and the vegetables we grow?'

'I'm pleasantly surprised,' Sula commented genuinely and remembered all the villages she had visited in the East of Bhan who seemed to follow pretty much the same policy. It was very unusual to find something similar here, in a much colder climate where one would expect people to consume meat over the winter to stay warm. But clearly they had found other ways without harming anyone. Although

Sula did not consume any animal products herself, not even eggs or cheese, and was against keeping animals in confinement she did however respect Felix and the villagers' way of life. They were really almost on the same page here, it seemed…almost.

***

'Remind me to help your people build a couple of barns so that next year you have more options to store your food in.' Sula said and Felix smiled warmly at that.

'Yes, it's indeed a great idea, thank you. Does that mean you'll stay?'

Sula took a sip of her tea and nearly choked.

'Only until the worst of the storms are over.'

Disappointed he poked a stick into the fire, staring in thought.

'Surely you can't be going to that cave? I still don't fully understand. Why that particular cave?'

'I like it.'

'But you don't hibernate?'

Sula laughed at that, 'Hmm, not really. I'd like to though, especially now!' And she yawned. 'I do tend to rest and of course the cold doesn't bother me if I'm in bear-mode.'

'Ah, but I don't think you'll be getting much rest with your new friend around. I'm sure he snores!'

They both chuckled.

Felix licked his lips and met her eyes, locking on.

'We don't own the land,' he said mysteriously to Sula. 'We just look after it for a while. To do that well is our obligation; to give something in return. Even though half of the world is covered in darkness, the other half sees the sun. Even the gloomy side will know its sunrise again. It's a constant balance. *You* can be our sun in dark times.'

She crimsoned at that, playing with her wooden cup that was empty now. Again he hit the right spot with his words. How did he know her name meant 'sun' in her people's language?

He saw what he had done to her and continued his flattery with renewed energy, 'You are an example to us. How you live in harmony with all life around you. If we look into your eyes we see heaven; a forgotten place for us. Maybe that's why people also feared you.'

Sula was speechless. She could only stare at the young bright man talking to her, sharing his thoughts, unique among his own kind and even his village that was ahead of their time.

'Even in my childhood days I used to wonder,' he continued. 'When travelling to other places with my family, seeing how other people lived, why they've lost their way; when and where? All of life seemed so at one with nature. We humans are searching in our own way; conquering; trying to find answers and making them up when we don't find them, but we always seem to grab only thin air.'

'We have a saying,' Sula said gingerly, looking hesitantly at Felix. 'When their stomach speaks; their brain forgets. When their brain speak; their heart forgets. When their heart speaks…they forget…everything.' her voice was so soft, like a mere whisper and it was very sensuous.

Felix smiled at her for Sula did not talk about humans like he was one of them. *That* was a great improvement. 'That's beautiful and very true, Sula.'

'People just don't live up to their potential.' Sula sighed.

'Maybe you can teach us?'

She looked at him thoughtfully only to see he was serious. She shrugged.

'Well, humans don't want to be taught or preached at. People need to experience things for themselves at their own pace and at the right time. Not everyone is ready to receive the truth. Besides…And I have learned that humans only tend to listen to those whom they *think* are wise, but often aren't; leaders and the likes. If people would listen to the *truly* wise ones and open their hearts to the truth that lies within their own hearts, something that cannot be taught, it would be a real start. To look around at the real world instead of the one they've created,' she stopped for a moment to think and held his gaze.

'Like you, Felix; you listen to your pieces of wood. Other people would say the pieces are dead, but you know they're not. Perhaps the spirit has left, but not entirely. Something is still there; you can *feel* it. Life has left its mark and it is exactly *this* that talks to you. You hear it and communicate with it to ask allowance for your vision.'

He smiled shyly at her and nodded.

Time drifted by deep into the night while they sat and talked in front of the cosy fire. And as they listened and contemplated life, a deeper understanding between the human and the half comyenti grew. Felix reminded Sula of her human side; trying to break through her bitterness and pain and she taught him to see through her eyes.

They were no longer two different species; they were of the same kind.

Chapter 8 Sacrifice

How is it possible,' Felix asked in the middle of the night whilst drinking and sharing a cup of delicious apple wine made with honey that he had managed to salvage from the barn. 'that they managed to wipe out the entire comyenti species? You're all so strong and intelligent; surely a human is no match for a comyenti!'

He remembered how fast she had made it to the cave and recalled her bear growl and how she had thrown him away from the giant and carried the heavy sacks of food home, all so easily and with such strength. And surely with their abilities to both defend and even attack their opponents they would have been invincible?

'It's not the first time this has happened. Humans have exterminated other species who were just as strong as us. The fact that we can only use one or two special abilities at any one time means we're no stronger than the strongest or fastest animal. We can only be one animal at any one time. Our enemies were many and in their hands they held something more powerful than claws, teeth, or wings. They had spears or bows and arrows, nets, dogs; giving them the ability to kill from a distance. That's what made you so dangerous.'

She decided against mentioning the comyentis' weakest point; what really led to their downfall and kept quiet.

Felix closed his eyes and felt so mournful he could almost weep. He turned his head quickly to rub his hot eyes, but Sula had already seen him. She moved a little closer to him so that her thigh touched his. She actually felt more relaxed, maybe because of the wine or maybe being in the presence of this caring handsome young man.

'Wave and Tiger,' he suddenly announced, breaking the tension. 'They're the only creatures I feel connected to and really love.'

'More so than with your family?'

He rubbed his nose and laughed at her. 'They are my family, just as my parents and sister.'

'Well, cats will never disappoint or hurt you, not intentionally anyway and they are easily forgiven if they are ever naughty.' And she tickled Tiger under his chin and he immediately started purring. 'They are easier to communicate with; even without words.'

'We have some more cats in the farmhouse, but these two are my favourites and together they are great friends whereas some of them can be a bit moody. The farmhouse used to be my parents', it's where I grew up,' and he smiled warmly. 'We've built a smaller house down in the village for them, so the old farmhouse is mine and my sister's now. She has her own house up in the woods. It's quite noisy with all the animals in wintertime, so we can't live in the farmhouse you see, but we do store things there, make cheese, and it's where I do my wood work. I build and fix furniture and I make my figurines. I do spend a lot of time there, that is why I only need this small house to rest and be myself.'

'Hmm, perhaps you can store some of your food supply in your farmhouse for next winter?' Sula suggested and Felix nodded.

Sula picked up one of the carved figurines, the image of the young man and the cat.

'So, this is you then.'

He nodded, 'I have to feed the goats in the barn in the morning there, so you can see the farmhouse if you like.'

She only smiled at him, so he continued, 'We have great summers here and all kinds of landscapes. I have travelled some, but I've never seen a greater country than this; under all the snow we have luscious woods, gentle mountains, a river with lots of wildlife in and around it and rolling green fields with many flowers,' and he grinned happily. 'And I haven't even mentioned all the kinds of fruit that grow here including the best cherries ever!'

'It does sound special.'

Enough to make you stay?

'I can show you around, weather permitting.'

They were silent for a couple of minutes before Felix said, 'You've not asked me if I live alone.'

She peeked around and shrugged her shoulders and rolled her eyes gesturing at his narrow bed.

'I can see you do.'

He crimsoned at that.

'Yeah, well.'

'You don't have many friends, do you?'

Felix poked in the fire.

'Not with many people, no, and not in Rosinhill, although I know everyone here; but that doesn't make me friends with them. I have my travel buddies, two close friends, who live days away from here though. I had thought about asking for their help with the food situation,' and he glanced at her, suddenly shy.

'And what about you, have you made some friends during your travels?'

'Some, mainly with non-human animals, though but the problem with me is that I can't keep friendships going. I have to fly, literally. And it's hard if you travel like me, you hardly ever go back to the same place twice,' she answered.

'So you've never been in love?'

The question came as a complete surprise and nearly made her jump as if he'd said something indecent. She stared at her empty cup in response and he could feel her leg tensing up against his. After a while she answered the very personal question in a quiet voice, 'Well, just once.'

He tried to look into her eyes, but the fire, which she continually stared at, burned low and it was becoming increasingly dark in the house.

'So you did meet a human? Did you have to give him up because of The Search?'

It seemed like a long time until she answered him, for a knot in her throat was building up.

Why now? 'Maybe, I…don't know…Oh, blast.' She turned her face away and he could see her body shake and hear her weep softly. He quickly laid an arm around her shoulders for comfort and she immediately buried her face in his chest, shedding tears upon his soft knitted woollen jumper. *Made from the wool of his friends the sheep; donated lovingly!* she thought with a hint of humour, but it didn't help her feel any better; if anything it made her feel worse. If only she could hate him! It would be much easier!

He stroked her hair softly and she could hear his heart beating rapidly.

What am I doing? This feels so good, and then moments later. *Who's weak now?*

***

Felix let her release her sorrow upon his chest; it was the most painful lonely crying he had ever heard. He reckoned she hadn't cried for a long time. Maybe she had buried a lot of her emotions in order to survive. A very human thing to do.

'That feels better doesn't it?' he asked softly when her breathing became calmer.

'I was wondering,' he asked to change the subject, as she dried her tears with her sleeve. 'Did you ever meet your father?'

'No,' she shook her head, looking slightly embarrassed.

'Didn't you ever want to?'

'Not really. My mother said he was a nice man,' and she laughed a little. 'Why, what's your point?'

'Don't you think a child has the right to get to know her father?' He made his voice gentle, without judgement.

'Yes, of course I do, that's why my mother gave me his name and told me where he lives or at least used to, I even got close once, but-'

'You're afraid of what you might find.'

She sighed deeply, 'Maybe,' *he is human after all.*

'But did you never miss having a father?'

They exchanged a long look, it made him feel dizzy, like he was under her spell. For a moment he thought he was asking her too many questions again as she still looked sad.

'My mother was a mother and father at the same time.'

It got slightly colder in the house. They could hear nothing else but each other's breathing.

'If you…reproduced with a human,' Felix carefully began, for he sensed she had lowered her guard. 'you could perhaps stay somewhere longer–'

'And give up The Search?' she asked loudly pressing her lips together in distress and knitted her brows.

'Not necessarily; maybe for a while. You must have thought about that. And there is the promise to your mother. With a halfling child new hope would arise and you wouldn't then be the only comyenti anymore, right? I reckon a child of yours will share your abilities?'

She looked confused at him, growing even more tired.

'Yes, it hopefully will,' she sighed. 'But naturally the bloodline will be thinner every time we reproduce with a human and will therefore die out eventually. That's why I can never give up The Search. I need to know if there are others out there, not just to reproduce with, but to know if there are more doing the same thing; searching, trying to securing the future of comyenti species or bonding with humans,' *like I'm doing now, stupidly?*

Felix touched the side of her neck lightly with his fingertips, making her shiver and burn at the same time.

So, it's possible…he thought.

'Did you know,' she quickly exclaimed. 'that my name means 'sun' in my language?'

'Sula,' he whispered alluringly holding her gaze. 'The sun is a symbol of light and hope in many countries.'

'Yes, the last hope of my people.'

He shook his head grimly.

'Too great a burden for one to carry I should say.'

She nodded. *But somehow it no longer seems so heavy,* 'I think…you have made it lighter for me. You've given me hope.'

'I have?' His blue eyes began to twinkle even in the dim light she could see, like two stars. She smiled at him. His face came closer to hers. His lips brushed hers lightly and she could feel his warmth and yearning for her, but he was a gentleman.

Oh, how easy it would be to just lose herself in him and let him give her what she needed. To be soothed, comforted, wanted and loved. A child…Her body ached for him, but her mind urged caution.

You've been lonely; it wouldn't be right to give yourself to the first man you came across and make the everlasting powerful Heartmerge!

Even though she somehow knew it was more than mere lust and the need to have child she felt for this man. He was so understanding and compassionate and very much how she imagined a comyenti man would be.

'We really need our rest,' she said nervously looking at his comfortable bed. She hated herself for breaking the spell.

Felix stood up, feeling embarrassed and stupid.
I'll have to be careful with her, very careful.

They prepared themselves in silence for the night. She could feel Felix's insecurity and shyness. She was also too tense and unfamiliar with men; she always avoided them as much as she could, trying not to get involved in anything like this and now it seemed that it had gone too far already.

I must leave as soon as possible. But she so wanted to be with him tonight, to hold his warm body close, to have him touch her and comfort her. She was not a fool; she had seen him looking at her in that special way and somehow she had a feeling he wouldn't mind if she used him to father her child.

There was one thing that bothered her deeply; she was not as young as him anymore. She still bled, even if she was nearly forty. What would Felix say if she told him her real age? She was twice his age for sure!

What am I even thinking of? I am not planning to do any of this!
"Remember the Oath," the voice of her mother sounded again.
'Will you go with me tomorrow to see my farmhouse?' he asked her

from his bed in front of the fire. It was dark, with only the bright stars shining palely through the only window. All Sula could think of were his eyes. It was freezing outside and they both sensed the weather was getting worse again.

'I would love to,' she responded honestly.

She could hear him sigh in relief.

'I somehow thought you would leave, especially given that the weather might be turning.'

'Really, and risk crashing into another bridge?' she joked and heard him chuckle.

'I was hoping you could stay the rest of the winter?'

She didn't answer.

Oh, no! I've been too pushy again! Felix thought too late.

'You don't have to decide now,' he quickly added. 'I don't want to pressure you, but it seems silly to travel in winter and be alone in some cave, no disrespect, whilst you could be here warm and comfortable with friends. If you would like some space we can always put you up at my sister's who is travelling south and won't be back until spring,' but when she still didn't respond he added, 'All I want you to know is that you will always have a roof, a friend and a bed to come back to.' Sula's heart almost stopped.

'Not... necessarily in that order...of course.' He smiled.

'Thank you, Felix...I really appreciate it very much. I've never experienced such true kindness before.'

'It was about time you did.'

***

I should have kept my distance,

Sula couldn't sleep; she had never felt this awake before and so...restless.

That was the plan, the promise, if I ever encountered a suitable mate, she said to herself. *I have gotten too close. But I am not like you, mother, I know that now! I can't do that to anyone!*

That evening with Felix had been so cosy, warm and honest, even if he was human. He was different, that was obvious, but who knew; what if it were just words to impress her and get her into his bed?

Why was she questioning her intuition? She was usually right about people. She never felt so close and open to anyone before, she found herself thinking again about his gentle sparkling blue eyes and supple hands and the way he moved them through his blond hair... His voice and slim body. It made her head spin. She felt her body heat up and her skin felt moist underneath the thick woollen blanket.

She felt herself trapped between two worlds. Her mother had always warned her that this could happen.

Well, I am after all part human! she retorted to herself.

She could hear Felix shift on his sheepskin bed on the floor whilst a storm started raging outside.

Comyentis were family people once. We were forced to live in solitude. It was never my choice, nor my mother's. Although I love to be alone with nature and wildlife, I cannot always shut human company out from my world. Not Felix, anyway,

She would have to sacrifice a lot to stay in his house, but not if it was just for the winter surely? To be with him...

When will you experience this again? It's not the end of the world if I stay a while is it?

Chapter 9 Heartmerge

The family farmhouse was not that far away from Felix's house and it turned out to be a nice morning stroll further up the mountain, away from the village. Rosinhill itself lay surrounded by fertile mountain slopes; now covered with a thick layer of snow. Felix explained that it was on those mountains where he let the goats graze during the summer and autumn months. He would gather them together late each afternoon to milk them if need be or sometimes he would stay the night in the pleasant mountains. He had followed in his father's footsteps. Felix also pointed out the cultivated meadows and vegetable plots close to the village surrounded by thorny hedges to protect the food from being eaten by both goats and rabbits. Then they came across the pens which gave the animals shelter from the snow and frost.

Felix showed Sula some of his neighbours' livestock as they walked further along on that misty morning. She saw cows and horses that were well looked after in their warm dry stables. Then he showed her a large oval barn which had a roof that lay so heavy with snow, it looked ready to collapse.

'As you can see, it needs a new roof in springtime; the snow has done too much damage this year,' Felix said to her as they went inside through one of the doors. Straw covered the floor and it smelled a little sour to Sula's enhanced sense of smell, but it didn't bother her too much.

She helped Felix feed the goats a combination of hay and clover while he threw away the old and trodden straw from the floor, replacing it with fresh supply that he got from another section of the barn where he also held his milk buckets and cheese making equipment.

'Did you know that goats are one of the oldest domesticated animals?' Felix asked her whilst working.

'Hmm, yes,' Sula replied a little moody and stroked one that munched, gently on the nose, remembering wild mountain goats happily jumping and climbing with great ease in the southern mountains. 'You must know, I don't agree with it,' she almost whispered, Felix wasn't sure if she was talking to him or the goat. 'People, keeping animals imprisoned.'

'I don't suppose you do, but we talked about this last night. Most of the year they have a pretty awesome life in the mountains. You should come back in the summer and see them jump and run freely! When the days grow shorter I keep them in fields closer by. At night I lock them in just to keep them safe; from wolves *and* giants.' And he grinned. 'I told you, I merely protect and look after them.'

He went about his work again.

There were a few cats inside, some had been asleep since they arrived, whilst others were trying to win their attention as they worked. Sula smiled when she noticed a big red one meowing very loudly at her while she communicated with one of the goats. She struggled to divide her attention between so many creatures at once. Comyentis were easily over-stimulated and so she learned the need to focus on one task at a time, lest she lose the use of her abilities. She had found out the hard way.

'You hear them, right?' Felix asked.

'Hmm, sometimes I receive words and sentences from pets that live very close to humans, such as yours. But from wild animals it's mainly images they send me; they show me things. Although after a Mindmerge I can't really tell what it is, neither of us has to make any effort, communication flows so easy, I wouldn't be able to tell if it's words we use. We simply understand one another.'

'I would give anything to talk to my cats and goats. What would they say!?' He sighed dreamily leaning on his pitchfork. Then he suddenly stared at her and asked, 'Hey, can you ask Gertie if she still suffers from toothache?'

Sula smiled, faced the goat to her right and after a minute or so gave Felix a satisfying answer. He had been studying her intently and she could feel his gaze without looking at him. With so many questions, he was bursting, but he had to contain himself, that much he knew.

'So when you merge your mind with that of another creature to adopt a new skill, what happens?'

'For a moment our minds merge and we become one,' Sula answered, looking up from the goat to Felix.

'One…And you can still think and remember who you are?'

She laughed and her eyes shone brighter. They were so beautiful and again her exceptional beauty touched his heart.

'Of course.'

'But you change only in the mind, not your body?'

'No, please!' And she shook her head violently.

'May I watch you one time when you do a Mindmerge?'

Her smile faded visibly from her face.

'Sorry, I don't do that,' she replied coldly.

Felix was disappointed but tried to hide it.

'Well, we're finished here,' he announced dryly. 'Will you help me remove the snow from the roof?'

'Certainly.'

And they went outside. Felix fetched two shovels and helped her climb onto the roof. The snow had frozen the day after it had fallen and after that there had been another fresh layer on top of it so it was just too heavy and couldn't come down by itself. A little ladder stood by the wall to reach it.

They started working on shovelling the snow off, working without a coat. It would have been hard work if Sula hadn't been there. Felix watched her in amazement lifting heavy shovels of snow one after the other without much effort. When they were almost done, Felix accidentally threw some snow on Sula's head and shoulders helped by a gust of wind. She jerked her head away while she yelped, spitting the snow from her mouth, 'Felix!'

'Oh, I am so sorry,' he said, a little shocked. But when she stood straight up and he saw her green tunic and purple vest with scarlet lining all white, even her brown leather leggings and black boots and her head covered in snow, added to that the annoyed expression on her face, he couldn't help himself but laugh. She narrowed her eyes in anger, but on seeing and hearing him, she soon melted like the snow. She took up her shovel and threw a large pile of snow on him yelling heartily.

'Revenge!'

They had a fierce snow battle on the roof until Sula suddenly fell and slipped a good ten feet at least, landing on the soft pile of snow they had just created below. She sank into it. That in itself caused Felix to burst out in more laughter, but when he didn't see her emerge he panicked.

'Sula!' He slid off the roof after her. 'Are you alright?'

She popped out of the snow and when he extended his hand to remove the snow from her head, she grabbed hold of it, pulling him towards her, so that he fell to the side on his stomach with his face in the snow. Suddenly she sat on top of him and buried him beneath a thick layer of snow. Starting to stand up, she smiled, but then she felt him roll over faster than expected and suddenly his hands were on her hips and he tipped her over, so she landed on her back.

He continued laughing and they were both throwing snow at each other hysterically.

Felix had to stop as he coughed, wiping the snow from his red wet face. They both stayed sitting with tears of joy rolling down their cheeks, catching their breath, but happy.

The melting snow had made its way via Sula's neck down her spine. It also felt cold and wet down her front; between her breasts. She stopped laughing.

'Great, my extra cloths are still wet from washing them this morning and now this! What am I going to wear?' She wiped her wet hair from her face.

He looked at her with tears still in his eyes and chuckled, 'I'm not sure unless you wear my clothes, but you would drown in them. Maybe–' But he stopped himself, biting his lip, cocking his head slightly.

Sula stared thoughtfully at him; trying to read his mind, which of course she couldn't. She'd never tried to link her mind with a human before, she wasn't sure she would be able to do as they would surely resist. It wouldn't work without asking first or without the special intimacy shared between two lovers. Maybe she had to try sometime, in order to understand them better...

While she gazed into his summer ocean-blue eyes she saw a sudden change in them. His pupils grew dark; in a wave of desire. He wasn't laughing anymore; he just stared at her with a yearning look. She suddenly felt so overwhelmed by his want for her, that she felt it too. Not knowing if it was her own feeling or his. He embraced her so closely as if just to warm her, but she knew better than that. He held her so tight while they both shivered.

Neither of them wanted to let go, so they sat there a while in their shared embrace.

'Come,' Felix whispered to her and gestured her to stand up, extending his hand to her. 'Let's dry your clothes at home.'

***

They walked back to Felix's cosy house where it was warm. He pulled off his jumper and shirt and hung them over a chair in front of the fireplace. With a naked torso he walked over to Sula, who didn't know where to look.

'You're cold,' he softly murmured and lifted her chin to look at him. She jammed her eyes closed for a moment, somehow expecting his lips, but heard him say, 'Let me take your clothes.'

She stared at him, not able to do anything, breathing faster, water from her wet clothes dripping on his floor; drip, drip, drip. He helped her out of her furry leather vest, standing behind her, but then she just stood rigid.

'Don't fight it, Sula. Stop fighting me.'

She felt him brushing her damp hair to one side and then tenderly kissing her ears, nibbling the earlobes, kissing her neck, slowly pulling her green tight tunic up at her waist. She felt his hands on her skin, warm and although slightly calloused, his hands were surprisingly tender and attentive.

Her tunic and leggings fell to the floor one by one and standing in her under wear, which was low at the front, showing her full breasts and the cleft between them, she felt herself getting more aroused. He cupped her breasts with his hands and kneaded them gently but urgently. When she did not protest, but moaned softly, he played with her hardened nipples. She bit her lower lip at that and felt her knees getting weak. He turned her round to face him and kissed her more passionately now. She placed her hands around the back of his neck, playing with his hair, stroking his strong shoulders. In one movement he lifted her up in his arms and carefully laid her down on his bed. When his hard body met hers, she felt his soft lips on the hot skin of her neck and breasts. She could do nothing other than return his passionate kisses and caresses for it was all she really wanted. He was the perfect mate for her.

Who's weak now?

'Am I,' Felix spoke when he stopped for a moment. 'your first then?'

'You are, Felix,' she panted.

He smiled his beautiful boyish smile and whispered alluringly in her ear, 'I'll be gentle. I'll show you what to do.'

'Have you…?' she asked hoarsely.

'Yes, but only a couple of times. She was a childhood friend. We dated a few weeks a couple of years ago. Trust me, I know what to do.'

She gave him a half smile at that. Now this was a first! In all other territories she was the expert, she possessed most abilities and had skilfully mastered them, having travelled and met many species whom she merged with. But in matters of the heart and physical acts such as mating, she had no clue. No one had ever taught her that! Finally Felix was leading her in the one thing he apparently was very skilled at indeed. With confidence and patience he explored every inch of her, slowly moving from one place to another, making her more and more aroused. But always waiting for her reaction and making eye contact; he suspected not every woman was the same and all liked something different. He found his way with her and she liked it a lot. In fact she had no idea it would be this good. With his fingers and his lips, he was certainly melting her frozen heart…

She knew that mating rituals with most species could be a lengthy process; especially the courting. Sula assumed she and Felix had done all that, and that the actual mating could be over within the blink of an eye. In this case it was certainly true; Felix did not waste any time, he did his best to hold out for as long as he could so that she would enjoy it too. He teased and touched her in all the right places and made her more and more ready. And when he entered her; he held her hands above her head lovingly, fingers intertwined, moving at first with gentle thrusts, then more persistently. It certainly burned her and hurt her, but it was a pleasurable pain, unlike anything she'd ever felt before and she found herself floating in it, reaching higher and higher. They were dancing, almost a rhythm. When he came first he cried out like a lion. His roar made her smile, he bit her on her neck too like a cat!

She felt his heartbeat close to hers; fast and loud, almost deafening. She dug her nails into his back, holding him close while he was still inside her. Felix had to catch his breath, but then continued to kiss her as he pulled out and slowly made his way down her body, kissing her toned but soft stomach, licking her belly button which made her moan. And when she felt his warm persistent tongue between her legs it was only a matter of a few heartbeats before she felt herself reaching for the sky; only flying could come close to that feeling, and she too screamed out.

***

When Sula awoke, Felix was still half wrapped around her body; as if he was afraid she might leave him.

I should go, she thought, even though her heart and body protested and wanted to stay in his warm almost familiar embrace.

It is not fair on him, but he knows I should. I'm not human enough to live here.

Silently she removed his arm and lifted his leg from between her legs and silently slipped out of the bed. The warm sheep fur tickled her feet in a pleasant way. Suddenly she felt as if Felix had defrosted her somehow.

It's the Heartmerge, I know it is!

She shook her head and stared out of the round window. It grew dark and she remembered the villagers had arranged a party for her that coming evening; they had insisted on it even though she tried to decline. She flinched with anxiety.

Sula tiptoed away silently from the bed. The clothes she worn that day still lay scattered on the floor where Felix had dropped them. She tried not to think about the pleasant moments just passed as she pulled her nearly dry clothes from the rack above the fireplace and got dressed.

When she pulled her dark cloak firmly around her, it felt like protective wings. She buttoned it up and hauled her rucksack on to her back. She looked one last time at the sleeping man in the bed. Softly she murmured, 'Farewell... Felix.' She turned quickly to open the door while pressing her mouth firmly against the welling tears.

'Is this going to be a habit?' she heard a familiar croaking voice from behind her. She didn't turn round, but instead stood numbly in the doorway with her back to him.

'Sula?' His voice sounded so utterly sad, she had to step outside and run.

'Sula!' She heard Felix calling after her helplessly but she didn't stop running.

He fell back on the bed in despair covering his eyes with his hands.

'Felix?' A small voice sounded suddenly from the door opening moments later.

He quickly sat up in hope only to stare into his twin sister's eyes. Feline had been away on her travels, like she always did every autumn and winter. Why was she back so soon? Not being able to think clearly, he dropped his head in his hands and grumbled, 'Not now, sis.'

Feline walked towards Felix after dropping a couple of oranges from a bag she had been carrying to sit beside him.

'Who was that girl I saw running off like she was chasing the wind? Was she the one who persuaded the giant to bring back our barn, what's her name...Sula?'

When he didn't respond, she shook her head, not understanding his silence, even though they were very close.

'What did you do to her, bro?'

He glanced at her with red eyes and got up, covering his nakedness with a blanket and stood in a corner of the room.

'I chased her away,' he scowled. 'That's what I did!'

'How?' she asked for she only knew her brother to be sensible and loving, most of the time.

'By being too eager and...stupid!'

'Oh, boy,' she tilted her head in the same way he could. 'Then... you must be in love.'

Brother and sister exchanged concerned looks. They looked so alike.

'Deeply.'

Feline smiled at him.

'Why don't you go after her, then? Come on!'

He returned her thoughtful gaze by saying, 'Because...I cannot cage a rare bird, sis. That... would be cruel.'

***

Sula had ran out of the village to the nearby woods. She needed air to breath, but when she got there, she felt so empty inside, she knelt down in the snow and cried. Her heart felt heavy and there was a tight knot in her stomach when she thought about leaving Felix. Every step away from him had felt heavy and near impossible. She already missed him...and never seeing him again was something she could not face.

So, this is love? Or is it just the Heartmerge doing this to me?

She never thought she could be affected this way. Her mother never mentioned this, so maybe her mother had never experienced love.

Oh, Felix, you haven't made my burden lighter! You have made it worse, for now I am caught!

She stood up and kicked a snow-covered trunk with her boot. 'No!' screaming out loud, she focused on the wolf.

'We don't belong here, you and I,' she said to the beast inside her. 'Even if...Felix is different.' she sobbed.

'I might be carrying his child.'

"Good, now leave!" the voice of her mother demanded on the wind blowing past her.

No! I don't want to run away like you did! Run and hide and all for this stupid search! I never promised you that!

Wearily she got up and closed her eyes to pray for a solution. The spirit of her mother wasn't any help. She said things that Sula didn't agree with.

But in her heart she'd already decided, from the moment she turned around to face Felix that first day at the bridge. She could have taken off without ever looking back, but something had held her back...

I followed my heart then; I'd already decided not to walk away, but can I hold myself to that?

Sula knew that she had at last found what she had been so desperately looking for. It had perhaps not only been a quest for her species, but also a personal one.

She had truly found a companion of the soul in Felix. A soul mate, maybe more than any other of her own kind could ever be, if she had ever found one, or ever would.

Not one of her bloodline then, but a kindred spirit; a bond stronger than anything else.

***

When she stood at his door her heart pounded so heavily in her throat, it frightened her.

All these new feelings, these new emotions made her feel dizzy.

Am I making the right decision?

But she didn't doubt anymore when she found herself face to face with her friend and lover after knocking on his door and seeing him. She could tell he had been crying and that hurt her.

They stared at one another, as if in shock. His hair and eyes wild, his expression unbelieving as if he couldn't believe she had come back.

But then a relieved warm smile came to his lips and fresh tears started to flow.

Whatever may come, I will be here for you, my love, always and forever, she heard him say in her head…

Sula's eyes widened in surprise; he hadn't opened his mouth! She listened again. Of course she would hear his thoughts. They had shared their bodies and souls; the unique Heartmerge for lovers. Although a mystery to her; according to her mother, who couldn't tell her anything since she herself had run away before she ever experienced the effects of it and thereby breaking it; it could last a lifetime if unbroken.

Sula had no idea if Felix was able to hear *her* thoughts yet though…or if he ever would, being human.

Why does she look so stunned, has she never seen a man cry?

She fell into his open arms and laughed and cried at the same time on hearing his thoughts again; a result of their deep feelings and their hours of passion.

Felix thankfully closed his red rimmed eyes and was barely able to breathe, for she hugged him so tight. But he didn't care, she had come back to him. At a loss for words and with a warm glowing feeling around his heart, he nestled his wet face in her neck most gratefully.

PART II Spring Tears

Tears, idle tears, I know not what they mean,
Tears from the depth of some divine despair
Rise in the heart, and gather in the eyes,

Down to the world unseen.

Chapter 10 Twello

Two little feet moved rapidly across the dark forest floor. Ferns and tall grass stroked against thin bare legs.

The small boy was no more than skin and bones but he moved sleekly like a cat in the night. He seemed to know where he was going and very determined to get there quickly. Only once did he stop and turn around to look back through the trees that he was about to leave behind, before going out into the open exposed meadow. He panted heavily and small plumes of hot breath met the cold night air. Tears gleamed in his pale blue eyes and there were smears of dirt on his face and skinny bare arms. His clothes were rags. He hesitated but only for a moment.

His brows knitted together in anger as he remembered something. Fighting back his tears he headed on, crossing the grassy meadow. Everything shone blue in the light of the thin new moon high up in the starry sky. It all looked magical in this light, but the boy hardly seemed to notice, for he had only one goal in mind. There it was, rising dark in front of him a few hundred feet away: The tower.

With wild eyes he stumbled over an unseen object and fell. A cold gust of wind lifted his hazel hair and his mouth trembled slightly before he found the strength to stand.

As he came closer now he felt his heart pounding like a caged animal in his small chest. Swallowing away his fear he stared at the high wall of the tower he had to climb. There was no doubt in his mind, he had no other option. Seeing the faces of his scared parents in front of his inner eye; he knew he had to continue.

He knelt down and crawled through the dense spring grass towards the black tower.

When he reached the stone wall he waited for a while in an attempt to slow his breathing down before pressing himself flat against the wall. He shivered both from the cold and anxiety.

He knew there had to be guards upstairs, they had told him that. Examining the stone wall with his delicate but long fingers he found the men had been right; the wall had big rough rocks sticking out of it slightly. An adult could not have climbed it as their feet and hands would have been too large to find a suitable spot to get a good grip. Yet it was perfect for a child; but not just any child. The men had seen the boy climb earlier that day. They knew he would be perfect for the job and for that reason had captured him and his parents.

Twello had always been good at climbing trees and walls; better than all the other children in the village. Silently he cursed that skill now. If it wasn't for him, he and his parents would still be safe. The only way to make it up to them now, was by climbing this tower wall and bringing back what the men wanted. There was still time. But once he had climbed the wall, what then? The men had given him instructions for that too, but what if he would be seen once inside? He was petite yes, but he wasn't invisible.

Searching, touching the rocks with his numb fingers, he found his way and pushed his weight up, finding suitable places for his feet to stand on. It took some time, and although he had until dawn, he was careful not to slip and fall.

All the muscles in his small body of six summers ached but he bravely ignored the pain as he made ascent, nearing the edge of the high wall. The wind blew harder here and he could smell that he got closer. There were definitely guards; he could smell the leather of their armour, their sweat, piss and beer.

Carefully Twello peeked over the edge of the outer wall, holding himself up on just two tiny rocks for his feet and two for his hands. He saw only one guard; standing solid with his face turned away from him. Twello saw the narrow hole in the inner wall that the men had mentioned, it did look small but he would fit through, he was sure!

Twello placed his hands and arms across the broad edge of the wall, placing one foot carefully on a corner of a rock before pushing himself up. Silently jumping over, he dropped to the cold hard floor, lying flat, never taking his eyes off the guard. Luckily any sound was muffled by the noise of a sudden gust of wind.

Quickly he made his way on all fours to the other side; to the actual tower, towards the hole in the wall. The turret of the tower itself was narrow and higher than the outer wall with only a few thin windows near the top.

He dove head first into the dark hole unseen by any guard. Twello crawled forward, feeling like a rat as he went, moving further through the oppressive dark gap which was almost like a tunnel. He couldn't see a thing but he just pressed on, knowing that it would lead to what he came for. The floor was wet and stank of damp.

After a few feet Twello heard muffled sounds and as he came closer the noise became clearer. He could hear screaming and the clatter of weapons. Blinded and on his knees, while using only his hands he found he couldn't go any further as the little tunnel ended. It had been closed up. A big rock now lay in front of the opening; however it didn't cover it completely.

A small beam of light seeped through the gap. It should have been open according to the men who had said it was some sort of ventilation outlet in the other-wise stuffy tower. With his fingers Twello tried to move the heavy rock to the side. Using all his strength he noticed the sounds were becoming louder. The gap had become a little wider and through the crack he could now see what was going on: men fighting, falling and dying in terror. There was no way he could go in there, even if he could manage to move aside the rock completely. He would surely get killed in the fight or…maybe he could use it to his advantage. The men might be too busy to see him. Yes, that was it; the fighting men were a distraction away from him. With new-found energy he pushed and pushed, when suddenly the rock moved to one side and he inched his way through the hole.

Chapter 11 The Wizard

Seeing more clearly now as the room was lit by torchlight, his eyes searched through the huge space. More than ten men were fighting just in front of him while more than a dozen lay dead. A large wooden table had fallen on its side and numerous chairs lay about broken on the floor. The men fought on with a clattering of swords, screaming at each other in the chaos. They were very much like the men that held his parents hostage, Twello noticed. Big brutes who were smelly and noisy.

One of the men had wanted to come along with Twello, saying that he didn't trust the boy with the task. But Twello had sworn to his parents, on his life, that he would come back to them; with the stone. The men would be waiting for him in the woods as they knew that he would return to his parents whether he succeeded or not.

Twello tried not to look at the fighting men and blocked their awful cries of terror from his mind. At the far side of the room, in a corner to his right, away from the men, stood a pure marble white pillar. On top of it beneath a glass bowl sat a dark green gem. Without hesitation he quickly hid behind the fallen table. When he thought the coast was clear he stayed as close to the cold floor as possible, crawling with his tummy touching the floor, and swiftly made his way over to the pillar. He had to crawl over a dead body and standing up he quickly looked back at the men and then at the stone in front of him before lifting the bowl up between his small hands and reaching inside for the precious gem. He was surprised at how little the stone weighed.

He heard an awful deep roar from behind him and felt a dull pain against the side of his head. Dropping to the floor he held on to the gem, his treasure, and he rolled over to see his attacker. A large beast of a man stood over him with the tip of his blade above Twello's throat.

'Give that to me boy!'

Twello pressed the gem closely to his chest with terror in his eyes, reluctant to give up his prize, frozen to the ground by fear.

'Have it your way then!' the man bellowed, raising his sword. The man's eyes grew bigger on seeing the green gem suddenly light up. The boy saw it too and his mouth fell open. Suddenly the man's body shook and his limbs moved like he was dancing; only from the expression on his face it was no dance of joy, but of pain. His jaw was clenched tight as he fought the pain, silently while his eyes bulged with a look of terror and disbelief. With his sword still clutched in his hands and with white knuckles he fell onto his knees beside Twello, eyes wide-open.

Twello moved backwards, keeping the precious stone close to his chest; thinking that it had saved his life! Then he saw another man where the other had just stood seconds before but this young man looked different than all the rest of the ones fighting. He stood there with grace and he seemed better dressed. He also had a different weapon in his hands; a simple iron staff. It still pointed towards the dead man as he eyed the boy up and down with a confused look.

A wizard! the boy thought, they hadn't told him about that! Ignoring the dull pain in his head he jumped back towards the gap in the wall. But before he could reach it he heard a terrible low sounding noise which caused a deafening pain in his head. He had to cover both his ears with his hands. The stone, which had dimmed in colour by now, dropped to the floor. The boy fell with it, covering the gem with his tiny body as if his life depended on it.

The tall man stood beside him, watching him curiously. He dropped the iron staff and looked with empathy in his slant green eyes at the boy. Eyes as green as the gem but with more depth and golden flecks. His bronze face was narrow and delicate almost like that of a girl, with high cheekbones and fine arched black brows, but his jaw was set in a fine strong masculine line. A black band covered his forehead and part of his ears. A few strands of his long raven hair fell over his headband. He looked more the part of a thief in his tight black clothes and long robe than a brute criminal, like the other men in the room had been; all dead now apart from the boy and the strange man.

The boy crawled on top of the stone with his whole body, clinging to it for dear life, fearing the man and crying silently over his fate.

'I don't want to hurt you. All I want is the stone,' the young man spoke in a soothing calm voice, deeper than Twello had expected.

Their eyes met; the terrified dark blue eyes of the boy and the kind calm but determined eyes of the mysterious man.

'Please don't kill me, please don't!'

The man sighed and knelt by him. The boy jerked away, watching the staff carefully. The man spoke to the boy in a comforting voice, 'I won't kill you. I don't kill small boys. Don't be afraid. It's the stone I want, not you.'

Somewhat relieved by this, the boy relaxed a little, still holding on to the stone, sitting upright.

'Not this one!'

'Look, boy. It's not a normal stone. I'll give you all the gems you want, sparkling and bright just like this one in exchange. Look at me. You know I can.'

Their eyes met and Twello saw sincerity and kindness in them.

'My name is Shazar, what's yours?'

A blink of his eyes and a swallow in his throat later the boy yelled, 'But I need this stone!'

Shazar shook his head. 'Not you as well?' And he pressed his lips tightly in thought. 'Can you walk?' the mysterious man asked as he examined the boy. Standing up, Twello nodded.

'Alright, we have to leave now, before more come.'

More? Were there more? Sudden fright again in the boy's eyes struck the man's heart and he helped the boy up, who seemed less afraid of him now.

'Please protect me against them; you will, won't you?' He had decided to trust the man. At least he had killed the 'bad' men.

Shazar glanced from the boy to the stone and then back. He had no choice.

'I will, I promise. Now come, stay close to me.' Grabbing the boy's hand, they made their way silently through the room into a hallway which smelled of urine. The man walked in front with the iron staff in his free hand carried like a torch.

Shazar wondered how a boy this young; so small and fragile had made his way into this well-guarded place. He had seen him run towards the small gap in the wall; was this the way he had come in? But what about the guards outside? He himself with all his abilities had barely managed to make his way through. And moreover, why would this boy need the stone? What question did *he* have that needed to be answered? Shazar himself had a very good reason to put himself at risk. But what about the boy?

Rumours brought him to Karashne; a small village by the sea, kept safe by the prophecies of the temple priestess. This priestess was said to have a special stone which helped her establish a link so that she could predict the future and tell the people what they wanted to know; the truth. The stone was called-not very originally-the Truthstone.

Shazar wanted one question to be answered and one only, no more. However, before he could pay a visit to the priestess, a week before his arrival, she had been kidnapped by bandits and presumed dead by the amount of blood found in her temple, although her body was never found.

The villagers mourned for their priestess but also missed the Truthstone with its helpful guidance. The stone had been in their possession for generations since the first priestess. They called for brave people to come forward to help win back the stone, stolen by the bandits of Malegesch and had raised an army to face the men who had killed the Count of Karashne and inhabited his tower. The army was soon defeated as was the second and the third, leaving the brutal bandits with at least a dozen men remaining. Another army was to be sent a few days later to kill off the last of the bandits and finally take back the stone, but Shazar wanted to obtain the stone for himself, before the army could, even though it was not really his to take. Shazar planned to return the stone to the village once he got his answer. The bandits were surprised he was on his own and were cocky, but soon paid for their mistake…

Shazar needed to concentrate on any sound, any smell; any indication of any men left in the tower. He had no problem with killing for the right cause and this certainly was exactly that, but he would only kill when absolutely necessary; which was debatable of course, for when was killing a necessity? But not for Shazar who had strict rules of his own for that.

As they made their way down through the tower, Shazar suddenly picked up a faint murmur. He stopped and pulled the boy towards him who looked questioningly at him and he urged him up the tower again. They slipped into a narrow side passage and halted in front of a door.

'Make no sound, you look out that way. If you see or hear anything, call me straight away,' he whispered and concentrated, closing his eyes for a short moment as he chanted almost soundlessly. 'Your mind, my mind, your heart, my heart, your strength, mine…'

Shazar put his forehead against the door and his hands. He sensed a human body behind the heavy wooden door and with better ears he heard a soft shallow breathing and even the faint beating of a heart. This person, whoever it was, was wounded. He could have easily have carried on and exited the tower but something in Shazar told him not to. And that instinct was not to be ignored.

Chapter 12 The Once Priestess

A few more chants and Shazar knocked down the door with a single light kick of his foot. The frame cracked with a crash. Twello looked back at it in shock. This was the strongest man he had ever seen! With a loud bang the door fell onto the wooden floor and gave way to a big cloud of dust circling up in the air. It blurred the vision of Shazar, but sharpening his eyesight he could see more clearly.

There was no time to waste. It wasn't so much the guards on the outer wall he feared, but the villagers of Karashne bursting in. He would have to return the stone to them, but feared he might not be able to let go of it himself that easily without hurting anyone.

Beyond the cloud of dust he saw a woman lying in one corner; her arms spread towards the door as if she had reached out to it, but had fallen down in her attempt.

She was barely dressed in rags of torn dirty clothes that once had been a fine and impressive gown. Now the bright green and blue was stained with not only dirt but also dried blood. Her limbs were bruised and her long blond hair tangled and grimy. The once priestess…

Shazar was shocked for a moment, for he had seen a lot of barbaric things in his life; but none seem to match this.

Watching the results of their crimes…

This woman who was thin, but not emaciated, must have lived imprisoned in this tiny dirty room with only a hard bed and no blankets. A latrine in one corner, an empty plate and cup, neither windows nor fresh air and she had had to endure whatever they had done to her for weeks. Her body must have been beaten repeatedly, because there were old and new bruises and cuts.

Tears stung Shazar's eyes at the thought of it all and the sight of the seriously hurt woman; human or not. He was glad he'd killed them.

Her face looked swollen and her pulse so weak Shazar feared she would not live much longer.

Without hesitating he carefully picked her up in his arms and lifted her over his shoulder and with a free hand he picked up his iron staff. Twello stared in awe at him.

'What are you looking at? Come on!' he ordered the boy to follow him and saw to it that he held on to the gem, which of course he did. Descending the winding stairs they didn't meet anyone until they left through the tower gate. Two guards came running over, but Shazar, for a moment letting go of Twello's hand, used his staff on them too and the men dropped lifeless to the floor.

The Tower was finally deserted and would be for a long time.*

~~~

Entering the dark woods they hurried on into the night with only the owls and other creatures of the dark as their witnesses. Twello couldn't see a single thing, but Shazar of course did; using his night vision. Walking confidently as he knew his way Shazar held on to the boy even though he still carried the woman. Twello could not escape his grip and could hardly keep up with his fast pace but he didn't want to stay behind either. He was about to object when Shazar finally stopped and laid the woman down on a grassy meadow underneath an old oak tree.

Give her strength, Shazar prayed to the tree as he placed his robe over her. He stood up to see to the boy who was about to crawl away into the darkness.

'Not so fast.'
'You promised not to hurt me!' Twello yelled as he tried to run.
'I did, so I won't,' Shazar answered solemnly as he held him by his narrow shoulders.

*Read *Chained Freedom*

'Then let me go or help me!'

'Help you with what?'

'Protect me when I give the stone to the nasty men. I'm afraid they will hurt me and my parents.'

'What men?'

'Those who keep my parents,' Twello whimpered and his bottom lip started to quiver.

'They'll free your parents in return for the stone?'

The boy nodded in the dark but Shazar had seen it.

'Great Yentil, what misery holds this world?' he cursed but his eyes grew softer as he saw the boy cry. His tears falling silently down his cheeks, bigger than Shazar had ever seen.

'I will help you free your parents,' Shazar said soothingly.

Twello's eyes lit up.

'You will?'

'Of course, and I never break a promise.' He placed his hand upon his heart with mysterious dark eyes and his voice was kind and honest.

The boy suddenly lowered his guard and hugged the man by his waist. Shazar was startled by this simple gesture and held his arms up in surprise. It was a long time since anyone paid him this much kindness. *Children,* Shazar thought with a pang in his heart, *even if they are human; are so genuine,*

Shazar stroked the boy's hair slowly, uncertain and not used to comfort a child, glancing at the unconscious dying woman, shifting his thoughts to her.

I have to help her too if I can. If this woman is who I think she is...

'You have to save the lady too, Mr Wizard,' Twello sounded concerned, as if he'd read his mind. 'Can you?' Twello looked at Shazar with so much expectation and confidence; he felt his heart sink at this innocence.

Well, let him believe I'm just that, a wizard.

Shazar knelt by the woman. He had no healing gifts apart from his

111

own survival skills and he was able to replace, if needed, his own limbs, if severed. He had the octopus to thank for that. He was sorry but he couldn't help her, even if she was human. He quickly tried to block out old painful memories, before they could disturb him again. Of all the powers he had he wasn't able to use them to save his own family...

He felt her wrist, there was a weak pulse and her face was ash grey apart from the reddish blue bruises. He stood up and sniffed for water. The boy never realised he had gone and came back, in the blink of an eye, with water to splash on the woman's face and arms. This was more important than his secret at this moment. For no matter how deep his hatred of the human race; he could not forsake women and children in need. It was men he had to watch out for; his only true enemy.

~~~

Shazar cared for the woman's wounds and rubbed her cold feet and hands. The boy told him his name and where he came from.

'How long did they give you, Twello?' Shazar asked whilst attending to the woman.

'Until dawn, Mr Wizard,' Twello answered with frightened eyes, worried.

'My name is Shazar, not Mr Wizard. Now, where is the place they are keeping your parents?' Shazar asked looking up now.

'At the other side of the woods; in a clearing where they have torches and a bonfire so I will remember.' He clenched his fists.

They could easily make it in time but Shazar felt reluctant to leave the woman to die by herself. Was he getting faint hearted towards people? Well, she probably wouldn't gain consciousness, so it would be alright he figured. He could save the boy's parents, kill the men, keep the stone and perhaps even come back to check up on the woman; or at least send someone for her. Yes, that would be the plan, for he didn't want to be involved any further than he already was. The stone was the most important thing now. It was the key to everything he lived for.

Just as they were about to leave, Shazar heard a faint murmur. The woman was coming to. At that very moment she opened her eyes, and even though it was dark, she knew she was somewhere else. In the fresh air! Slowly she breathed it in. Staring up she saw branches and the night sky, stars! Was she free at last? Had she died? Why was she so cold? It wasn't supposed to be cold in the Afterlife. Looking down at her body and feeling the hard cold forest floor she smelled oak leaves. She noticed there was a warm woollen blanket on top of her. Well, that was certainly a change. Then there was a soft rustle and she could make out a face in the faint light. The lips moved saying, 'You're free.'

Free…

She raised her brows and blinked a couple of times, trying to move away from the man staring at her, even if he did have a kind face.

'Go away,' she managed to say with a husked cracked voice.

Shazar knelt down by her and the boy came to sit beside him. They waited patiently for her to recover. Shazar offered her some water from his flask. She blinked her eyes a couple of times and refused. He tried again; her throat and mouth were dry but this time she swallowed. Her chest moved irregularly up and down underneath the blanket and her breathing sounded raspy.

'Who are you? Where am I?' She quickly glanced around but she could only make out dark trees around her; she could hardly see a thing in the light of the crest of the new moon.

'Take it easy, you're badly hurt.'

'Mr W…er Shazar freed you and brought you to safety,' Twello spoke with big eyes gesturing at Shazar.

She glanced at the boy and wondered what was happening. A man and a boy in the woods? This man freed her?

'The door was… solid wood,' she whispered as talking clearly hurt her. 'I've…tried many times, even when I was still…strong.'

'You should have seen him! He is so powerful and a w-' Shazar held a hand to the boy's mouth and gave him a warning look. The boy held still instantly, fearing him.

But then she remembered the ruckus downstairs and her own cries for help and hoping it had been a rescue team. Her memory was blank from there on; so she must have blacked out. Her throat was still dry as paper and she felt it itch. Starting to cough she tried to sit. Shazar helped her. At his touch she flinched so he moved back instinctively with the palms of his hands towards her.

The young priestess continued coughing and he gave her some more water. She drank until the coughing eased off.

When she could speak again with tear stung red eyes she stared at him.

'You came… for me?'

'I carried you away from that dreadful place,' Shazar said softly. 'Now lie back and rest some more. Are you in pain?'

She shook her head, even though her whole body ached, but she was getting accustomed to it. Pain had become her trusty friend.

She is strong for a human, Shazar thought.

'Are they dead?' she asked in a dull voice.

'They are.'

She closed her eyes a moment and said thanks to her gods, but not to him.

'Where are the others?'

Her cheeks had gained some colour and her green eyes shone fiercely as if she was still fighting demons.

Shazar and the boy exchanged looks.

'It's just us.'

'No, I mean the villagers; where are the others who helped you?' She sounded restless and uneasy.

'I needed no help.'

'That's true.' The boy nodded proudly for being there and having witnessed the scene. Now he had something to tell his parents about.

Incredulously the priestess stared at them. She knew how many bandits there had been.

Suddenly she spotted the stone; her gem, dark this time, in the boy's lap. Her mouth fell open.

'You found it,' she gasped.

Twello glanced at it and back at her face.

'I don't know how to thank you,' she spoke without moving her eyes from the stone, 'but I'm sure you'll be properly rewarded by my people.'

She stretched her hand to the gem as emerald green as her own eyes with the light of the moon on it. The boy immediately wrapped his body around it. She knotted her brows in confusion.

'I know it's a beautiful stone, boy, but you can give it back to me now. It's *mine*.'

Twello looked at Shazar for help.

'That is true, but I am sorry, my lady...' Shazar spoke calmly, not knowing what to say next when he saw the hurt in her eyes. The priestess stared at him a short moment with empty eyes, then a look of understanding appeared before she answered in distress, 'I had not thought the villagers to be this cruel; to save me first and then to keep the Truthstone from me because I am no longer...', she added in anger, lower lip trembling, 'You should have let me die in there!'

'Better to die whilst free,' Shazar spoke with his eyes clouded. 'Anyway, the villagers and their business are of no concern to me. Only the stone matters.'

'What? You two are simply thieves who came for the stone just like...them; not for me at all?!'

'I suspected you were still alive... Ashanna. It's been months and the villagers did send armies, but these rough savages were stubborn and strong.'

'You're telling me? The Truthstone made them blind, blind for power! They defended the thing they thought was going to give them just that! Just like the villagers who think the stone more important than me. Of course I should have known...' her voice waned and she looked up at the trees.

'They had found so much blood in your temple,' Shazar gingerly spoke. 'That they presumed you were dead, Ashanna. If they had known–'

'Blood… yes, they wounded me alright. As for the villagers….All this time I thought they respected me, honoured me. Me; the oracle, the priestess, the guardian of the Truthstone…while it was the damn *stone* they worshipped, not its reader; its link to the world. They needed my abilities. Not me at all,' she whispered with such sadness Shazar felt it in his own heart.

'You are the only one who can hear the stone.' He glanced at it; he had not yet had the opportunity of examining the precious gem himself. For a human to communicate with a stone was highly unusual; even if it was not a normal stone. Only *she* was able to hear the stone as a priestess and that intrigued him; *she* intrigued him.

'Without you it is just a rock, right?'

She nodded and stared from Shazar to Twello in the dusk of the night.

Twello rubbed the green gem like a pet. Shazar had seen it glow in his hands, so he knew it was more than just a rock outside of the priestess' hands. He didn't need her.

'You keep it, for all I care! I don't want to see that thing again for as long as I breathe!' And she tried to grab it from the boy to throw it away. Twello backed off and the priestess fell on her stomach on the forest floor. There she lay crying, her whole body shaking. It had been her gift and curse; this stone.

Twello looked worried but Shazar shook his head as if to say not to worry as he placed a soft hand on her shoulder. Ashanna shook him off, not caring about her gown, or what was left of it, coming undone.

'Leave me!' she whimpered and he and the boy sat down a few feet away.

'She is mad,' Twello said with big eyes.

'No, not mad, but hurt, very hurt,' he put an arm around the boy.

'and her wounds need time to heal and not just on the outside.'

'But we must go soon!' Twello whispered.

'We will, I promise.' Shazar crossed his heart like he had done before.

Chapter 13 The Truthstone

'They did try to rescue you. Not just the stone,' Shazar explained. 'Save your petty story, please. I know better than that. They know I'm...violated and worthless to them.' Ashanna's voice was cold and distant again as if he knew she had to be in order to survive, for that was what she was doing still.

'Then... you're no longer able to hear the stone?'

'What's it to you? Oh...I get it.' She narrowed her eyes at him with loathing.

'No! I'm sorry, I'm just trying to understand this oracle thing,' he responded apologetically.

The priestess tried to avoid his olive green eyes with the golden specks. It was as if he could see her clearly even in this dim light. She however could only see the contours of his face and body and those kind eyes; dark but very green. They reminded her of her stone.

They were seated under an oak tree. Ashanna had calmed down and regained some strength. Shazar made movements to leave.

'They will find a new priestess just as easily,' she said staring into nothing.

'So there are others who can—' Shazar started.

'No, we are very rare! It will be hard to find a new priestess, but she will come. There has always been one.'

'You are upset.'

Ashanna tried to read his face and in doing so narrowed her eyes.

'You would be too if they placed the stone in the centre instead of you as a person. My body and wits have been used and abused in a poor excuse to get me to tell.'

He swallowed away the knot in his throat.

'Yes, human – er… men can be cruel. So the villagers will come after you to get their stone back?'

'Not me, *only* the stone. They need it to help find a new priestess,' she sighed.

'Well, we have to get going now.' Shazar stood and called for the boy who waited impatiently nearby, biting his nails. Shazar quickly explained where they were going.

'But we won't leave you here of course,' Shazar said whilst packing the few things in his rucksack which he had hidden, including his iron staff, and hauling it on his back; it looked heavy.

'Why not? Don't tell me you need me to answer one of your questions for I won't!'

Shazar ignored her. She had more life left in her than he'd realised.

'I don't think the villagers will be that harsh on you when they find you. You have always served them well and after all it wasn't your fault. You merely protected the stone. But I am surprised there was no one to guard *you* in your temple.'

'There was never any need for that. Everyone *knew* that I was the only one who could communicate with the Truthstone. These outsiders thought there was a secret I was hiding from them, but there wasn't. The stone only works with the chosen one linked to it. I never protected the stone. I was trying to save my own skin, though rather poorly I'm afraid.'

'Hmm. They…hurt you because they could not find out how the stone worked, even though you told them that?'

She nodded. 'And I can't lie as long as I am bound to the Truthstone but they didn't believe me. They didn't believe I was the only one who could work with it. I wanted to prove it to them, offering to answer any question they might have. But they wouldn't give the stone to me, saying it could be a device or weapon in *my* hands.'

'So they feared you; that's why they hurt you.'

He understood that all too well. It had hit home; all of this. His kind was used and abused like this in order to get the magic out of them. Feeling a connection with the priestess, he walked over to her with

Twello by his side, wanting to do something to make her see that he understood. He extended his hand but she ignored it, turning away from him.

'It's a male thing,' she said through clenched teeth, her anger rising, misunderstanding his gesture. 'Power and dominion that sort of thing. That's why the stone chooses its *own* owner, or link as we prefer to call it. And those have all been women throughout time. So it would be in safe hands.'

'Knowledge is power.' Shazar nodded.

'Something they could never possess without me. Instead they were killing me while I could have answered all their questions. All of them.' Tears were shining in her eyes.

He held his silence for a moment out of respect before he asked, 'All?'

She sighed at that, rubbing her dirty forehead and he was sorry he asked.

'Within reason, but sometimes vague and in riddles, but trustworthy.'

He was silent again for too long, because she felt him thinking. He looked away, embarrassed.

'Of course *you* have a question too. That's why you came, didn't you? Not for me, not for money or fame but to have one question answered.'

'I did.'

His honesty struck her. 'Well, no such luck for you there I am afraid,' she said with a tight face, holding her emotions in. 'Good luck with your quest.'

'With all due respect, I would never force you to give me an answer to my question. Surely you need time-'

'I will *never* answer *any* questions again.'

'Why? Is your link with the stone broken now because of your loss of your er... maidenhood?' He was sorry he mentioned it, for it made her feel awful and the memories were still so fresh.

'I...' she stammered, *Say yes, say yes! To make him stop asking!* But she

120

found it hard to lie, even now that she was allowed, for she no longer served the people of Karashne. But there was still a link and he suspected it. Why was there such a stupid rule that she could no longer be a priestess then? He dared not ask, but surmised it was yet another of the primitive rules found all over Bhan.

'I don't want to keep you from going, please leave,' she mumbled.

'You still have a link don't you?' Shazar did not need her himself, for he trusted he could establish a link with the stone himself, but he would not let her think that either.

He gently took her arm. 'Please come.'

'No. I will answer all the questions you have and after that leave me alone.' Ashanna said suddenly, too weak to refuse.

'I'm most grateful, but the boy's parents don't have longer to live than dawn, so we must go now.'

She stared back at him. 'You can't make me come with you. I'd rather die here.'

'You don't mean that. Look, I don't want to hurt you. I want you to be safe whether you believe me or not. Just in case the villagers won't be as kind.'

'Who said I will allow them to find me? I will go…that way.'

Shazar smiled faintly at her courage and stamina.

'Same direction we're heading!'

'Then I'll go that way!' And she stood up and started walking slowly through the trees in the opposite direction.

Twello urged him to come and pulled at his breeches, but somehow Shazar would not let this woman go. With all his heart, he couldn't.

He was right, for she stumbled; too weak to walk after a few steps. He lifted her up over his shoulder.

'What are you doing?' It sounded soft, but still strong. 'Let me go.'

One stroke of his hand and a whisper, 'Sleep.'

And she fell into a deep slumber while he carried her effortlessly.

~~~

'How many men are there, Twello?' Shazar asked while walking.

'Three.' The boy stared with big eyes at him. The man grew higher and higher in his awe; he was his personal hero now and he wanted to be just like him when he grew up.

'Pah! That should be easy.'

They made their way to the men's camp without need of the boy's directions as Shazar could smell them from afar.

They looked at the small camp amongst the trees. There was an old haggard brown tent and a fire with one man seated and one standing, on the look-out, waiting for Twello to return. Their horses stood nearby and looked nervous because of the smells of cooked meat on the fire. It nearly made Shazar gag as he was so sensitive to such smells. Not just because it was human flesh he smelt; the men were cannibals, but any meat had the same effect on him. Shazar feared the worst for Twello's parents.

He covered Ashanna with his robe, to keep her warm and hid her well. Then he thought about the boy. It was too risky to let him approach these brute men by himself. They might kill him on the spot. No, Twello would have to hide and wait. He told him so. Twello entrusted him with the stone. Shazar placed it in his rucksack and took his iron staff as he concentrated, unafraid, breathing slowly, watching the two men near the fire.

Jumping in front of them he pointed the staff at them and even before they could respond they were electrocuted, dropping dead to the floor.

'For Twello,' he whispered.

The flap of the tent opened and a third man, ran out growling, grabbed a crossbow and confronted him. In one heartbeat Shazar stood next to him and touched the brute with his staff, which was not a weapon or device, it only looked that way to outsiders. Shazar had no need for weapons. The staff was merely for show, running the electricity coming out of Shazar's hands. He didn't want people to know his secret. And that was only one of them. The man fell to the ground, dead.

'Good old faithful electric eel, you make it so easy!'

It was from *that* creature that he gained the ability to deliver the lethal strike. But he had used up most of his energy as it took a lot of strength to be able to do this. In nature the electric eel would be able to issue such a powerful strike only once before requiring some time to recharge. Shazar had broken contact with the eel now but still felt drained.

Quickly he stepped into the tent. It was dark and smelly. It had the stench of death and with a pang in his heart he instantly knew he had come too late. Sharpening his sight he saw the sad scene of two lifeless bodies; a man and a woman, Twello's parents.

Great Yentil!

Why hadn't they waited? It wasn't dawn yet. Once again mankind had proven not to be trusted; never to be bargained with, but the boy had had no other choice. Guilt struck Shazar's heart; what if he had been quicker, would they have lived?

What was to become of Twello now? Shazar knelt down and felt the woman's neck; she was already cold, killed early in the night. He would have been too late anyway, even if they hadn't rescued Ashanna. Twello's mother had been ravished, by the look of her and afterwards her throat had been cut. The father had been heavily beaten before he had been stabbed to death. Their limbs had been cut off and were missing. The sickening smell of the meat outside became worse. It reminded him of other times long past.

The boy was not to know how his parents came to meet their end, or he would grow up with hate in his heart. He was too young. Shazar had been young himself when he witnessed the loss his parents to brutal men.

Feeling for the boy and thinking about Ashanna as well, he returned sadly. How could he soften this heavy news?

~~~

'No! You're lying! You gave the stone, mum and dad are safe!'

'I'm so sorry Twello, those men lied to you! They took your parents' lives shortly after you left! Trust me, there is nothing you or I could have done. Do you hear me? Nothing. It's not your fault. Those men were evil but I took their lives in return.'

Shazar held the boy gently by his thin shoulders. He knew Twello would feel guilty, blaming himself for not speeding up and returning with the stone. It might haunt him for the rest of his life, so Shazar had to keep repeating it, in the hope that he wouldn't.

Twello became uncontrollable and kicked and punched the man in his stomach and chest, but Shazar felt like iron to Twello so that he hurt his hands and started to cry heartbreakingly.

Ashanna woke at the sound and stared questioningly at Shazar. He sighed and briefly explained. She said nothing but walked over to the boy who by now was hitting a tree. She gently laid an arm around his shoulder and knelt down before him taking him in her arms. Feeling the warmth and softness of her body; missing his mother, he wept loudly until he could weep no more. Ashanna wept with him in silence, both for him and his loss and for herself and the injustice of it all. The boy crawled into her lap like a baby and wept himself to sleep. Ashanna held him and stared into nothingness, stroking his hair.

Shazar had watched them out of concern, keeping an eye and ear on the surrounding woods. The animals were silent as the night moved into day, most had been scared off by the noise.

Chapter 14 Teardrops

'**W**hy do men kill?' Twello asked Ashanna with red rimmed eyes, when he had woken up.

'Because they can,' she replied with wise knowing eyes.

The stone lit up bright green while she spoke; the same colour as her eyes. She spoke the truth.

Ashanna held the Truthstone in her hands as if weighing it. It felt so familiar and yet so strange.

So much suffering over such a small rock.

She had communicated with it almost daily; the gem being her only friend but now it would not answer her question: how to get rid of her disturbing memories. The stone was too close to her and could not help her except by responding in a vague reply.

"Time will heal your wounds and time will fade the memories", it had replied. Time, of course, she could have said so herself. When she was old and senile perhaps. By that time she might have half-forgotten these terrible months, but for now? What could she do to block the horrible memories? What could she do to forget?

"Love is the answer. The child needs a mother. The woman the child, and the nomad will bring salvation", she got in reply which made her frown.

Later that morning over breakfast Twello was quiet. He had mentioned he had no family or friends that he could live with. He and his parents had just moved to a village not far away from the Tower but he had never liked it there, nor did his parents. His father had a carpenter's job which brought in enough for the family to live on, so they had stayed. But now that they were gone, it was just him.

Alone, like me. Orphaned, Shazar thought. *And Ashanna.* Shazar stared at her, feeling sorry for them both. Trying to distract them he said, 'You must be a wise woman to have all the answers to those burning questions that we all have.'

Shazar disturbed her and brought her out of thoughts. She looked up holding a dry piece of bread in her hands; she forgot she had been eating. They had eaten a simple breakfast of old bread and berries. Ashanna noticed Shazar hardly ate anything.

She saw him now in full daylight and she tried not to stare at him all the time. He was beautiful in every way; smooth bronze skinned without so much as a hint of stubble on his chin or above his mouth, which was strange, as she had not seen him shave. He was gracious in every movement. His body was slim and muscled, his facial features delicate with high cheekbones, arched dark brows and a kind mouth. His manners were genteel and patient and he was softly spoken. She had never known that a man could be all this. She had only known the rough farmers and fishermen from Karashne who came to her temple in search of answers and more recently of course, her kidnappers. Whilst in her temple she led a solitary life in order to avoid distractions from her work. She had seen boys over time change into tall hairy overweight men. Just like the brutes that had captured her. She looked away. Shazar was a man too. Although she should have been wiser than to think all men evil. But at this moment all she wanted was to be was alone, away from everyone.

'I'm not,' she said at last. Shazar looked at her as if he'd forgotten what he had said to her but then he remembered.

'But you must have asked the stone a thousand questions and know the answers?'

'I have,' she responded coolly.

'And?'

'None are to be shared. *You* are not a priestess!'

Disappointed, he rubbed his chin.

'Wise is the one who acknowledges that there is always more to learn…through experience,' she spoke.

'Very true, but you must have gained a lot by now from the people who came to you, through their experiences and the answers the stone gave you?'

'I wish I hadn't.'

He frowned at that.

'If I could wish for anything it would be total... ignorance,' Ashanna said with pursed lips. 'It would be so much easier. If I look into the eyes of a small child or a simpleton I feel... envy.'

Shazar nodded gravely, understanding this too well.

'Things do make more sense now, even pain and suffering. I know the true reason for that now,' she spoke. 'I know the truth.'

'Violence has a reason?'

She bit her lip, trying not to answer, thinking hurt too much. She had never known she would experience such violence herself, for she had never wanted to know her own future like so many of her patrons had.

'Not really, no. People are both good and bad. Both sides are represented in each of us. There are situations that bring out the best or the worst in us. It's up to us which we choose to be and we have to accept the consequences of our actions. One can only appreciate goodness or happiness by understanding both sides. By experiencing the dark side, once in a while, or sometimes for an entire lifetime. It can't be day all the time, night is also required. Balance keeps the world alive and also us. People don't always see it that way. They get bitter or angry with their fate not understanding that we can change our own fate. It takes strength and courage to be good, to do good in darker times. But those who do survive can become enlightened and teach others,' she chewed her lip and Shazar saw the pain in her eyes and felt it.

'You see, people are not punished for their deeds, but *by* their deeds. They punish themselves by the life they live now or in the next. To know *that* is a great comfort to me.'

She had said her last statement through gritted teeth, remembering the brutes in the tower and their actions.

'They get what they deserve hmm?' Shazar asked.

'I don't care if you believe it or not, I know!' she said with a pursed mouth, looking away.

'No, on the contrary. Besides, the Truthstone told you and you are a Truthteller; that's proof enough for me. It's just that you are different from any person I've ever met, Ashanna. More advanced and much wiser,' he said kindly, smiling with surprised eyes at her.

She would have blushed out of embarrassment normally but she was still too battered and in shock for his flattery to affect her. In order to survive she needed to let go mentally and be somewhere else, anywhere but in her body. She still felt that she wasn't really there, still floating and light headed, although she started to notice things around her. It felt very much as if she still witnessed it from the outside, looking in. She tore her eyes away from his reluctantly and remembered what the stone had answered, *"The nomad will bring salvation"*. Would that be Shazar?

'I was more concerned from the victim's point of view,' Shazar said. 'What about them, Ashanna? Like you, what did *they* do to deserve pain and suffering? Bad karma as they say in the Eastland?' *And why you?* He really wanted to add, for he really wanted to understand fully.

Ashanna just stared at him, unable to answer, too distracted by his features, by him being there; her mind felt blank. She shook her head. He understood her silence and nodded kindly, not wanting to pry any more than he had already.

She felt the stone warm in her hands. Her lifelong friend and her foe. She hadn't been able to lead a happy life with it; she was good and had done only good but now she had come to know evil. She had no need for the Truthstone anymore really, but to live without it would be such an uncertain life. But it had to be done and she knew it. It was time for her to start living. She couldn't bear to look at it anymore. And in an instance she threw it forcefully away. It landed in some bushes a little way from where they sat.

'They'll never find it!' she exclaimed with triumph.

Shazar had followed her throw with his quick eyes. He still needed it but didn't like to mention it to her. He needed to keep his secret to himself for now. There was no need to involve her and cause her more trouble.

Ashanna stood, looking at the boy who slept again. Twello got feverish and he mumbled and wept in his sleep.

'Take good care of him,' she said, needing to get away. The boy's cries upset her too much. In a way the child and his hurt were the very image of her own tormented soul. Thinking that the child in her had died a long time ago when she first started to receive answers from the stone, she now knew it wasn't so; the child in her had just been asleep. When the brutes took her away and tormented her daily they had torn away the controlled wise priestess who understood the reason why. What was left was a wounded child, weeping inside her, without parents who could comfort her.

'What?' Shazar replied in shock.

'Thank you for saving my life,' she said with modesty, although she wasn't sure if she was happy about it or not.

'But where are you going?' he asked with concern painted on his face.

'I'll head southwest. I have an aunt living there.'

'Can you not return to your temple?'

'I'm not welcome anymore or able to do my work there. I am no longer pure you see. Those are the rules, even though none of it was through my own choice.'

Shazar silently cursed the people from Karashne for their cold hearts. He touched his headband which covered most of his ears; his black almost crimson hair fell loosely over it.

'And you can't live in the village either?'

'How can you even ask that?'

The shame and the looks of sympathy from the villagers would be too much for her to bear. Her face showed this.

'Your aunt it is then. But what about the boy, would he be welcome there too?'

'He is *your* responsibility, you found him!'

'But I don't know anything about children! You're a woman and I…I'm a nomad.'

She raised her brows at that comment, forgetting what the stone had advised her before.

'You'll do fine.' She turned away and got up to leave.

The boy woke up and started crying when he saw her leaving and ran after her. He hugged her tightly around her waist and she froze at the touch. She hadn't expected him to attach to her so quickly.

Shazar smiled smugly.

~~~

'It looks like we're stuck with each other for a little while longer.' Ashanna spoke kindly to the boy, ruffling his brown hair.

'He sure needs someone right now. I am glad you have found each other.' Shazar commented, glad not to be burdened with the child himself. There was no way he could have cared for someone that young whilst continuing with his search, living a rough life in the wilderness.

He packed up his things quickly and nodded at the boy, apologising in his mind.

'Goodbye, stay close to her. She will protect you from now on.'

Twello stared at him disappointedly because Shazar would leave him but he understood, for a wizard would have many more important things to do than to look after a boy.

'Take these.' Shazar walked over and handed Ashanna a small package.

'What's this?'

'It's an ointment of healing herbs for your bruises. I applied it earlier when you were unconscious. It needs repeating tonight. They'll heal sooner that way. Do take some rest soon though, you're not fully recovered yet.'

Silently she took it from him, trying to avoid his eyes with the orange and yellow flecks in the green of his irises like shafts of sunlight. They seemed to shift in colour and the green sometimes seemed darker, almost green-brown. Was that possible? Would that make him a wizard, like the boy had mentioned earlier? How else could he have rescued her from all those men? She was too tired to think about all that now.

She stood so close to him now that suddenly she could feel the presence of the gem nearby… Shocked she stepped back only to see it shining green from within his rucksack, she could see it shining through the fabric, as if it was calling out to her, however…she couldn't hear its subtle voice.

'You took it again!'

Shazar stared at her questioningly but she grabbed his rucksack from his back and upon opening it tore the stone out of his bag and showed it to him. He closed his eyes in shame. He thought she wouldn't notice. How wrong he had been.

'I need it, I told you,' he almost whispered.

'Why? I told you it won't work without me!'

'I saw it glow once in my hands!' Twello interrupted.

'What?' both Shazar and Ashanna echoed loudly.

The boy crimsoned and felt smaller than he was.

'When?' Ashanna asked him kindly, calming him with her voice.

'In the tower when a man wanted to kill me, just before Shazar came to rescue me.'

'In your *hands* you said?' she asked him.

Twello nodded.

Shazar was glad that she was too occupied with the boy to worry about why he would have taken it.

'It only shines when the stone picks out a new priestess or in answer to *me*,' she said confused, her eyes filling with tears. 'I was too far away at that moment and had none of the physical contact required,' she glanced at Shazar. 'You *and* the boy were there.' She now looked at them both, deciding which of them had the gift. But surely it had to be the boy as Shazar wasn't a *virgin* or was he?

'There is only one way to find out,' she said and placed the stone in Twello's hands. After a few breaths in time it started to shimmer. They were all speechless.

'Im…pppossible!' Ashanna stuttered after a moment, staring at the boy and the stone. Twello's face was unreadable.

'Only *women* are chosen as Priestess of the Truthstone. Unless you're a girl?'

Ashanna looked Twello up and down, whose eyes narrowed in anger.

'I'm not!'

'Perhaps it was time for a change,' Shazar said.

She turned with confused eyes to him.

'Well, it doesn't matter anyway,' she sighed. 'for we're going and so is the stone.' And in one movement she took it from him. The stone stopped glowing immediately. Disappointed and hurt she tried to hide her tears. A boy, what was the stone thinking! She wanted to throw the gem away again, and this time she would choose a roaring river. It would take hours, or even days to find it, Shazar thought, perhaps never, if it reached the sea. He was quicker this time and grabbed her wrist hard enough so that she dropped it to the floor.

'Let go of me!'

Ashanna hit his shoulder hard and when she found out he wasn't defending himself she hit him again and again. It felt good to release her anger and pain onto someone else.

Exhausted she finally stopped, realised the goodness in this man and started crying. Shazar gave Twello an apple and ordered him to go and sit underneath a tree by the river.

'This will only take a moment. It will be alright, you'll see,' he calmly mouthed to the boy, so Ashanna wouldn't hear.

~~~

Shazar let the woman cry and when she wept softer he put his arms around her. At first she fought him again, trying to escape his gentle but firm grip, then he spoke to her softly as a father would to a child. She started trembling and understood that he meant no harm.

'There now. Just cry, Ashanna, let it all out. You're not alone anymore.'

She held on to his arms and cried on his shoulder, wetting his black woollen tunic.

'It's over. No one will hurt you ever again.'
'How do you know?' she sobbed, childlike.
Because I will see to it.
Shazar wished he could promise her that but he had his search. He was weary of it, now more than ever. The nomad in him fought his constant desire to settle down somewhere with a woman like her. But no, that could never be. She was human.

'Listen, where I come from we have a saying,' he began in his low gentle voice. 'that the World Sea is the gathering of the tears of the Moon and the Sun. When Bhan sprang forth from the Sun, the Moon couldn't stop crying, because it meant that from now on the Moon and the Sun would be separated for all time, whereas before they had been one...'

Ashanna had stopped crying and she listened.

'The Moon and the Sun missed each other so greatly that they chased one another day and night forever only catching the mere reflection of each other. But they could never reunite again. The ash and fire that their separation left on the lonely planet, their child, upset them so much that their tears sprang forth. *That* was the birth of rain. In those early days it rained for days on end, forming a rich salty sea, spreading more and more until the whole world was covered by sea. This intrigued the Sun and Moon greatly, however separated they were they would watch the reflection of the sunrise and sunset in the great sea and the reflection of the moon and stars. They stopped crying, for all that they saw was too beautiful to be sad about. They also noticed that the Sun was warming the sea so that life started on their child Bhan. Algae, seaweed, sea stars, fish. The moon gave the small beings a soul. More complex they became and more diverse and richer in shape and numbers. Scented flowers and dragonflies so delicate and the colours of it all! Witnessing this, the lovers praised this fact and smiled down upon the lower beings, their grandchildren. No longer were they sad and no longer did they cry from sorrow. The Sun and the Moon had accepted their fate and rejoiced in the life they brought to the world below. After some time the World Sea dried up slowly and land emerged so that the creatures could inhabit it making the world even more diverse. For years and years it went well, but then natural disasters started happening. Over time there were ice-ages, earthquakes, landslides, volcanic eruptions and the Moon and Sun saw the creatures struggle with the fierce laws of nature. Sometimes they interfered, settling things, trying to save their favourites. However soon they understood, for the Sun and the Moon needed to learn as well, that these minor creatures were only a part of the greater universe. Moreover the sun always shines behind the clouds and will rise again after a dark night. Good things always came after a disaster, so they learned to just let it happen,' he paused a moment taking a deep breath.

'When it rains the sun weeps for this mere fact; those are hot tears, hot rain during summer days. When the moon cries; cold tears. Their tears *always* bring new life and help to sustain it. Without water there is no life. So you see, rain, tears are good and it's just as important as dry days. And were it not for the droplets of water, the sun's rays could not create a rainbow,' he made his voice even softer when he concluded, 'Your tears eventually will bring something good, even though you can't see it now.'

~~~

Never in her life had Ashanna been comforted like this, not even by own her mother. When she was a child her mother had been distant from her and always seemed so busy and her father was always at sea, being a fisherman. She had only been six when the stone had called to her after the death of the previous priestess, and from then on her training had begun. Her parents visited her only once in a while, and the stone soon taught her everything. The villagers provided her with food and shelter. As the years went by her parents had begun to look up to her, like the rest of the villagers and look down on themselves, being simple people. They were ever so proud of having such an important daughter. She hadn't thought about them for years as they had visited her less and less and she had no time to pay them a visit, for her work had always been very demanding and tiring.

Shazar had comforted her. Not only did his story fit right in with her belief in good and bad and the all-important balance, but she thought to herself how her own parents could have been more to her if only they had had it in them. They were probably never comforted as children themselves, so as a result they hadn't known how. That saddening thought was replaced by Shazar's presence. He had been a parent for her, just now. The way he had told her this pretty little tale. She, a wise woman being taught by a man. That had never happened before, only the stone had taught her. She had begun to regain her trust in men, in people. He had done that for her, although he didn't know this yet.

Ashanna leaned back and avoided his eyes, drying her own.
'That…was kind of you.'
'Not a big deal. You may seem a tough priestess but you're fragile, just like everyone else.'

She smiled for the first time and he noticed through the bruises and stains that she had a lovely face, though not overly attractive with her nose perhaps a little too long and her eyes a bit too close together. She had very bright intelligent eyes, and she had the most beautiful smile. He found himself thinking again that it was a pity that she was not of his kind. She was lovely both within and without and she had similar powers to him. If she could do a Mindmerge with a stone; she might be capable of other things, most humans couldn't. That stirred an interest in Shazar.

She seemed to be aware of herself for the first time and said suddenly, 'I'm going to have a proper wash before I leave.' She stood and walked over to the river's edge.
Shazar just nodded at her.

He saw the stone lying on the grass and quickly picked it up. Now was his chance. He didn't want her to find out he was different, that he was probably able to hear the stone as well.

That makes three. It will be the end of her!

He also didn't want to hurt her feelings by still wanting his question answered, even though she had no idea of the importance of it.

Let her think I don't care for that anymore. She needs healing. She mustn't find out that I have her stone again,

He concentrated and closed his eyes in order to begin the Mindmerge, 'Your breath, my breath, your mind, my mind, your soul, my soul…' He began the chanting.

The stone started to shimmer…

Chapter 15 The Chosen One

'You can make it shine too?' he suddenly heard a small surprised voice: Twello!

Annoyed, Shazar looked up. He had forgotten about the boy.

The stone shone bright green in his hands, awoken, ready to be spoken to.

'Of course, because you're a wizard, right?'

'Right.' Shazar smiled warmly at the boy, genuinely touched by his faith in him.

'Can't we keep it?'

'I'm afraid not. It's already brought too much trouble. Best to get rid of it.'

Twello nodded fast, holding his breath. 'But I can hear her.'

'Hear who, Twello?' Shazar asked curiously, for that was special indeed.

'Calling me, saying my name. It doesn't frighten me, it sounds a bit like…mummy.'

Tears suddenly filled the boy's eyes again. Shazar pulled him towards him and put his arm around his tiny shaking shoulders.

He sat there for a while with the boy until Ashanna came back; all washed and clean. She not only looked better but she felt better as well. With Shazar's blanket around her, draped like a dress with a knot over her breasts, her hair hanging wet on her shoulders, she held her wet washed rags in front of her.

Shazar's blood suddenly ran faster through his veins. He tried to ignore it and instead looked down at his hands where the stone lay.

He felt weary and had stupidly forgotten about it for a moment. It was too late. When she glanced at him she saw the stone in his hands glowing brightly in the fading evening light…

'The boy,' she spoke with wide eyes. 'and now you as well? Is… e…everyone a…able to talk to it now?' She was so stunned that she stuttered again.

He sighed and bit his lip, shaking his head, thinking fast. He had to tell her at least something, that much he owed her. She already suspected he was a wizard, so let him be that.

'Come, sit down beside me and I'll tell you how it's possible.'

She did, but she sat a little away from him, keeping her distance. He had spoken with the stone in his hand, the fool, and told her that he was a wizard. But at that moment he, of course, lied and the stone *knew* when a lie was told and dimmed immediately. That was how she knew.

'Did you really think you could fool me this easily?' Her voice was icy, but her eyes still showed feelings, feelings of disappointment and hurt.

'He *is* a wizard,' Twello said in protest, knowing he had to defend him. 'I saw him kill all those men with just an iron stick and he made a very loud inhuman noise which hurt my ears when I tried to run away with the stone! And he kicked that door in with just his feet like…like a bear or something.' Twello spoke rapidly.

Ashanna listened to the boy's fast flowing stream of words. Shazar kept quiet. He didn't know what to do, but fear ate at his heart; old but somehow still raw fear. She saw it and was a little puzzled.

'Inhuman, huh?'

The boy nodded happily because he had silenced the argument.

Silence indeed followed.

Then Ashanna picked up the stone from Shazar's hands and placed it in Twello's hands, asking the boy if he could ask it if Shazar wasn't human. Twello looked at Shazar who silently nodded and only then did the boy obey.

'He isn't human!' Twello exclaimed in shock. 'I hear the stone say it in my head!'

Ashanna was too shocked to ask what he was then.

'Now you know,' Shazar spoke quietly.

'I knew it,' she mumbled. 'somehow I knew you were no ordinary man. This kind, soothing, understanding, wise…beautiful.'

Shazar had expected anything, but not this. She wasn't afraid or at least she didn't show it and he had seen fear in her eyes before and so his own anxiety eased off a bit.

'You don't need to explain. You must be tired of that and afraid of those who mean you harm, even though you are strong,' *but why did he look so afraid?* 'Your secret is safe with me,' was all that she said despite her curiosity.

That surprised him, for they always wanted to know didn't they? Well, he and his family had avoided humans since he was born as much as they could, so he wouldn't really know. He never had to explain before either. He and his brother had killed everyone who found out and Shazar had continued to do so, even after his brother's death. If his headband came off or if anyone had seen his eyes change when defending himself *they* were soon dealt with. There had never been any personal contact and yes, he was still a virgin. But that wasn't why he could communicate with the stone; comyentis could link their minds with anything with a soul if properly trained…

Until he met Twello and Ashanna he never had any human contact. The Search had not taken him to look amongst humans. Comyentis would not mix so there was no need to.

~~~

He had been surprised how easily she took it all in and he tried to read her mind, but of course he couldn't, not until there had been a very intimate connection established, the sacred Heartmerge. A Mindmerge would also be possible, but since humans had nothing a comyenti could use, it was never done. However the Heartmerge was all the more out of the question; for not only did comyentis mate for life with only one chosen mate, they mated solely with other comyentis. Shazar had been told this by his parents and grandparents who were all gone now. Mating with the enemy, humans, was strictly forbidden by the elder comyentis.

He needed to trust her but could he?

'I'm honoured to know you, Ashanna.'

She turned towards him. 'Well, likewise. You're a powerful man, being strong *and* caring; that's what all women want, believe me: I know.'

He grinned sheepishly.

'Are there more like you?' she asked perching down beside him.

'I wouldn't know to be honest.'

Ashanna stared at the stone which lay on the grass. Well, he was opening up to her and genuinely so. She trusted that much on instinct. However empty it made her feel, she had to make it without her stone. She was on her own now; a life without the stone. Just her and her faith in herself. But she wasn't ready to face the world on her own yet. That troubled her, and the boy, could she care for him? She knew that she could, for the stone had taught her that much over the years; through her answering the villagers' questions about their children, their development, their need for structure, love and safety; their tantrums and what guidance they needed. *"The child needs a mother. The woman the child."*

Her mind shifted to Shazar again.

'You mean, you're the last?'

'That remains to be seen.' He stared hopefully at the stone.

'Why didn't you tell me this before, I would have understood!'

'I don't normally trust people with my secret, Ashanna. I have to kill all those who find out.' His eyes darted away, ashamed.

Her face paled visibly and she swallowed away her fear.

'Don't worry, I have a policy too. I don't kill women and children.'

'Oh,' she sighed relieved.

'But you do have to promise me that you'll keep it a secret. Can you promise me that?'

'I promise.'

There was no doubt in her eyes. She would do anything for him now, her saviour.

'Well, go on then,' she coaxed him. 'Ask the Truthstone. You don't need me anymore. Can you tell me how you do it at least?'

'Everything has a soul. I listen, Ashanna, like you and many others could do as well, if they tried hard enough. I suppose you, as a human, are a sensitive Hearer or Seer with the Sight, as they are called in some cultures. Both you and Twello. There are more like you and you have a hard time among your kind; just because, like me, you are different in your sensitivity. Being different means you're often misunderstood. You were lucky to be worshipped as a priestess, in some cultures you would have ended up on a fire.'

Ashanna swallowed hard and looked at the boy.

I must protect him, she thought for the first time, feeling something again.

He saw her fright.

'In the South you'll be safe. But to be sure you must keep a low profile. Never show your gift to anyone you don't trust. You had better keep it to yourself from now on to be on the safe side,' Shazar said.

'You mean you think I could have told the truth *without* the stone?'

'That and much more. You often have dreams that come true don't you? And often *know* what people think or are trying to tell you, even if they haven't even opened their mouths? Sense of direction? Sense of right and wrong?'

'Yes, how did you know?'

He almost smiled.

'It comes with the territory,' *A pity I can't train her. She could teach people, educate them to think differently; to use their own abilities in different ways.*

'I myself have the same and more, much more. My people… link with animals.'

'Animals…but you look human.'

'We are all animals, I'm simply a humanoid but I don't like that term much. 'Non-human animal' is much better, believed to have been born on a planet very much like Bhan. Many millions of years ago we took a different path in our development than your kind. We are what you could have been.'

She noticed him touching something around his neck, she hadn't seen it before. It was some kind of necklace with a metallic round object as a pendant.

'I hope we meet again,' she spoke gently and Shazar wasn't sure if she was referring to herself and him, or her kind and his in general.

He picked the latter.

'It's… better to keep the species separated,' he said apologetically.

'Oh? Didn't you just say you link with animals?'

'Yes spiritually. We stay away from people for obvious reasons.' He grimaced.

'But wouldn't there be a better understanding if you did mix, living together in harmony?'

'Pah, that would be impossible! Humans were our downfall and it could happen again. Their jealously and greed would kill us. Or worse it could lead to the disappearance of my kind *into* humans; our enemy. They might mate and create halflings. Our kind would be truly doomed!'

Chapter 16 Mindmerge

Shazar was alone with the stone. Ashanna was busy washing the boy down by the river that evening, before turning in for the night, as it turned late and nearly dark. Shazar built a fire and sat near its warmth, which he didn't need for himself but he did like the smell and sight of it. It was an element and an ancient one; it put him in the right mood. Chanting he started the ritual, opening himself up to his surroundings, but to the stone in particular.

He spoke in his mind this time, *Your mind…my mind. Precious gem, I need to know. Are there more of my kind; the comyenti, living in this world?*

The stone lit up and like a heartbeat it pulsated.
'Yes,' it answered him in response.

It surprised him and his heart leapt with hope. So he wasn't the last one. There were others! Other comyentis; Mindmergers with animals, having shared and 'given' their abilities to create Mindmodes and Mindskills.

Where are they?
Silence.
He asked again.
'Here and there.'
Here and there? How is that possible?
'They travel.'
Of course; like me. How many are there?
'One and a half.'

Shazar rubbed his chin at that, shocked to find out the harsh truth, but puzzled at this strange number. *How can that be possible?* But there was no reply to that.

Where does this one and a half comyenti live?
'In Northland near the Balla Mountains.'

Of course! The only safe place, where giants used to live so that people would stay away.

~~~

'I tried for hours,' Shazar said the following morning at breakfast, looking weary. 'But it remains vague, what does it mean by 'one and a half'? A whole one and a half one? Or no arms, no legs, a mutated one?' *Or a halfling?* That was his worse fear.

'The stone didn't reveal it to me, only that the gender is female and that she or they live near the Balla Mountains in Northland.

'Hmm, it has happened before that it answers vaguely, but perhaps this is for a reason, which you'll have to find out for yourself. At least you now know where they live.'

'Yes, of course I'm glad there are more of my kind; *that* at least is hopeful and I know the location!'

He closed his eyes against the bright sun light for a moment. It glittered on the river surface like fire… Images came to him and Shazar thought about his brother who had not lived to know this. He died two decades before in a fire when they had set light to a human village. *That* had been their revenge at the time in exchange for all the comyenti lives lost and their slim future. The whole human race their enemy.

He was wiser now but his brother had tried to save a baby left in one of the burning buildings; for they never killed women and children if they could help it. The baby lived, protected by his brother's scorched body. No animal ability could have saved him from that.

How ironic; a comyenti saving a human. The hunted saving the hunter.

'How come there are so few of you left?'

Shazar awoke up from his thoughts and stared at his black boots. The stone had been buried by the edge of the river; they had given it back to the earth it once came from. Ashanna had thanked it and cried like she would have at a loved one's funeral, but the stone's spirit didn't mind the prospect of the rest it deserved.

'We were thought to be dangerous to the human race,' Shazar said to her. 'Being different and strange in their eyes, we were thought to be a threat. We have powers people can only dream of but we were never a violent species; until we had to defend ourselves. We never used our skills on any living being without respect, only for our own survival and enjoyment. Never to hurt. We lived in harmony with all around us respecting life and the animals and trees. We fled. We never take away an ability of an animal; it is given to us in a mutual agreement to protect the animals' life if needed. They will call us when the time comes. Wherever we are we have to obey; for that is the deal,' he swallowed before he continued. Ashanna forgot about her own problems for a moment, feeling for this man and his history, intrigued as well. 'When the first of us was slain, the war began. At first we didn't want to fight them; they were barbaric but still part of the animal kingdom and surely still developing. We didn't want to interfere but rather fled to avoid contact. Instead they chased us, hunted us down like pack predators, my grandparents told me. Apparently we tried to reason with them, to make them understand that we would be no threat to them and keep to ourselves but, them being lower beings, they were not ready to understand. We killed many but *that* only worsened the matter. You see; had we not they might have lost interest in us. Now they had even more reason to blame us for everything. We were captured, tortured, slain and killed in numbers throughout the years, all over the entire planet.'

Ashanna had not known about his species before, having lived an isolated life with not much knowledge of the things outside the temple. It had not been her concern. Now she felt like she had been living in a shell. Moreover she felt a link to this man as he, or at least his kind, had been treated unjustly like her.

'But according to Twello you are very powerful and strong. Then how–'

'They were too many,' he replied quickly, known that the question would come.

'Our kind lives longer but produces less offspring and we mature more slowly. Humans are always greater in number, like ants. Perhaps *that* was our downfall. Perhaps we too should have bred in numbers.

Only to see our children slain…We only defended ourselves and our birthright; our lives, yet it didn't help much. Humans seemed to adapt better than we did. Perhaps that's why they're so successful overall. But,' he hesitated. 'We… get stressed really easy and overwhelmed by people and their reactions; their noises, their smells sicken us. It weakens us.' He hesitated again before he concluded, 'That's what made us vulnerable and weak.' *We cannot use our abilities when stressed or frightened. It's a miracle we managed to kill at all…*

'That is a horrible history, Shazar. You must hate us very much.'

'Hate, that is something only humans are capable of. It was their hate for us that got us killed. Now we stay away from them, like a wolf when he smells a human village. But we loathe them alright. It grew in our hearts, our blood and bones over the years. It remains in our instinct,' *but here I am, talking to one! And not only that, I raided a human building, and left one alive! No, I saved a woman and a child; there is no wrong in that! Even if they are human and have the potential to do evil…*

Nothing more was said. Ashanna wasn't capable of soothing Shazar but she knew she wasn't the one he needed. He needed his family with him. He was so focussed to find others of his kind and would not want her around. It was a surprise he had helped her escape at all. Although he had shown kindness to her there was also a kind of darkness in him. Perhaps because she had been hurt by pretty much the same type of people that hurt him and his family he felt he needed to help her?

Shazar had not mentioned the name of his kind, so she couldn't tell anyone what he exactly was; even if she did promise to keep the secret, one could never be certain. And Ashanna had not asked.

~~~

The next morning after breakfast they decided to pack up.

'Why don't you come with me to my aunt's house to rest and get your strength back before going north?' Ashanna spoke gingerly.

'I suppose I could pay you two a visit in the Southeast in the near future but not now. Was it near Randaria you said you're aunt lives?'

He smiled at Twello who smiled back a little.

Ashanna nodded, 'Yes, she has a hut in the dunes set a little apart from the village so quite safe for you,' and she sighed, 'I do hope you'll find your kind!'

'Somehow I have a good feeling about it.'

'So do I,' she said with a half smile. 'Don't forget us.'

'I won't.' He smiled back.

There was a certain tension in the air, Shazar felt it and didn't know what to think of it. Did the woman feel bad about him leaving her?

'Don't be afraid, Ashanna. It will be alright, you'll see. When you find your aunt and make a living for yourself and the boy, your confidence will grow and time will heal your wounds. The nightmares will lessen in time.' He had heard her mumble in her sleep, waking with sweat on her troubled forehead.

"Time will heal your wounds and time will fade the memories."

'Sure,' she replied, squeezing her mouth tight, not really believing it.

Shazar sighed. Even though he had been able to comfort her before, when she cried, he didn't know how to deal with these courtesies. He hardly remembered how to act in social situations, having stayed away from people. He'd always acted on instinct and followed his heart.

He remembered to shake her hand though. Her lips parted in response and she took his so human warm hand in hers.

'Goodbye for now,' he said and laid his other hand on top of hers, before letting go with some reluctance and turning to the boy. 'I will pay you both a visit, that's a promise.'

Shazar ruffled Twello's hair but the boy shook him off and hugged him by the waist. Twello knew how to say goodbye properly, 'I'll never forget you, Shazar.'

Tears welled up in Shazar's eyes.

'You better not, for I'll be back. Your parents are so proud of you. You stood up against evil and that is never forgotten.'

'I didn't save them. They're gone,' he said in a tiny voice, still holding the man closely.

'You did! Even though they're no longer here physically, they are watching over you, keeping you safe and will remain in your heart and in your memories. They're truly free now and *you* have to make them proud with what you do with the rest of your life,' he took the boy's chin in his hand and stared into his pale blue eyes. 'Never stop fighting against the wrong in the world and try to do the right thing, Twello. Never stop living. Never stop caring. And…look after Ashanna for me, yes?'

Twello nodded, although tears dropped down his cheeks.

'Take care Ashanna. Same thing goes for you.' He gave her an uncertain half smile. She nodded back, fighting back tears. She had started to feel again after thinking she never would.

'Good luck, Shazar.'

She turned to the boy and as Shazar hitched his rucksack higher and left the camping spot, Ashanna and Twello soon would leave as well, he saw her putting an arm around the boy saying, 'I know this story about tears…'

~~~

Shazar smiled and grabbed the straps of his rucksack pulling them tighter, touching his head band, feeling it was in place to hide his unusually pointy ears from the rest of the world.

It would be a long road, but he was patient. He would search high and low in the Balla Mountains. The stone didn't reveal the exact location. He did not ask the Truthstone if he would ever succeed. He could have done so but he wanted to let the future remain as it would be and thus make life more interesting; a surprise.

Well, and with *"one and a half"* comyenti wouldn't it be just that?

PART III Summer Struggles

The morning
feels cool and crisp.
Smells of the fragrant earth
reek the air,
Hear- the twitter of the birds,
I SEARCH FOR YOU THERE
In the bumble of the bees,
the slow opening of the rose
when the bee kisses the petals,
the exuberance of the thunder,
the flash of the lightning,
the lash of the sea waves
on the pebbled shore,
I SEARCH FOR YOU THERE
The rapturous glow of the moon
the twinkle of the stars,
the rise of the dawn,
the flame of the afternoon
the closing shades of twilight
I SEARCH YOU THERE
In the velocity of the tornado
the pitter-patter of the raindrops on my rooftop,
the sway of the leaves of the tree
the lustre of the diamonds
the flow of your poetic verses
I SEARCH FOR YOU.
On my heart with folded palms
in devotion I pray for your wellbeing
But still,
I'M SEARCHING FOR YOU.

ANJALI SINHA

Chapter 17 The Halfling

A warm summer breeze blew through the bright green canopy of trees. Beech, oak and pine stood spread about. Underneath lay a carpet of fern and blueberry.

A wood warbler sang its cheerful song overhead. A sudden disruption below caused it to stop singing and fly off.

There was a slight rush from the parting of ferns and a soft low thumping sound of two small feet; hardly a disturbance to the peace of the summer wood, however added to that a high pitched child's exited squeal and it was alarming enough for the shy birds to flee on rapid wings.

The child continued to squeal and laugh, running extremely fast until she entered a clearing. She ran towards a figure lying on a blanket with their eyes closed on the grassy meadow.

Presently the dark haired tanned woman looked up, resting herself lazily on one elbow, smiling warmly at the child running towards her.

'Mummy! I was faster again!'

Sula opened her arms, caressing the little girl on her back with tender hands. Holding her at arms length, Sula looked proudly at her. The blond girl's blue eyes shone brightly and intelligently and her laughing mouth showed her little white teeth. The sun had darkened the few freckles on her tiny nose making her olive cheeks a lovely rosy apple colour. Her ears were slightly pointed and stuck through the strands of hair.

The only piece of clothing she wore was a pair of orange shorts that were full of mud-and grass stains. Her feet were bare and splattered with mud as well, as were her knees, but the mother knew well enough that this child proved hard to keep clean during the day. The young girl of nearly five autumns looked so happy and proud that Sula didn't worry about yet another piece of clothing to be washed. In fact it was better in the summer when the child could run around half naked and did not stain too many clothes as she would in the other seasons. She reminded Sula of herself at that age. She would do anything in the world to have her feeling this way for as long as possible.

Before the confusion starts.

The dazzling woman smiled at her daughter with shining emerald eyes.

'Fay, you amaze me every time! Now, where did you leave your father?'

The girl grinned gesturing over her shoulder to glance at the woods behind her. A young handsome blonde man approached the sunny clearing, heavily panting and leaning with both hands on his bare knees. He too was bare above the waist and sweat shimmered on his toned torso; only dressed in short brown linen breeches. They both stared at him, laughing at his exhaustion.

As soon as he saw them Felix looked up and quickly contained his weariness; laughing slyly as he walked in a fake relaxed fashion towards them with opened arms. His firm stomach and hairless chest shining like bronze in the sun. When he'd almost reached them he suddenly said in a teasing voice, 'Who said the chase was over?' And made a dash for Fay. She screamed high pitched, giggling, attempting to run away but this time her father was faster and lifted the little girl up, roaring loudly.

'I'm going to eat you!' He bit her softly on her upper leg. At that the girl screamed more. Her mother chuckled at the infectious giggles of her daughter and looked with amusement at the scene.

After spinning her around and around, Felix finally put her down to stroke her fuzzy shoulder length hair with a couple of small braids.

'That wasn't fair daddy!' the girl objected suddenly looking up at him seriously.

'I got you, didn't I?' he replied laughing.

The young fair father, who also had small braids in his hair, leaned over to his stunning wife to kiss her on the lips before letting himself fall beside her. Felix, who laid on his back with the sun reflected in his blue eyes, looked up at her and said, 'She is getting faster by the day, Miss Sula! Already she outruns me.'

She smiled down at him, laughing at his special term of endearment for her, referring to when they first met.

'Of course she does. She's my girl!'

'She sure is! No doubt about that,' he said smiling with his eyes closed against the bright sunlight. It was late afternoon and the warmth felt pleasant now, not oppressive any more.

'But she definitely has your good looks,' Sula added sweetly and lay down beside him, putting an arm around his bare suntanned chest with her eyes suddenly dark and yearning. Felix gasped when he saw it and grinned at her.

'Oh, really, you think so, huh?' he joked and heard Fay laughing stretched out on the grass, throwing her legs upwards so that the sun would shine on the soles of her feet, wiggling her toes. A butterfly landed on her biggest toe and the girl giggled and waved her short leg in the soft wind like a tall stem, imagining her toes to be the flower.

The little family spent every summer travelling; staying a month in one area, camping here and there, taking every day as it came. In Fay's first summer they had undertaken a light four days walk towards the sea in Westland. The second year, they had set out to go deeper in the mountains to see the numerous lakes in the north, a little closer to home. The third year they travelled to Eastland with its long stretches of plains with flocks of reindeer and meerkats inhabiting the unusual shaped rocky land with its endless caves and steppes. Last summer they strolled through the warm Midland with its woodlands and enormous clear lakes with little bird islands.

This year they'd let Fay choose where they should go and she said she wanted to see the mountains, deciduous woodlands and open steppes in the Northwest where wolves still roamed freely despite the many wolf hunts. The rest of the year they travelled frequently too; short distances in the gentle area where they lived near the small village of

Rosinhill and its hilly meadows and friendly forests, lakes and rivers and surrounding mountains.

It would have been a great sacrifice for Sula to give up her life's goal altogether; the search for others of her species, but her love for Felix made it easier for her to settle down. She called it her 'small sacrifice' and after a couple of moons their child was conceived. Fay Rosinhill was that child and with her a new era was about to begin. Through her the species would or could live on.

Sula Comyenti, known as Sula Rosinhill in the village since their blessing and to keep her safe, had not given birth to any more children.

Back in the meadow, not knowing yet what a heavy burden she carried, the girl slept carefree between her loving parents in the shade of the protective beech trees. Felix and Sula soon fell asleep too, cuddled up against each other.

Chapter 18 One and One

Like a soft breeze *someone* moved amongst the ferns and blueberry bushes across the forest floor towards the grassy meadow. With the sweet scent of resin in his nostrils, he stood completely still beneath a large pine tree that marked the entrance of the wood. Taking a sharp breath at the sight, he pinned himself to the tree so as not to be seen. The sweet sap of the pine was almost overpowering now, he tried to focus on his hearing and eyesight instead.

He had heard and seen the small child running earlier; drawing his attention and although it was just a flash of her, he instantly knew she could not be human. *No* human child could run that fast at such a young age. He *knew* he had to follow her. He was on the right trail.

Shazar had been silent like a cat in his chase so that the man following the girl had neither seen nor heard him, and neither had the child. They were both laughing; too wrapped up in their own game, so he knew she was not in danger. The man chasing her was no threat. The girl seemed unaware of any dangers, though.

No doubt the man's fault. A human? What is he to her anyway? Shazar thought with loathing.

Dressed in black and standing with his back exposed to the heat of the sun which he was used to, being born and having spent a lot of his time further south, he hugged the tree. The heat seemed to bother him suddenly or was it anger? Sweat trickled down his neck and between his shoulder blades.

He patiently waited several moments. He observed the young girl, the man and another sleeping on the grass. He suddenly found himself having a vision of other people; his own mother, father and baby sister lying on the grass similar to this. However this was not a happy vision:

they were all covered in their own blood… slain. Rage and sadness overwhelmed him at the memory and he clenched his fists tight. Blocking the thoughts out, throwing them back into his memories of long ago he regained his stature and tried to relax.

Yes, relax, for there is hope still. One and a half comyenti…

Walking slowly, softly, making no sound he came closer to the three people on the grass meadow; a man, a woman and a child. He stood over them, taking a good look at them with his slanted green eyes. The young man seemed handsome and healthy looking with a suntanned muscular body. Unmistakably human, strong and seemingly flawless. He quickly directed his eyes away. The girl had his fair looks, but she had very different ears; high and pointed at the tips. Pine needles were tangled in her blond hair. Shazar touched his own ears under his headband. His skin felt itchy and damp.

His gut feeling had been right, the child was a halfling. He bit his cheek at that, annoyed.

Well, I suppose I've found the half part. Now, for the woman…she must be the 'one.'

Shifting his gaze to the sleeping woman he held his breath. Her ears! Yes, she was definitely comyenti; full comyenti he guessed, so yes: one. His heart leaped, for that was more than he could have expected. A half comyenti female child and a grown female, her mother without a doubt! He had searched for a couple of months since leaving Ashanna and Twello, combing out the Balla Mountains, but without any luck. And here they were…

The female was stunning. He only vaguely remembered his own mother and she had been beautiful. On seeing this young comyenti woman stretched out on the grass, scarcely dressed in a dark pine green dress his heart leaped up. The colour of her skin was the same as his; bronze. Her dress was open at the neck, and a small line of sweat trickled between the cleft of her full breasts. Sweat circled her neck like a necklace of dew. He raised his eyebrows; she wasn't using a cooling technique? Well, he was and even he sweated in this heat, but then again it was more his emotions that caused it. He tore his eyes away from her body and focussed on her face: her pointed ears, her long black eyelashes, her arched eyebrows and when he saw her mouth a little open he felt his legs tremble and his knees weaken.

His breathing had become faster and he felt his heart almost burst out of his chest. He wanted to cry out from joy, *I have found you! I can call off the search now! Mother, father, brother and sisters, finally. Your deaths will not have been in vain!*

But he could not, not yet. He could not wake her or talk to her. She wasn't alone. Shazar could see why she picked the human man but he could not fathom why she had stayed with him. Didn't she know the horrors of her history?

Better to wait for another moment to meet her and ask; that would be a special moment. He would not let them out of his sight. No, he would watch their every move.

He closed his eyes for a heartbeat, concentrating on his Mindskill and in the next heartbeat he sprinted off; as fast as a hare, the branches of the trees closing behind him.

Sula awoke at once, jamming her eyes open, sitting up, immediately sensing a presence. Suspiciously she looked around, feeling a stir in the air, unable to grasp what it was.

There had been someone here, right here.

How foolish of me to think we're safe!

She concentrated on the smelling sense of the wolf and sniffed the air around them. Yes, she could definitely smell it had been a being large enough to be human. However… it didn't smell much like human. She frowned and sniffed again. Not a deer, nor lynx nor a bear. It smelt unlike any other creature she'd smelt before; however it did smell vaguely familiar. She stood silently; alarmed and confused, staring at the grass, kneeling and searching for any footprints. But the grass had already been flattened so much that any other footprint would have gone unnoticed.

How foolish of me to fall asleep on such an open meadow, making us so very vulnerable!

She woke her family up, coaxing them to leave the clearing and look for a suitable camping spot. She didn't tell Felix about a possible intruder yet or the chance of them being followed and he did not suspect. He wasn't able to read her thoughts after their Heartmerge but she could. Only comyentis could, she found out.

She could mind read with her daughter, them sharing the same blood, and their relationship was very close and easy because of it. There were hardly any misunderstandings between them but sometimes Sula had to block her thoughts from her daughter, if she wanted some privacy. Felix had always been a little envious of this but was also proud of having such a special little family.

It would only worry Felix if she told him about their visitor and she kept it well hidden from him and even from Fay.

They chose a camping spot deep in the woods and they had their dinner. Fay soon dozed off in her soft bed made of fern leaves and moss beneath a blanket, after Felix had told her a bedtime story. Sula lay beside her daughter spooning her, more protectively than normally and pretended to be fast asleep when Felix gently put a warm hand on her waist underneath the blanket. When she did not respond he caressed her hair and kissed her in her neck, whispering, 'Sleep well my love.'

She felt a little guilty for leaving him out but she had to do this on her own. She waited for him to fall asleep, listening to his steady shallow breathing and feeling him stir occasionally in his sleep.

Soundlessly she stood, then rearranged the blanket over her husband and child. Next, she opened her senses in all directions.

~~~

It was a moonless night and therefore utterly dark but by the light of the stars she used the night vision and precision of the cat and moved

157

sleekly and silently through the trees. She would go back to the clearing, only a few miles away, and start tracking the, by now, old trail. Already she knew deep in her heart that she would not have to look far, for someone had been following her...

Sula whiffed him clearly behind her now, close. He did not seem to be interested in the camping spot. Good, so he would not be a threat to her family...yet. It was her he wanted, that much was clear.

She smelled him nearby and walked slowly, using all her senses. It was only a matter of waiting for him to show up now.

A small movement of leaves in the bushes a few feet away from the meadow and a whisper, 'Don't be afraid, I mean no harm to you or your... *family*.' There had been a slight odd sound in the man's voice when pronouncing the word 'family' as if he had difficulty saying it, but he sounded kind enough.

'Show yourself,' she whispered defiantly back, stiffening and ready for an attack, even if he said he meant no harm.

Slowly he slipped out of the bushes holding his hands up to show her he had no weapons, knowing she would fear those. Under the light of the stars, using her cat-vision, she saw a handsome slender tallish young man dressed in black. His black hair reached his shoulders and his green slant eyes stared directly into hers; wide with curiosity.

'Who are you?' she asked angrily.

'Look at me thoroughly and you will know,' he answered and he used one of his hands to slide aside a few strands of his hair; shining almost blue in this hour of the night. Her heart sank when she saw his ears; pointed at the tips, bigger than she had ever seen, but beautifully shaped and proportioned, just like the rest of his almost feminine or genderless face. She would have sighed but she was in too much of a shock to respond. When she saw his eyes she recognized her own in his; something Felix could never get used to; the irises shifting with colour; sometimes deep jade, a moment later emerald, sometimes even shifting to tangerine or hazel, depending on her mood. This man's were bright grass green at the moment with specks of peach and lemon, glittering like the sun on water. One could quench ones thirst just by staring into his eyes alone.

His mouth and eyes showed a friendly smile when he saw her reaction and took another step forward.

'Sister…'

His intimate tender voice startled her.

'Sister?'

'Yes, we are the same and by calling you sister I acknowledge that we are both comyenti. It is a way of greeting one another, sister, brother…'

'Brother…' she softly spoke impulsively and tried out the, to her unfamiliar, word on her lips. She'd never had a brother before. As she spoke she saw his eyes growing watery and a tear running along his pale cheek.

She swallowed hard and she felt a bit dizzy. For so long she had been searching for others of her kind and now that she had lessened her efforts she had found one, or rather *he* had found her.

'How…did you find me?'

'That was easy; the halfling child was to be heard from miles away, and since people hardly ever stroll these woods, I got curious.'

Shivering at the clarity in his voice Sula stared down at her loose flannel nightgown and hugged herself to stay warm in the chilly night. She didn't have to be cold for she could easily use the spirit of the sheep to stay warm by its imaginary insulating woolly coat, but the man held all her attention for now. However, he had seen her shiver and that made him frown. He wore tight fitting black leggings, laced up black boots and a roughly woven black shirt which was open at the neck and rolled up at the arms. His arms were tanned and muscular. She noticed he wore a dark string around his neck, but she couldn't see the jewellery attached to it.

'Come, let us talk.' He gestured her to sit beside him on a tree trunk. She hesitated only briefly, reading the relieved face of the stranger. She sat down beside him, holding his gaze. She felt odd. She had imagined many times what it would be like when she would finally meet another comyenti; what she would do, how she would greet him or her, what she would say. But now that moment had come she felt frozen and numb.

He seemed sincere and patient, for he was excited as well, although he had had more time to prepare himself.

They sat silently next to each other in the darkness, very much aware of one another, not knowing where to start.

'My name is Shazar… and yours?'

'Sula,' she replied in as level a voice as she could manage.

"Sun',' he translated the word with surprise in his voice. 'A good name.'

After that silence again.

Her hands were in her lap and glancing sideways at him she moved one of her hands towards his elbow that was leaning on his knee. He looked at her and swallowed hard, giving her his hand. She squeezed it tight and embraced him suddenly, crying her old tears on his shoulder. He held her close and wept silently with her.

Chapter 19 Brother

'I was born in the South-East in the Shanzarian Mountains,' Shazar explained to her in a steady voice, after the ice was broken between them. His voice had a slight lilt to it, almost an accent, but it was like a mixture of languages. 'Hence my name, we nomads tend to do that, to remind ourselves. I've been travelling Bhan since my early teens. How old do you think I am?'

Sula took a better look at him with her cat eyes. His smooth beardless face looked young, with hardly any lines, with its high cheekbones and strong jaw, yet his eyes were calm and wise. They confused her. He looked ageless.

'Thirty, thirty something.'

He smiled at her with a big grin, showing perfect white teeth.

'Fifty seven.'

'Impossible!' Her eyes grew bigger.

'I'm telling you the truth, I wouldn't lie to you. I can't guess your age either. You look in your middle twenties but I suppose you might be older?' Shazar looked intently at her eyes.

'That is true,' she answered. 'I will be forty five this autumn. I always wondered how I remained younger looking. The food, the water, the mountain air? My mother never told me. She herself had always looked the same to me and I was sure she didn't use the ability of any animal to do so. I mean she could have used the ability of any long living animal such as the giant tortoise,' her face suddenly looked thoughtful. 'Both me and my mother have tried to Mindmerge with a certain type of jellyfish so we would be able to live longer. They can turn the clock back all together over and over. Have you ever tried this?'

Shazar shook his head smiling.

'I find it very hard to reach their mind as well but we might have to keep trying. If we could do this we would be immortal, like them.'

'But even if we could I'd be afraid to use it! What if our minds changed back into the foetus stage all together?'

'Even in a Mindmode we still keep our identities!' he argued.

'Yes and our bodies are never physically changed by using a Mindskill; we fool our bodies. But my point is, if we truly wanted to be immortal we would have to 'be' the jellyfish all the time!'

'Hmm, we don't know about that. Perhaps we only have to go in the jellyfish-mode when our bodies show signs of aging? But yes it could prove very exhausting or…fatal.'

'Not even that. You said it yourself how hard it is to reach a jellyfish's mind. They are so different than mammals, even from fish. They're almost the same as floating plants! It's impossible to make eye contact and I don't think they have a brain as most animals which is essential to make the Mindmerge. I'm worried if we ever succeed and have to stay in a Mindmode too long it could cause us to lose ourselves all together, to lose who we are. My mother lived with wolves for a couple of years and she used their abilities a lot, she told me she was in wolf-mode so often she started to forget her comyenti side. She even started to behave like a wolf and even develop a liking to the hunt and that is very unlike any comyenti! When she met my kind human father she tried hard to change back. After all, she had to mate. She did change back all together but it was a struggle and she had copied a lot of wolfish attributes. So she always warned me not to use any Mindskill for too long a time,' Sula swallowed hard remembering her mother. 'She died from a fever when she was fifty eight. That's twenty four years ago now.'

'Hmm. She might not have known everything. We can reach up to two hundred and fifty years if we manage to stay safe, just like a giant tortoise! Some comyentis have even claimed to have reached three centuries. Few of our time knew this, because it rarely happened due to the killings. We look younger because we age more slowly. We reach full adulthood when we are about twenty.'

She opened her mouth in surprise.

'I did have my first cycle late.'
'Not late; late in human terms but on time in ours.'

Sula bit her lip and thought fast, her eyes darting from side to side.

'I'm sorry about your loss, Sula. Your mother…what was her story then?'

'She fled as a child when her family was killed. A pack of wolves found her and raised her. Luckily she remembered her duty and had had some training from her parents to pass on to me. But her memory of comyentis was clouded,' she looked up at him with her hands folded in her lap and added, 'She was so young. I'm interested in what you know? You've searched most of your life like me?'

He nodded.

'The Search; a comyenti necessity. The last ones made the binding promise and we cannot forsake it and not only because it's done under the Comyenti Oath.'

'Yes, the Comyenti Oath; if we break our promise we lose all our traits, abilities and skills, so it is said, my mother knew that. But I never just searched because I gave her the promise.'

'Nor me. Oh, but the Oath is very real by the way. My parents knew someone who broke a promise and became…human. Even so, The Search is more than that; it is our duty,' and he glanced at her. 'I have travelled every deserted place that I could find, knowing a comyenti would seek a safe place, shielded from humans. From the west to the east and the South to the north, the north being my latest search,' Shazar said.

'So have I and I have especially searched the north thoroughly the last four years, since I live here.'

Both looked sadly at one another.

'Either they hide too well or…we are alone,' Sula stated plainly.

Shazar gently took her hand in his and looked at her without blinking his eyes.

'Sula… we *are* alone. We are the last.'

'How do you know?'

He briefly explained his encounter with Ashanna and her Truthstone and the answer the stone had given him.

'So it is true,' she started sobbing.

'I knew you were out there somewhere, though. I've always felt it,' he

163

comforted her. 'Even though you travelled, like me, we tend to hide too well to be found. I have found you and for that I am more than glad. The Search indeed is over.'

Sula looked at him and saw his misty eyes admiring her, looking so pleased. She did not know how to deal with his overwhelming sense of joy.

I have found you… it resounded in her head when she thought about it. His face showed no sign of hair and Sula vaguely remembered her mother saying that comyenti men had no beard or moustache growth and never needed to shave. He was ridiculously handsome.

She was of course in one way relieved that The Search was over too, yet sad that there were no more comyentis other than the two of them, if his story was true and if she could trust him. But she had to: he was comyenti. They didn't lie, there was nothing wicked about them.

Yet, unlike him; her life had moved on and she was married now, had a child and was happy.

'You seem to know more about our common history than me. What do you know?' she almost demanded of him. But he smiled and told her what he had been told by his grandparents and parents and she in her turn what she knew from her mother. It seemed Shazar's family believed they did not spring forth from Bhan and he showed her the pendant hanging around his neck underneath his tunic; a simple round metallic object with a hole in the middle where the string fell through.

'It belonged to my father's father who received it from his mother, I believe, but the family was scattered early. They had to live in small numbers spread about as that was safer. So we don't know everything and nothing is written down so our legend is lost too. Only some uncertain tales remain.'

Sula looked at the round coppery piece with strange symbols carved upon it and touched it. It felt warm and smooth and she could feel power radiating from it, almost like electricity. She could see Shazar's pulse in his neck and feel his warmth. He stared at her and she reluctantly let go of the pendant. Ruefully, he looked down.

'It is not a metal made from this world and even though we are not sure any more whether this tale is truth or fiction, this pendant is some proof of our origin. All the rest is lost together with our ancestors.'

'So we might not be related to humans or to any other animal...' she mumbled, more to herself, and frowned.

'Quite likely not. Although our bodies, oddly enough, seem to somehow match with those of humans. You wouldn't be here otherwise. I guess we must have a similar development or perhaps our circular world was very much like this one with the same origin, born of the same sun and moon. Maybe we are able to mix because of our abilities. When we do a Heartmerge we do a Mindmerge?' He shrugged his shoulders and looked uncertain. 'Our home world might even be close but we know so little of the heavens other than that the stars are spheres of flame just like the sun but smaller, we spin and so does the sun.' He sighed, looking up. Sula followed his gaze, thoughtfully, her mind all over the place.

How did we come to be here?

'Have you...any children?' she asked him after a lengthy silence, wanting to think about the future, not the past.

He looked down at his hands.

'No, I told you, you and I are the last. There have been women but I knew it wouldn't be wise to mate with them.'

'Why not? I don't understand.'

He looked sternly at her, remembering Fay all of a sudden, 'If we mate with humans we risk our bloodline becoming thinner and not only that but also our unique traits and abilities will be lost eventually. Did no one tell you?' He shook his head, realising that that wasn't likely. He should not be angry with her.

'Only after generations... I presumed we would be lost altogether; but how can we truly know? I am a halfling and I possess just as much magic as my full blood mother did,' Sula responded strongly.

'Magic?' Shazar retorted raising his eyebrows, shaking his head, his eyes darting from side to side, thinking.

'You know what I mean.'

'Of course, your mother mated with a human,' he slapped himself on the forehead nearly forgetting. He had heard her say it but it hadn't

165

really sunken in. 'You are a halfling,' *"One and a half"… If she is the half, who is 'the one' part of it? What about the child? She surely is… one quarter?* But then again Shazar didn't think the Truthstone would have been that technical about it. A sudden insight hit him. What if the stone had really meant one *adult* and a *child*? Shazar had always believed the answer referred to a full comyenti and a halfling, but with Sula technically speaking, having had a human father so being a halfling and Fay a quarterling, why had the stone not been more accurate? Ashanna did say that the stone could answer vaguely and it had been right about the location, so Shazar left it at that.

Sula nodded.

'When my mother did not find any other comyenti male she had to give it a try to save our species and it worked. I think I can do as much as she could, skills wise. What about you?'

'I am a true comyenti,' he mumbled somewhat disappointed by the fact she wasn't a full comyenti and had human blood running through her veins. He should have prepared himself for something like that. This felt like a blow to her and she narrowed her eyes to him and his comment.

'I don't feel human and I don't feel comyenti and I envy you that you do!' Sula raised her voice at him.

'Ai! I am comyenti and know nothing else. I saw my family being assassinated by humans and my brother and I fled…until he too was killed.' His voice became soft, almost a whisper. He left out the fact he and his brother visited many villages after the death of their parents and wiped out most of the human males out of revenge. Shazar had realised a long time ago that this perhaps had been their lesson; a hard one at that, but a lesson all the same: never to become like your enemy as it will only bring more hurt. And it never brought his loved ones back.

'I am sorry for your loss.'

'As you should be. They were your family as well. All comyentis are family.'

Does he mean as in 'related'?

'What does it feel like being a 'true comyenti?' she asked out loud somewhat sarcastically.

He stared long at her, trying to read her mind but of course he couldn't; not until they had shared the special bond of mating. He wasn't a close relative either; otherwise he would have known what she was thinking.

Shazar looked skywards again, at the glittering stars and the woods around him. Dew clung to the trees, grass and leaves, making the forest shimmer under the stars. He smiled alluringly.

'One with my surroundings; the trees, the animals, we are all connected and part of the Great Spirit,' he glanced at her, suddenly aware of her again, frowning. 'But you are both, that must be hard for you. Knowing what they did to us and to the world around them without any respect.' Shazar's face showed pity for the woman. He himself would have hated his human part, perhaps she did too. If she was a true comyenti in her heart she would have.

'Oh yes, at times it can be hard.'
'Why have you stayed with this man?'

For a moment she thought she heard her mother speaking, he had the same judgemental tone in his voice as she had had at times or would have had if she had lived to see the day her daughter had married a human male, instead of running away with her full belly like she had done.

'I married him after I was with child.'
'Yes but why?' he asked her in shock, realising she might have made the Comyenti Oath in marrying Felix; she would have had to promise certain things. Had she?
She could tell he didn't fathom it and blinked.
Upset she flashed her eyes at him and her green irises changed from dark to light and back and specks of orange flashed from within. Shazar was delighted to see it and almost felt tears in his eyes at remembering the last time he had seen it in a person; his brother.

'You ask me why? You who probably never loved anyone deeply enough to make you stay anywhere!'
'Love,' he locked onto her eyes, shaking off his memories. 'How can

a comyenti *love* a human after all they did to us? They have our blood on their hands and are still riddled with prejudices and superstitions which will take decades to eradicate, if it's even possible! They are narrow-minded, violent and ignorant. Humans are not to know we are still alive!' *We have to kill every human who does!* He shook his head, rubbing his neck, trying to calm himself down. 'Look, I know how awfully lonely it can get during The Search, so you mating… well I suppose it could be forgiven *if* you had taken the necessary precautions…and I *even* would have understood if you got yourself pregnant to continue the line this way, but to stay…' He looked at her with slits for eyes. Sula was too stunned for words at being treated like this and she thought her mother had been judgemental!

'Where do you live with this man, I hope not close to other humans?'

'I live in the mountains near a lovely village with my family and warm and caring people for neighbours.' she answered him in a neutral voice, gathering her thoughts and her temper, trying to stay aloof.

He let his head drop in his hands and grumbled.

~~~

'You cannot be serious?' Shazar asked.

Sula thought about Rosinhill and its people. They were simple farmers and craftspeople just living their lives like generations before them had with their hearts in the right place. They had welcomed Sula and made her feel special and needed. Felix's twin sister Feline and their parents were also dear to her heart and they had made her feel very welcome and loved. That was what she needed as well, for she was an orphan. Even though she was an adult; she needed family. Even her mother had had her wolf pack for a long time and after that her daughter for company. Sula had been on the road for nearly twenty years on her own before she had met Felix, only in the company of animals, never people. She had been full of wrath and loathed people alright but Shazar was more extreme than she'd ever been and she had been able to change.

'Talking of narrow-mindedness,' she sighed, reflecting his words. 'Felix and his people are not responsible for his entire species! He's different and absolutely not a murderer or someone to worry about!'

'You have become weak, Sula, more human than comyenti.' He narrowed his eyes which shone emerald under the starlight.

'Who ever said that comyentis are supposed to hold grudges and live like cold hearted hermits on a mountain top? Where is that written or who has ever said that?!'

'Hmm, I like your temper. It reminds me of myself. Yes, no, we are full of feelings and they are at times hard to control. Living like a hermit is certainly not the answer! It is easier to close our eyes and ears to things than to close our heart against our feelings and the emotions that come with it; especially for us sentient beings. It is a gift and one we should use. We do not only hear; we *listen*, we do not only look; we *see*. But it is still a choice even for us. We can choose to feel or walk away. The love bond or Heartmerge, as you no doubt know we call it, is a very powerful one, but not impossible to undo. Speaking of feelings... already I have feelings for you Sula.'

She stood up, holding his gaze with angry eyes at his last words.

'You do not! You only see a potential mate in me to bear your children.'

He looked up at her.

'Of course that as well. But they will be 'our children', Sula. I have saved myself for you. All that time I was looking for you, you were already inside me. I feel it clearly now. Together we will make sure comyentis have a future. Please listen to me. Your little girl is not the answer, for her blood is now even thinner and weaker because of this feeble human and when she mates it will only thin out further. No, we *together* can produce many children and *they* will secure the future of the comyenti.'

She swallowed away her anger at his direct shallow words before she answered, shaking uncontrollably 'Even if I could, for I have not conceived after Fay, I wouldn't. I already have a family.'

'You still think like a human, Sula. You had Fay, what, four years ago? Comyenti women can have children until they are *seventy* and they are fertile again only *four* years after having had a child… not sooner. They can only get pregnant during that fourth year. When is Fay's fifth birthday?'

She bit her lip at that, *seventy*? She had not known that. Absentmindedly she answered, 'The first night of the waxing moon after the equinox in autumn.'

He stood up and moved to face her, gently taking and holding both her hands. She was too stunned to withdraw.

'Think about it, Sula. I know you will need time. Just remember you and I have an obligation to fulfil and we cannot let our own personal feelings come between them. We are sentient beings but we are also intelligent and have to find the right balance and do what's right. Do you want us to die out? We cannot keep mixing with humans until eternity. You know it! We will be gone, lost and our unique skill can never survive for three or four generations. It will be harder to master with every generation, trust me. I am a full comyenti and you half comyenti, our children will be whole again.'

Chapter 20 Decisions

After they had parted Sula lay under the stars for the remaining of the night just thinking. She no longer was the last one, she never again needed to feel misunderstood or lonely inside for even the bond she shared with Felix could not live up to the bond with another comyenti. After generations and decades of seeking, The Search finally was over…

Two hundred and fifty years…Never have I suspected it to be possible, a terrifying thought suddenly flashed through her like lightning with the bolt painfully striking her heart, *I will outlive Felix by many years...*

She stared at her husband, fast asleep, unaware of what had just occurred and what it meant to all of them now.

Her eyes moved towards Fay who lay stretched out on her back, cuddled up between them. She was too small to understand the burden of it all. They had chosen to wait until she was old enough to tell her she was not completely human. But of course she already knew she was different than other children and because of that Sula had asked her not to use her abilities in public nor mention it. Fay wouldn't, for she had seen the fright in her mother's eyes when she had asked it of her.

Sula started Fay's training slowly just as her own mother had done with her from age five which Fay nearly was. Fay harmlessly linked with their animals; cats, goats, Feline's horse and her grandfather's dog resulting in her communicating with them and behaving and feeling like them, thinking it was a game. They had become her closest friends and she already seemed fonder of animals than other children her age. They seemed years behind Fay and she felt it. Soon Sula would start teaching her to link minds with various animals properly. Then she would be able to use and control their unique abilities and be able to communicate with them as well.

It was true that Fay would have a difficult life growing up amongst

171

humans and she might experience a sense of alienation and loneliness when with them. She might even develop her human side and neglect her comyenti one, detesting it, as it would make her too different to ever be part of a human society. Sula would have to ask the girl to keep silent throughout her entire life just as she had had to among the villagers; as friendly as they may seem.

When it was time for her to leave her parents to find her own place in the world Sula would ask caution of her, since humans could never fully be trusted even if they did think that comyentis were extinct.

"We will be gone"…she suddenly heard Shazar's words in her mind. All this time she thought that *her* child would secure the future of the comyenti species and now this man said it would only lead to them *dying* out? But how could he know? He didn't know that for sure, did he? He certainly hadn't known halflings before. As far as she knew she was the first. Sula painfully remembered however how her mother had worried about the time it had taken her to master flying. It might be even harder for Fay, perhaps dangerous if she lost the Mindmode whilst flying; she could fall to her death.

Mixing with humans could also result to in a better understanding and a chance for people to see comyentis in a different light.

It is the unknown that humans fear most.

Nevertheless, mankind could be cruel and unpredictable as Sula knew very well and Fay could expose herself to many dangers if she stayed amongst them.

Sula sighed. She couldn't look into the future, but she hoped times would change for the better. *And not just for us…*

She let the thought cross her mind to build a comyenti village somewhere where no humans could ever come and start a large family with Shazar so that her kind; her new family, could live in safety. They would never again have to face another human and their problems. But she let that thought go just as easily, for that would be almost impossible. Not only for the fact that people had penetrated almost every corner of the world but the thought of losing Felix…and Feline.

She was dragged back into her thoughts again. She had come across rare remote uninhabited places, but they would be too harsh to endure because of extreme conditions. They would have to use the survival abilities of several species non-stop, giving them no rest. No, that wouldn't do and it wasn't the answer either, hiding away.

We could grow stronger and become a better opponent, she thought determinedly but then she looked at her sleeping husband and almost heard his voice in her head saying a familiar line: *"I am not your enemy..."* *Not you,* Sula thought defiantly. *But many people would still try to kill us if they found out we're alive.* She had never stopped believing that. *They would kill me as easily as they kill any animal,* she therefore felt more related to animals and knew their fate lay close to hers. Only worse, she felt everything they felt; being sentient meant that their pain was hers. *If only humans had this skill everything would be different.*

Fay moved in her sleep and Sula looked at her as she tore herself away from her thoughts. *What have I done? What burden have I put upon you? How could I have been so irrational, so...heartless? I should never have got pregnant in the first place, I should have left. I should have stayed away from humans rather than putting such a heavy burden on my offspring; to live in this barbaric world where there is hardly any harmony or peace with Bhan's children,* But when she looked at her beloved sleeping child there were tears in her eyes. Then she looked at Felix and she knew she had never been happier, for he and the village they lived in were different. She couldn't imagine a life without him, Fay, their cats and their goats. They had made her complete and given her so much in return. *But that is selfish; to feel happiness while Fay will one day fathom the burden...I of all people should know that. I was angry with my mother, my people, the promise; all of it, even though I obeyed; I searched...and had a child. But by meeting Felix I changed. I learned,* Sula hoped with all her heart that one day Fay would find understanding and love like she had. And moreover, knowing that their species might be lost if mixed further with humans, she wouldn't have her make the comyenti promise, the oath, to continue the line.

It will stop it here and Fay will truly be free, something I never was. Shazar is our new hope.

Chapter 21 Thoughts

'*Y*ou've what?' Felix said more than startled, staring at her with big eyes, his normally coloured cheeks suddenly pale.

Sula felt herself flush and stammering at his reaction. But then his eyes gleamed with tears of joy and he hugged her close, smiling. His voice was filled with happiness when he said, 'But that is wonderful for you, my love, wonderful!' He held her at arm's length, gently cupping her face in his hands.

'You've met another comyenti! Your dream, your life's search has finally brought you a result!' And again he hugged her with all his strength, almost choking her. She hugged him back, closing her eyes.

He does not yet fathom the meaning of this...

'You must be thrilled!'

She smiled at him but concern was painted on her face and he saw it.

'What ever is the matter?'

She shrugged and shook her head. 'It's so sudden. I didn't expect it.' She glanced up and looked at him in his eyes.

'No, I can imagine but then again what did you expect?'

'Well, not on our holiday, I suppose.'

'But love, that's one of the reasons we travel each summer. And to *be* found, well that's even better. Now, where is he?'

She knelt by the river to fill her water bag and looked over her shoulder at Fay playing, near the camping spot.

'He said he would give me some time to get used to the idea. He must be around here somewhere.'

'Oh? Is he as shy as you were in the beginning when we had just met?'

She smiled at that. 'No, he just doesn't want to interfere with our family.'

Felix knelt beside her, staring questioningly at her, searching her face for any sign of explanation.

'Well, tell him he is welcome and that he doesn't have to fear me.'

'I already did. Look Felix, I just need some time to realise the magnitude of this. He could only tell me that we are indeed the last *two*. Him and I.'

He blinked his eyes a couple of times.

'Are you sure? I mean: is he sure about that?'

Sula nodded.

'How?'

She explained Shazar's story of the Truthstone and what it had told him. Felix believed in oracles and magic, so he nodded without further questioning.

'I'm sorry, you must be devastated. And there is me going on about how thrilled you must be.' He touched her shoulder softly kneading it. He kissed her on the top of her head and held her closely. She could not cry, not yet at least.

After a short while he stood.

'If you need me I will be near the camp. I will er…prepare us some breakfast.'

Smiling gratefully at him with love in her eyes she nodded. He was always so understanding. That was what she loved about him from the day they met. Somehow he always seemed to know how she felt even before their intimate bond.

~~~

After breakfast she went for a walk along the river by herself and tried to clear her mind by listening to the sound of the babbling water. She rested on a rock. It reminded her of the river in Rosinhill, so dear to her and Felix. It wouldn't be easy to fall in love with Shazar; he was very attractive, but she wasn't sure about his character. But one good thing was that in order to have his children she wouldn't have to love or even like him. He only needed to father them and perhaps she could still remain in Rosinhill. But still, she couldn't betray Felix like that even if he ever agreed to it. She was married to him and had given Felix her vows and with that, unknowing to her husband, her binding Comyenti Oath. She had never explained to him the true meaning of the Comyenti Oath, she didn't know herself whether to believe it or not. Although she had never sworn to never leave him; that wasn't a part of their marriage rite. She had however promised to love and respect him and to stand by him, in good and bad times, for the rest of their lives.

He was a very jealous husband. Sula was much loved and desired by many in the village and as much as she stayed away from people, they of course knew where they lived and she had had to send away many an admirer. Sula's thoughts drifted back to Shazar; she doubted they could all live together in harmony. She felt a sudden sensational rush through her body at the mere thought of that. Her having two men, now that would be something!

As if ever!

"You and I have an obligation to fulfil and we cannot let our personal feelings come between them," she heard Shazar's words resonate in her head. In one motion she threw a stone in the water and it made a loud splash just like Shazar had done by coming into their lives, ruining everything, leaving the surface rippled and disturbed.

She couldn't let him go either, now that he was here, could she? That wouldn't make sense.

Perhaps I can have a child with him and stay married to Felix. Shazar would have to leave us in peace and perhaps only visit once or twice a year.

Sula shook her head, watching the slow flow of the river and a dipper sitting on a rock in the water, shaking his head too. He was ready to dive into the water again but before he did he shook his head again. The only bird to walk under water. She smiled at the little creature, thankful for its sign.

No, you're right little one, for as much as Felix is understanding, I doubt he will ever go along with that!

She loved him so much but she sometimes struggled with his possessiveness over her. She knew it was his protectiveness and his love but at times it was a little too much for her. It worked like a prison. At those times she needed space to breathe for she felt trapped. Being on her own for twenty four years prior to meeting Felix she had developed a certain sense and affinity for freedom and independence. Once in a while she still very much craved this. It was a need for her survival and sanity it seemed.

Usually that meant going for a stroll in the woods or a flight to the ocean, flying with the speed of the swift just below the clouds with her blood racing through her. Only then did she feel alive. After those moments she felt much better and whole again but more importantly, her inner peace restored again and her state of mind calmer.

Like any couple they quarrelled every so often. Just raising their voices, never any violence though, only harsh words; which could hurt like knives all the same. But when things went really bad between them Sula would pay a visit to her sister-in-law, Feline, to talk. She was always such a good listener, never judging and always so patient, so calm and gentle, never hot-headed nor overpowering.

There were so many thoughts raging through her head she just couldn't get them organized.

Sula needed help. She needed Feline to talk to. As always she would know what to do. Although it did concern her a little.

I miss her company.

~~~

Sula stretched her legs and walked back to their camping spot. It was already afternoon by the time she re-joined Fay and Felix at the little warm lake they were swimming in. It was hot in the open spot in the woods by the lake whereas Sula had stayed in the shade all morning.

First she studied the two people she loved most of all in the world before she stripped herself bare and joined the splashing father and child.

Their eyes met and time seemed to stand still for a moment. That amazing silence again as ever when Felix and Sula looked at each other; a sign of true love…

Fay played in slow motion in the shallow water. Felix's laugh had frozen as he saw his beautiful wife entering the lake. The water closed in around her shoulders as she swam towards him, smiling alluringly. He blinked slowly, drops of water on his long eyelashes, the sunlight on his light hair and in his clear blue eyes, the water glittering on his bronze skin. He grinned, suddenly feeling shy, as she finally reached him. She rose from the water, placing her arms around his neck, not letting go of their gaze and kissed him gently. He kissed her back, holding her.

Chapter 22 Stubborn

I have made my decision.' Sula spoke in a steady voice meeting Shazar the following morning.

On the edge of the woods where they stood he watched her in anticipation, standing so close, almost touching her, waiting patiently for her to continue. The sun shone in his eyes and he wore the black headband that covered his ears. She wondered where his belongings were or if he had any. She hadn't seen him carry any rucksack or even a bedroll.

He won't need anything, living like an animal that lives off the land, using their abilities to stay warm and dry, Sula thought, remembering herself when she led a nomadic life. She however did carry a rucksack with some books and personal belongings; no doubt Shazar would scold her for that too as it was very human to be attached to things.

'It is for the best this way,' she said meeting his eyes. 'You must agree with me that it is,' she almost whispered, feeling slightly guilty but she owed him nothing personally. 'We must part and you must find a human female to mate with and continue the line and perhaps you will find love as well. Maybe our children can come together one day.' *Oh, Bhan, I'm passing on the burden!*

His eyes narrowed and his mouth thinned, waves of both anger and despair flaring his face.

'How... can you talk like this? After all those years of searching?' He shook his head, his throat felt thick with shock.

'It's for the best. It will only complicate our lives. I'm married, Shazar, and I love my family!'

'Sula...Sula, your mind is clouded by your affection for the man. I won't judge you anymore for that. You promised your mother, didn't you? The Comyenti Oath...'

She blinked at that. *How did he know?*

He nodded understandingly. 'You needed to mate. With this child a new future for the comyentis would come; that's what both you and your mother believed. But you were both wrong as I explained previously! You have been lonely, never really fitting in with either animal kingdom or human world. But now that we have found each other you need never feel alone ever again. You can undo the bond, the Heartmerge, you know. It will be hard, but necessary.'

How arrogant is he! 'No,' she said simply, frowning. 'There are other options. I have thought about it!'

Shazar regarded her for a long moment. She was so beautiful, like no human woman could be, and he knew he was better looking than her handsome man was but it shouldn't be their looks that mattered to either of them. It was the principle of things.

She had softened and forgotten the importance of their mission.

Weak like a human!

'There are no other options,' he answered her matter-of-factly.

She sighed. He was so stubborn, even more than she was, and it would be hard to convince him.

'I understand that it must come as a shock for you to find another comyenti already bound to another man.'

'Bound? You are not *bound*, Sula! A comyenti does not let herself become bound to anyone. Only humans do that sort of thing. True, swans and wolves mate for life among other animals, as do *we*. But *our* bond is different to those strict chains of humans. You have forgotten the ways of the comyenti… or don't know them! I could teach you. You are a free solitary spirit and with me you would stay free. Even free to see what's his name…Felix. I would never claim you.'

She studied his almost feminine features and the fixed expression of his dark green eyes.

'I'm married to Felix. I took my wedding vow.'
'You mean your Comyenti Oath?'

'Of course.' She showed him her wedding band on her left hand; a silver ring with a tiny scarlet heart that shone bright in the sunlight.

'Ai!!!'

'What else did you expect after five years of being with Felix?' She shook her head in annoyance.

'He proposed to me after Fay's birth,' and she smiled, remembering. 'during my pregnancy. He always somehow feared I would leave but wisely didn't mention the subject of marriage, although it's highly unheard of around here not to marry before the birth of a child. We were the talk of the village but Felix, proud as he was, respected and loved me already so much. Instead, he gave me the opportunity to settle in.'

'Hmm, human rituals are nothing but folly! Marriage, pah! Empty and meaningless and adultery is very common amongst humans. No, our Heartmerge is sacred and comyentis mate for life. We don't need rings or other symbols as proof of that!'

'Don't lecture me! I cannot. Besides…giving up my life as I know it and my Heartmerge with him would be…like dying.'

'Then…he has made you happy…'

'Yes!'

Sula tried to calm herself down and stared up at the strong beech tree near her; the sun through its leaves, giving them an almost yellow colour, touching its smooth grey bark. Her heartbeat slowed right down. Trees did that to her.

'That's good but you and I know it won't last. He can never fully be a match for you like I can. You will lose him anyhow. You will outlive him by more than a hundred years. *That* is a long time, Sula. Have you talked to him about it?'

'I have,' her voice sounded fragile and tired. 'He knew that this day could come and however hard it is for him in some ways he supports me in whatever choice I make. Felix loves me.'

Shazar sniffed and brushed it off. The guy wouldn't be a threat to his plan anyway. He was no match for Shazar.

'Let me spend some time with you,' he started. 'make you see-'

'I cannot! I have already made up my mind, brother! I am deeply sorry, but for what it's worth, I still want you to be a part in my life and learn more about our heritage from you. I know so little.'

He looked startled. He wasn't letting go of her now that he had found her and he certainly wouldn't settle for less than to be her partner, her mate, her lover, or at least the father of their children! As if she read his mind she said, 'I did think about the possibility of you and I having children together and thus ensuring a strong comyenti line,' Sula sighed. 'I know I owe it to our species, all those that died,' She rubbed her forehead. 'I wouldn't have to leave Felix. I told him and he said he would accept it. What do you think about that? We would still be thinking about the future of our kind, we wouldn't have to love each other. And you could see your children once in a while.'

He bit his lip.

Well, at least she will have me mate with her. I could show her.

'Sounds reasonable, but couldn't you…love me?'

'My heart belongs to another. I told you. It hasn't got to do with me being married to him or any bond,' she touched her heart. 'It goes deeper than that. It was already like that before the Heartmerge-'

The Heartmerge! It suddenly dawned on her that a bond between her and Shazar would be formed if they tried to have children; a bond she really could do without. He would be able to hear her thoughts! But before she could open her mouth to ask, he said, 'I…I have to think about your suggestion.'

She nodded gravely, 'I have another one as well,' she started, her eyes calmer now. 'If you would find someone to love and mate with; a human female I mean, and start a family with, *my* children; mine and Felix *and yours*, half comyenti, could continue the line. For if I do give birth to *our* children they would also have to mate eventually with a human again, since there are no other comyentis. They can't possible mate with each other so what difference would it make in the end? I think we have a better chance in continuing the line if we both mate a human! Gradually there would be more comyentis; halflings yes, but coming together better and at least raising their families and spreading our kind. We will see to it that they keep their abilities alive, even though it might be harder to master the Mindmerge, we'll teach them. Fay is managing the Mindmerge already really well,' she looked at him intensely. 'We won't have to be alone and even better we will be linked together by our connected families; growing larger and stronger. Building a new comyenti civilisation.'

It was silent for a long time, Shazar lost in his thoughts and Sula staring at him trying to read his mind.

She does have a point. But she wouldn't be mine. His heart sank to his feet. Since when did he become so selfish and possessive? He admitted to himself that he would be disappointed if he could not be her partner, even if it was all for the higher purpose. Comyentis mated for life; it was in their instincts, so it wasn't so strange for Sula not to want to let go of Felix, nor Shazar to be able to let go of *her* that easily.

'No, not with halflings,' he shook his head. '*Our* children would be comyenti again.'

She sighed. 'Even if we have *ten* children together; they will *all* have to find a human again to make babies with and they too will be halflings or quarterlings or whatever! What is the difference? It is inevitable, Shazar! Why are you so against halflings, because we're mixed with humans, your enemy? They will still have our abilities, they won't be anything less! I have grown to accept certain things and by loving a human I have risen above myself, but above all I've found the strength and kindness in my own heart to free myself from any hatred and bigotry! So can you, Shazar,' she added a bit milder.

'Our children, mixed with humans, thus *combined* will be the future!'

Shazar's face was one full of horror and his eyes were shifting colour rapidly.

No, I won't stand for it!

~~~

Shazar still fumed inside and could not accept her proposal.

'Shazar, I don't want to lose you altogether but I think it's for the best if you go along with my idea!'

'What? Finding a human female, mating with her, having *halflings*, my *halflings* mating with your quarterlings or even *humans* again?' His face crimsoned at the thought. He felt embarrassed and hurt.

'Not all humans are as bad as you think. Back in my village-'

'You live in a human village?!' His voice rose.

'Yes, no, well only on the outskirts of one, I thought I told you-'

He stood up with warning eyes and a tight jaw.

'You *must* leave that place before they hurt you!'

Sula licked her lips. 'Must I?' With her own eyes bearing nothing but anger now, glaring at him, she spoke, 'You do not command me! The Rosinhillers are friendly animal loving people. They do not suspect I'm comyenti. They know I am different, but so are Felix and his sister-'

'It is only a matter of time before they will find out. They always do!' He shouted.

'Even if they do, I don't fear them nor should you. They have become my friends. I will show you.'

'I don't *fear* them, I *despise* them!' he said with narrowed eyes. 'You seem to have forgotten our past, all the lives that were lost at their hands!'

No, it certainly wasn't fear she saw in his eyes, it was hatred all right.

'In a group they are dangerous and I won't come with you to this village, nor will a child of mine ever set foot there! I will raise my children *with* you somewhere else. We can travel and stay safe. We were already nomads before the killing started,' He now looked at her with pleading eyes and said in a softer voice, 'Please think about it. If you are going to have my children you can't possibly *stay* in a human village?'

'Didn't you listen to me? You can't keep living in the past with hatred in your heart. *That* surely is not the comyenti way! Also we're more than our bodies and no one controls me or my body! My idea is the best for the security of our future. Besides, we can't have *our* comyenti children interbreed with one another! Surely you do see that?'

He grumped at that.

She raised one eyebrow. 'It's wrong, unnatural and selfish! The burden you put in their shoes! What and who are we to do that to anyone? What happened to you that you started to think this way?'

He stood tall and shouted, 'Genocide! That's what happened! To see your only family getting slain and burned in front of your eyes and still to this day hearing your baby sister's cries for help in your ears!' His eyes were filled with tears now.

'I know and I'm sorry, Shazar. That must have been horrible, but those evil people who did that are all long gone. So are we...' she mumbled and looked sad, shaking her head.

'No, they're still out there, Sula! People who think and act the same and they would do it all over again to us! I'm not looking for trouble, not anymore, but I know that if we were with more comyentis living close to humans, history would repeat itself all over again. I've seen what they do to other animals, and so have you. They haven't changed! You can't possibly be safe in this village, sooner or later they'll be the end of you.'

'Look, we can't bring our people back, not the way you want to! If your sister would have been alive today, you wouldn't even think about having a child with her, would you?'

His eyes narrowed, he sniffed but he saw what she was getting at.

'Then stop thinking this way. I love where I live and I will not give up my life. I'll discuss having your child further with Felix, although I really don't see what good it will do and I'm sure that won't be the end of it. And he or she will grow up with Felix and I, which I know you don't like, so *you* must respect *our* decision in the end, Shazar. You must!'

He dropped his head but gave no reply.

Chapter 23 Opponents

'So, how did it go?' Felix asked, looking up at Sula. He sat in front of the tent he had built with Fay, carving some wood.

Sula shook her head. 'He still won't come to meet you.'

Felix continued working on his wooden figurine, Fay who sat next to him, watched his hands closely.

'Rude, but well I suppose it is hard for the man to realise I have taken his one and only potential mate.'

She flopped down beside him, knowing he wasn't as relaxed as he appeared to be. That he was carving wooden figurines indicated that he had a lot on his mind, because working the wood de-stressed him.

'He just has his mind stuck on one idea that he hardly listens to what I have to say. He is more stubborn than I am.' And she briefly told her husband what had happened.

He stopped carving, holding the knife firmly, he read her face and quickly came to the conclusion what had occurred.

'Maybe I should have a word with him. Your children interbreeding with one another, sick bastard! Besides he can't expect you to run off with him and leave us behind! You have made a life, found a home!'

'No, Felix. I have to do this myself. I mentioned the ideas we discussed, but he said he has to think about it.'

'Think about what exactly? What right does he have and who does he think he is?'

'Er, the last comyenti?' Sula replied. 'And I'm only half of one.'

He grumbled at that. 'He is nothing more than you! If…you hadn't met me…would you have-'

'Oh, Felix, I know it must be hard on you. I won't let you think this way. Here and now is all that matters. He cannot come in between us, I won't let that happen.'

He hugged her and held her longer than he normally would have.

'What's next then?' he whispered in her hair.

'He will let me know.'

'It's your body and your life, *our* life we're talking about,' he got upset. *And you're my life,* he added in thought.

'Yes, but his dream is shattered.'

'Hmm, it's not his dream either; it's the *comyenti* dream and what would he have done if you'd been a man? He would see that the best shot you have is to both mate with a human female to continue the line and join your children together later on. Simple as that!'

'I agree honey, it should be no different now that I'm married, except for the fact that I am not a man.'

Felix grinned sheepishly at her. 'Thank the Great Bhan for that!'

She punched him teasingly in his side and they laughed together.

'Mummy,' Fay said suddenly. They had forgotten all about her, she had been listening all along. 'Tallon said he wished he was a girl like me.'

Sula looked at her questioningly.

'Why, sweetie?'

'To make his mummy happy. She wants a girl. Tallon has four older brothers and they all make his mommy crazy he says with their fighting and making the house look like a mess. So he wants to be a girl for her.'

Sula chuckled at that. 'Well, I can imagine, but Tallon mustn't worry about his mummy, darling, nor should you. You're too young for that.'

And she realised again what madness she found herself in. Putting children on this world was not something to be thought of lightly and their future and the burden they would have to carry.

~~~

'Do we have to wait for him?' Felix said sighing. 'Fay is getting restless.'

'*You* are getting restless,' Sula corrected him.

'Well, that too. We still have a long walk back.' He thought of the animals, his sister took care of while they were away, as well as their crops and Sula's garden. It was hard work for her on her own, but she was helped a little by friends in the village or his parents, but they were getting older.

'I can always fly you back, you know that,' she laughed and added, 'Perhaps he will walk back with us.'

'I thought he didn't want to interfere?'

'Yes, but it will be a good lesson for him to meet a kind human and learn something from our family.' She winked at Felix.

Felix smiled at her. 'Hmm, so that he might change his mind and go and do the same or see that I'm not a bad father, good thinking, love. I will pack our things.'

~~~

Sula's hair hung loosely around her face, clinging in damp curls at the base of her neck. It was already hot, she could easily cool down using the ability of the elephant but she usually decided against it. She tried to set the right example to her daughter so as not to get too dependent on their skills.

She glanced at Fay and a shaft of sunlight glinted in her eyes, making them sparkle in the green shadows. Fay was as always amazed by her mother's beauty and once more her heart was touched. She drew near, almost cautiously, as the forest light caressed her mother. They stopped by a river and her mother undressed and laid their clothes down beneath an old gnarled pine tree. Pine needles were tangled in her wavy hair, and the white remains of a sticky cobweb clung to her arm. She knelt down in just her underwear. Her hand was cupped around a single bright orange blossom of a yandala, blooming in the shadow of the old tree. It was an orchid type of flower but with only one single flower on its single stem. Its petals were exquisitely shaped; orange with yellow stripes. Its heart was ruby red with yellow pollen.

'Oh,' Fay exclaimed. 'It's beautiful.'

Sula smiled at her, close to tears at finding the flower here.

'And very rare,' she added softly, sitting back on her heels, her hands resting on top of her thighs. The sunlight cast a hard gleam in her eyes, and they glowed like those of an animal caught at night in torchlight. 'Like you, Fay,' and she paused before she said, 'My mother; Almaz, your grandmother, showed me a yandala once and told me it only flowers every four years,' *How coincidental! Shazar told me comyenti women are fertile every four years!* 'And not only that,' Sula continued in a mysterious voice. 'It relies solely on a specific bee; the billbee, for its pollination.'

'The billbee.' Fay giggled.

'It's called that because of its bill-like long mouth; but it's really just a long tongue.'

'Just like a butterfly! But mummy, what if the bee doesn't find this flower?'

'Well, bees have a very good sense of smell and sight and will travel miles to find their flowers. This one has a very strong fragrance. Here can you smell it?'

Fay inhaled whilst closing her eyes. 'Mmm, yummy!'

'But if the bee doesn't find her…then the yandala will eventually die out.' Sula concluded.

Fay nodded sadly and Sula wished she hadn't mentioned it to her, even though there might be another yandala around, growing nearby…like Shazar…

What would mother have said about this all?

Sula turned away her face, thinking about her mother whom she so missed and hid her face from her daughter as well as her thoughts. Fay could tell and this frightened the girl a little. Sula sensed this, so she quickly distracted her by freeing herself from her underwear and jumped in the river. Fay soon followed and they went on with the business of washing themselves with their self-made jasmine soap. Fay splashed her mother, trying to cheer her up, which worked and now they were both laughing.

Suddenly Fay stopped, looked up and asked, 'Mummy, who is that man?'

Sula was shocked to see Shazar standing on the other side of the river, watching them.

Quickly she covered her breasts and dipped down to her chin, glancing to Fay, luckily the child was in the water up to her shoulders. You never know, for all she knew he might have his hopes on her daughter if he had heard their conversation from earlier. When she looked again he was gone.

The sick coward! He won't come here but he can watch!

She decided not to tell Felix since it would only anger him and she knew he kept all his emotions inside for her and Fay's sake.

Instead they left the spot, but she hoped that he would reappear and confront them instead of following from a distance.

He did follow them, both Sula and Fay sensed him, but he didn't show himself.

It was only when they reached their next camping spot which they planned to stay at for just one night that he appeared again. Felix and Fay were building the simple tent and Sula tended to the fire alone. Shazar took this opportunity and approached her slowly.

Without looking up at him she said, 'What took you so long?'

He raised his chin at Felix, who had not spotted him yet, being too busy with the tent. Shazar did not wear his headband tonight.

'A fire?' he said questioningly. 'Why do you have a fire if not to cook meat?'

Sula looked up at him, annoyed. 'I told you we don't eat meat. It's to boil the water for our tea and porridge.' And she rattled with the pans.

'Tea, when you can drink fresh water? Porridge?'

'Look, I don't want a discussion with you about our lifestyle. We make porridge with oats, dried fruit and water. Fay and Felix love it. At home we have goats milk but only for Fay. And we love herbal tea; it is healthy and soothes the mind. If *you* just eat leaves and berries, that's your decision.'

Shazar wasn't fazed.

'It is the comyenti way,' he responded. 'We eat everything raw; we steer away from cooked food. In fact I hardly *ever* eat; you *know* we don't need to. As you probably also know kangaroos can live without water

190

for up to five years and cold blooded animals need less food than mammals. I can go into marine iguana-mode and live off vegetation that would not keep a rabbit alive and I would still flourish. So could you.'

Sula grew annoyed.

'You sound just like my mother!' she snarled.

Shazar just grinned at that. 'I would have loved to have known her.'

She stood up suddenly and walked towards him, grabbing his hand. His eyes grew bigger in surprise, but he did not protest as she gently urged him toward the tent, towards the human.

'Felix, there is someone who wants to say hello.'

He looked up from his work to stare at the handsome man. Shazar's ears were so much bigger at the tips than Sula's or Fay's were. Yes, he could understand why Shazar kept himself hidden from people. They wouldn't understand his strange beauty and above all his ways and abilities; knowing Sula's all too well.

'Hi,' Felix said with a strained voice and came to shake his hand. The stranger did not withdraw but took his hand in his, feeling the strength of Felix, squeezing his hand; was that a warning? Shazar had to admit she had chosen well. He nodded in greeting, letting go of Felix's hand as soon as he could.

'You are welcome to join our little camp and the warmth of our fire and food.'

'I have no need for such things,' Shazar retorted, a bit too harsh for Sula's liking.

Had she once been like this?

Felix smiled, taking no offence. *Definitely a comyenti*, he thought bemused to himself.

'Suit yourself,' he answered calmly.

'Shazar, I want you to meet my daughter Fay. Fay, could you come here please?' Sula said.

Looking up from her play area underneath a tree, where she had been watching a trail of busy ants. She eyed the man intently and came running towards her family.

'You are the man who's been observing us,' she said with narrowed

191

eyes, then frowned her little pretty brows when she noticed his ears.

Felix frowned as well and stared questioningly from his daughter to Shazar who did not flinch and then to his wife who coloured slightly and shrugged.

'Hello, young lady,' Shazar said to Fay.

'Hello,' she said and gave him only a small smile, still staring in wonder at his pointed ears.

'Can I look closer?' she asked innocently and he knelt so that she could. He didn't mind. He stared with soft eyes at the girl as she touched his ears gently.

'They are huge! Will mine be that big one day?' she asked him, knowing she and he were related somehow.

'No, Fay, more like those beautiful ears of your mother.' he answered, pointing at Sula with love in his eyes. Felix noticed it and flinched.

Fay stared at Sula's ears and smiled warmly, touching her own ears at the same time.

'Okay.' she said nonchalantly and ran away again.

Sula sighed, watching her daughter leave, apologising for her.

'She is like a sparrow; one moment here, the next gone.'

Shazar smiled lightly. 'You have a lovely daughter, Sula.'

'Yes, *we* are very proud of her,' Felix said a little irritated, stepping in between them, wanting to entice Shazar's attention away from his wife.

'I'm making us all some supper,' Sula said. 'Please Shazar, I know you don't need much food and can do without it for a long time but we would like to share our meal with you. It's a social thing as well, you know; sharing food, just like most primates do. It would be an honour if you would stay a while.'

He stared back at the woods he belonged in and then at the woman he needed. She was his future, so it wasn't hard for him to decide. Slowly he nodded.

Sula smiled relieved. *So far so good. This is not an easy step for him.*

They sat around the fire that evening, eating a simple meal of pancakes and blueberries and drinking mint tea. The atmosphere was surprisingly relaxed, even though Shazar didn't say much, just listened to

Fay telling little funny tales. After Sula had taken Fay to bed, something usually Felix did, she returned hastily, not wanting to leave the men alone for too long, immediately sensing the mood had changed while she had been away.

'You must have seen a great deal of the world?' Felix asked, sipping his hot but refreshing tea. The evening was warm and oppressive and Sula knew a thunderstorm was on its way. Dark clouds were forming overhead as they spoke. She knew they would be safe tonight and dry, as those clouds would move on, but tomorrow they would surely need to seek shelter.

'I have,' Shazar answered him plainly.

Felix watched him closely waiting for him to share an adventure with them, but he just locked his mouth and closed his eyes as he inhaled the scent of the mint tea, leaves that he had seen Sula pick that morning. He had to admit; herbal tea was indeed very soothing.

'Sula, you must tell him the story of the magical flute.'

Shazar looked up and stared expectantly at Sula, ignoring Felix. She smiled sweetly at her husband.

'I don't know if Shazar wants to hear about my adventures, Felix.'
'Oh, but I do, Sula,' Shazar objected.
'Well, there isn't much to tell.' But to ease the tension somewhat she started to tell him the story of the enchanted flute that a group of nomads carried along with them; it had been stolen from a sea witch in the west. The nomads weren't able to play a tune on it as she soon found out but she knew somehow there was magic at work and curiosity got the better of her. She followed them through the desert and along the plains, for she knew they had plans to sell their stolen goods at a market in a nearby city, including the flute. Sula had waited until one night when the group was asleep but as she was about to take the enchanted flute, one of the desert men woke up. He spotted her holding the instrument; the moment she laid her hands on it, it started to play. It had called out to her!

Sula found herself very vulnerable at that moment; enchanted, shocked and confused. The men acted quickly and tied her hands so she couldn't escape. But they soon spotted her unusual ears and shifting eyes and immediately backed off; thinking her some sort of evil in the shape of a beautiful woman. They came at her again and although she tried, she couldn't ward them off. After they had beaten her half to death, leaving her bruised and half-conscious, she realised that they were taking her to the city in their wagons to try and sell her along with the flute.

'It came to the moment they had packed the flute along with the other things to sell and I had to really concentrate in order to regain my strength,' Sula said. 'They did not expect me to be that strong for a woman but I used the force of the elephant to knock them all down and pretty soon I had them all tied up inside their own wagons.'

'You didn't kill them? Shazar asked confused.

She glanced with disgust at him. 'Of course not!'

'But they used violence against you!

'I didn't know it was 'the comyenti way' to kill?' she asked sarcastically.

He lowered his head and mumbled, 'For the protection of our kind we have to kill everyone who finds out about us.' and he glanced sideways towards Felix whose eyes grew a bit bigger at that. Not afraid, just startled.

'What? My mother never told me this. Is this *your* Comyenti Oath, the one you vowed to your family?'

Shazar shook his head, 'If it was; no man would be safe around me.'

A short silence followed and they both could see Felix thinking to himself.

'What's a Comyenti Oath?' he asked his wife quietly.

Now it was Shazar's turn to be startled. 'He doesn't know?'

'Later, Felix,' she sighed. 'Later, let me continue my story.' And she finished, telling about the flute and how she knew which box they had packed it in. She had quickly found it and carefully wrapped the box in an extra piece of cloth so as to shield her ears against its content, as she didn't want to get overwhelmed and enchanted again. She remembered an animal that could shut its nostrils and ears to protect itself from insect bites; the pangolin, an anteater. Then as quick as the cheetah she left the city, sprinting at top speed and when she reached safety, about half a mile away from any man in the Shadow Mountains she went into antelope-mode to run deeper and longer into the lonely mountains. It was there she unclothed the box and opened it.

'Why hadn't the men been enchanted like I was? I asked myself,' Sula said. 'But I knew it was because they hadn't truly listened to the flute and they couldn't play a decent tune on it. Of course being a comyenti is half the trouble; we listen, whether we want to or not.' She smiled a half-smile.

'Why did they want to sell it?' asked Shazar.

Sula looked at him in a mysterious way. 'Because it had belonged to a sea witch and therefore they knew it had to be something special and that they could get a good price for it even if the beautifully carved instrument lacked a good sound. Magic sells. The man who had woken up that night, when I tried to steal it, heard it too; so he knew it had to be magical.'

She told Shazar she had wanted to find out what the secret of the flute was. Sensing it wasn't evil magic, she tried to make a connection with it. It had a soul just as she expected and it asked her to help it.

'So I did. I played a song on it; a specific song and found out it was a good flute, and that the others simply hadn't known how to play it. It was that very song that set it free.'

'What did you set free?' Shazar asked, observing her.

'A little girl.'

Shazar frowned and leaned forward curiously.

'The sea witch had entrapped the little girl in her own flute after she had refused to play a song for the witch. She had heard the girl playing on the beach, and the witch loved music. But the girl had been too frightened to play for her so the witch cast her spell, saying that "Only The Song Of The Seagull played on the flute will set her free" and from then on she was cursed. The girl had been trapped inside the flute for nearly thirty years; having to play for the witch whenever she commanded. Over the years as the witch grew older, she'd forgotten all about the cursed girl and so she lay in wait all that time for the moment someone would listen to her crying out in distress. When the witch died and all hope seemed lost, thieves came into the witch's home and found her body. They took all the valuable things they could find from her hut. They were the travelling desert men.'

Sula had promised to protect the girl who had not aged over time. They set out to find the village of her birth on the shores of Cohel in the west. Her parents were old and white-haired by now but they were still alive and filled with joy as they welcomed their girl home. They had grieved so much for her over the years thinking she had been murdered and they wanted to thank Sula for rescuing her. All Sula had asked in return was that they showed respect for all that lived and be especially kind to all the animals that lived by the coast and in the sea. Her parents were fishermen, so she could not ask of them to give up their profession, but she did teach them how to make a different kind of net; so that dolphins and small sharks would no longer get caught in their nets. The parents said Sula was welcome there anytime and the girl gave her the flute that she had been captured in as a thank-you for everything that she had done. At first Sula had refused, since it had such a sad history, but the girl insisted; saying it would be a reminder of her courage should Sula ever doubt herself in times to come and whenever Sula played that flute she would think of Marin, the girl she had rescued.

'I'm not a great musician but the flute has a special place in my home now and my heart,' Sula smiled, staring distantly up at the stars.

'That is some story!' Shazar's thoughts went immediately to Twello; the boy he himself had saved, and wondered how he was faring. Sula and he were very much alike in that sense; never thinking twice to save someone, even if they were human. For children they would both go out of their way even though it sometimes meant risking themselves. That was the strength of the comyenti; to show compassion. However he himself had tried to stay out of human affairs as much as possible.

'It was risky and you got yourself hurt,' he said softly.

'But nevertheless I always prevail.' She made an appealing movement with her eyes, smiling.

Felix grinned proudly at her with love in his eyes.

'She certainly does, wait until you hear about the time she came to my village and-'

Shazar suddenly squeezed his tea cup too hard and it broke; spilling what was left of the tea over his clothes, as well as pieces of broken clay. Sula and Felix stared at him, incredulously. He apologized, trying to wipe his black tunic dry with a handkerchief.

Sula bit her lip, for she sensed his sudden anger and stood up.

'I am sorry but I am tired and will turn in for the night now. I will see you in the morning.'

Both Felix and Shazar stood, as was custom. Felix was surprised he even knew how to show some respect for a lady but Sula had already walked to the tent.

Shazar opened his mouth, following Sula with his eyes but Felix shot him a warning look and he wisely refrained. Felix sat down, threw another log on the fire and said, 'Sit down Shazar. I have something to discuss with you.'

Frowning Shazar followed Felix's instruction and stared interestedly at Felix, looking him in the eye in a way he had not done before.

'I know what you want from her and I can't say I blame you,' Felix started out plainly. 'If I were the last comyenti male and she the last comyenti female I would probably be after the same thing. The fact that she is amazing, intelligent and stunningly beautiful; the dream of every man, makes it even easier,' he pursed his lips together. 'But you see if *I* were in your boots; *I* would back off the moment I saw she was happily married. Even if it would spoil everything you always hoped for. You spoke of personal feelings to Sula; that she had to forget about me and her life with me and leave her home-'

'Just to try to make her understand the importance of-' Shazar interrupted.

'If you would let me finish, please,' Felix replied sternly, but very calmly, whilst refusing to look at him. Felix tried so hard to stay composed to keep his anger under control.

'I see you looking at my wife with interest and lust,' Felix stated.

'Now, wait a moment-' Shazar appealed.

Felix narrowed his eyes at Shazar.

'No, I won't, for I recognise the signs. I do not have to be a comyenti to see that! Now, if she decided to go with you, however painful that would be for me and Fay, I could understand.' *I've always known, feared, that day could come.* 'Or have your child, but she's made it clear to you that she doesn't want to. She gave you an option, so... do you accept it?'

Shazar did not answer, fuming inside, coiling his fists staring into the flames of the fire. *What is he to me? How dare he treat me like this!?*

Felix sensed from the expression on his face that Shazar did not agree with him.

'I warn you, Shazar. If you hit on my wife I-'

'You will what?' Shazar's eyes suddenly glowed like embers as they seemed to burn into Felix's. 'You know you are no match for me,' Shazar said through gritted teeth. 'Pah, you are not even a match for Sula! I don't know what she sees in you, but it must be something to hold her attention for so long! I assure you; she will come to me sooner or later.' He stood. Felix's eyes were firing back at him in rage, he also stood with coiled fists in front of his chest as if ready to fight.

He will not come between us! Was all Felix could think of. *Over my dead body!*

Shazar growled, almost like a wolf, from deep within his throat, his eyes glowing yellow! Sula's eyes could change colour from emerald to dark jade, depending on her mood interspersed with orange. Shazar grinned wickedly at him with those yellow eyes. When he noticed Felix's shock reaction, he turned and shot off towards the woods.

Felix followed Shazar's leaving; standing rigid and cursing him under his breath. He then started kicking sand into the fire, demanding him to be gone from their lives, wishing he had never come into theirs in the first place; comyenti or not, this was going too far.

Chapter 24 A History Lesson

I just want him gone, Sula, seriously. Before I do something I might regret!' Felix hissed the following morning while Fay was getting water at a nearby stream. Grey clouds were starting to form and the wind picked up, meaning it would probably rain soon.

Sula looked at him, surprised, because although passionate, he was not normally a violent man. He kept outside the tent for most of the night in anger, taking watch and protecting his family from the intruder in their lives, before finally slipping inside in the early moments of the morning. He had waited patiently for them to wake up, to share breakfast with them. Waiting for the right occasion to share his worry with Sula but only once their daughter was out of ear shot.

'What happened last night?'

'That arrogant bastard thinks you will go to him freely and that I…I can't possibly hold your attention throughout your long life. No, he thinks he's perfect, he's comyenti after all and he thinks you will choose him over me!'

Sula took his shaking hands in hers, calming him with her eyes.

'Honey, please don't worry. He is not a threat to us. I love you and you alone.' Her words calmed his raging heartbeat and slowed his breathing a little. He inhaled the morning freshness and could smell the coming rain. His senses were so much better since she had taught him to open up more to the world around him and to listen…truly listen.

'Yes, but for how long?' he asked with big eyes.

'What? What we have will never change; true love never does.' She smiled kindly at him.

He sighed, accepting this, for yes he knew she loved him, but still fear gnawed at his heart. 'Just be careful, love. I don't trust him.'

'Well, he is comyenti, so he *has* to be trusted,' *He has to promise first via the Comyenti Oath…* 'Yes, his thoughts and emotions are upsetting for us but it is humans who are violent and whom he despises,' she added.

I am human, Sula!

She sighed at that and nodded back at him, having heard his thoughts.

'I know but you're different,' Sula smiled at their old joke as did he. 'He won't come between us for the very fact that you are my partner, even if you are human. Moreover he will have to respect our bond!'

Felix raised his eyes at that, as Shazar hadn't shown much respect at all so far, but before he could say anything further he saw Fay coming back with the water and he quickly concluded, 'I will do anything needed to defend my family, Sula, *anything.*'

'Just as long as you promise me you won't kill him, you mustn't do that,' she whispered, suddenly afraid.

'You know I can't kill and I know the importance of the continuance of your kind, but he has to stay away from us. I will give him some time to think things through, but in the end he will have to respect your decision!'

She nodded, 'I will make him understand.'

~~~

It rained heavily for the whole day and the little family sought shelter in a nearby cave. They hadn't seen Shazar all day, but Sula sensed he was around somewhere. Lightning flashed outside the cave followed by rumbles of thunder.

Inside they were playing mind games to keep themselves busy. However Felix looked worried and his mind wasn't completely there with everyone else. He would stare at length at his wife from time to time and she would beam back at him, telling him over and over in his mind not to worry.

*All I want is for you to be happy…*he said in his mind to her.

I am happy, my love, and she hugged him closely.

The following day the weather cleared up and they continued their journey home. The evenings were warm again so they set up camp in an open valley away from the trees and midges, only three days travel from Rosinhill.

After dinner when they had put Fay to bed the two parents sat outside the tent in silence, cuddling closely together, Felix's arm around Sula.

'You don't have to protect me all the time, Felix. I can take care of myself.' But she couldn't blame him really.

'I have to take a leak, I'll be back in a mo,' he said to her whilst getting up. He disappeared behind a bush, with his face turned towards her, so that he could still keep an eye on her. Sula rolled her eyes and shook her head mocking his concern and went to stoke the fire.

She thought she heard a sound, so she looked up from what she was doing. She couldn't see anything so she looked in Felix's direction but he was no longer there; she heard a ruffle from inside the tent.

'Are you turning in?' she asked him whispering so as not to wake Fay up, but got no response. She stood, felt a little uneasy and so walked over to the tent. When she opened the door flap she saw her husband lying on his tummy beside Fay, half wrapped in their blanket, his eyes closed. Kneeling beside him, she listened to his steady breathing. *Asleep.*

Sula rubbed the bridge of her nose while she thought. He did have a little too much of that home-made wine of his! She knew how that made him sleepy but she was a little surprised about him saying nothing to her before he went to sleep. That was odd. Sure enough he was asleep so she decided to join him but before she did she went outside to put out the fire. As she spread out the embers to disperse the flames she heard someone approaching. Looking up she saw Shazar!

She inhaled and caught his scent. He smelled different; better.

'Shazar.'

'Ah, Sula,' he said as he walked to greet her. He looked stunning in the waxing pale moonlight. His hair caught the dim light, so that it shone almost blue. His eyes were dark jade and glittering like stars. His black shirt open at the top; she could see the nape of his neck and his collarbone. She caught another whiff of his musky scent. She felt her heartbeat faster as she smelt his sweet perfume; so appealing, it made her head spin. He came closer and said in a low voice, 'I knew you would come to me.'

'I didn't,' she shook her head. 'Looks like you have been waiting for me.'

'Always Sula, but now you are here. That lost time doesn't matter anymore for you and I will have an eternity ahead of us.'

'No, Shazar, th…tha-' she stumbled over her words.

'Ssh, don't speak, we have been talking too much, that is not the comyenti way. We feel and *know* without words. A single comyenti thought or series of events shown to another in the mind can prevent misunderstandings and save lengthy tiresome explanations. Moreover, language or vocabulary does not have to apply.' And he touched her cheek gently. She shivered but she wasn't cold. He smiled longingly at her, his teeth white in the pale moonlight.

'You know this to be true,' he said.

She had indeed experienced this with her mother and with Fay, for they were family and therefore they shared the telepathic bond. She should have had it with Felix through the Heartmerge, but it only worked from one side. That had saddened her. Conversations weren't always easy with him. She understood *him* perfectly well and could *hear* what *he* thought; sometimes it was things about her and sometimes they were unjust thoughts to which she hotly tried to explain things to him with words. That was still not easy, as she was used to being understood from a young age, without having to use words; without even having to speak and waste her breath. Thoughts always came easier to Sula than language.

Shazar must have known this and was getting to her somehow by stepping on a heartstring. She couldn't seem to think clearly anymore.

He smelled so good; all she wanted to do was nestle her nose in his neck and inhale him and hold him close, like a flower or a pet. Sula stepped nearer. They stood face to face, but she jammed her eyes shut; fighting him with all her power but she somehow couldn't. In panic she thought of an animal that could shut out all sense of smell, but before she knew it she breathed him in again...

She felt drunk. His mouth was too close to hers but he didn't brush her lips. She closed her mouth on his in an impulse and breathed in more of his enchanting scent. Now she could feel his soft lips touching hers gently. They kissed tenderly and he held her close, caressing her neck and her long dark strands.

It seemed to go on for ever, until Shazar broke the spell and led her toward his tent and a blanket on the grass in front of it. She sat down and he took his shirt off before he touched her hair and pressed his lips on her forehead, her cheeks, her eyes and mouth, everywhere. Next he unbuttoned her shirt and as she lay half naked with Shazar kissing and touching her she wanted to whisper a name: Felix. She realised it wasn't him and she opened her eyes to see a dark haired man making love to her and not her fair blue eyed familiar husband. What was she doing?

'No!' she objected with force and he stopped to stare at her. 'No, Shazar! This isn't right.'

'It *feels* right, Sula. Don't you feel it too? You are one, from what the Truthstone told me, it doesn't matter that you had a human father. *We* are one and the same. I... love you.'

She shook her head at that and the hairs on her arms stood on end.

'No, no. You don't know me at all and I don't know you.'

He came closer with his face above hers, and she smelt his perfume again, bedazzled.

'But we do, we are the last, we do know each other. Soon we can read each other's minds.' He kissed her again, but she objected, seeing Felix's face in her mind all the time. *Felix...*

And she felt the love she felt for him burning in her chest, flowing through her entire body. But this man...all she felt was desire yes; but love no, only lust and that wouldn't be right. Not like this. If he wanted to mate to conceive it would have to be on *her* terms.

She shook him off her and she stood up, buttoning up her shirt and with one last look at him she walked away, leaving him half naked on the blanket, startled.

~~~

Inhaling the fresh nightly air, she seemed to wake up a bit. Suddenly she felt a grip on her wrist. She stared into the green eyes of the other comyenti. She opened her mouth to speak, but he shook his head.

'Don't.' His eyes looked determined as if to say, "Enough has been said," and he embraced her again. However this time she fought him off with anger.

'I said no!' And she ran away. But not to her tent, for she wouldn't want to mix Felix up in this. She didn't want him to get hurt either!

Your heart, my heart, she spoke in her head beginning to speak to the spirit of the antelope inside her. *Your heart, my heart, your breath, my breath, your spirit, my spirit…your mind, my mind…*

He caught up with her, even though she at one point used the running speed of the cheetah; the fastest land mammal on the planet. He ran beside her; using the same ability, smiling at her. The valley seemed to stretch on for ever and she couldn't hide from him, so she stopped, out of breath, panting, cooling herself down and slowing her heartbeat.

'What do you want Shazar?'

'The same as you. I am a suitable mate for you, Sula and you know it. One and one, Sula.'

'I don't know why I kissed you but I shouldn't have. I am married and I don't want this.' She wondered how it had been possible. It was so unlike her, she wasn't even attracted to him. Then she knew how; he must have been using pheromones of some animal.

Her eyes narrowed. 'You despicable man, how could you?'

He grinned boyishly. 'Easy. It was only natural. Admit that you liked it, I could tell.'

She grew crimson and anger was building up inside her, her eyes started shifting. But Shazar stayed so calm, so self-assured he didn't worry in the slightest.

'How could you use pheromones on me?' Sula asked again.

'I know I shouldn't have and believe me I wouldn't have used them, but that man of yours is sticking to you like a thistle; never letting me close enough to make you understand that you and I belong together. Besides I wouldn't be using it unless it was necessary. I have to admit, your bond with him is strong. But for the sake of our future, Sula, please let us finish this.'

Grabbing her around her waist, he used the pheromones again on her. She closed her eyes and her nose against his scent, now that she knew what he was doing to her. She shook him off once more but he grabbed her again and held her in his arms with all his strength; she fought him wildly.

It was comyenti against comyenti now; a creature she never before had to fight. It was indeed a fierce battle; he tried to throw her to the ground while she kicked and threw her fists at him but every time he was quick enough to escape her blows. They didn't use any animal abilities as there was no time to chant. Shazar had no intentions of hurting her. All he wanted to do was to hold her, to touch her. She felt it; she felt his desperation and his selfish reasons so she didn't care anymore, for if this was the comyenti way she didn't want any part of it.

How wrong had she been about him!

Nearing exhaustion she fell to the ground and before she had time to get up he was on top of her at; pinning her down, using his pheromones drugging her. She became weaker and fought him less, but it was her will against his. It went on for over an hour and she slowly lost strength. She came round suddenly. She must have passed out at some point. Laying on top of her he nearly knocked the air out of her with his weight. She had to push him off her and he rolled onto the grass, facing away from her. Was he crying?

They both sat on the grass, heavily panting, ruffled and shaking.

'I don't want to fight you, Sula,' she could hear him say with a sob, his eyes glistening in the pale light of the moon. 'I want to love you, if you'll just let me.'

She almost felt sorry for him…almost.

'I can't! I told you! I believed you to be kind and understanding at first but you betrayed my trust.' she muttered with narrow eyes.

He stared at the angry woman, rubbing his jaw where she had hit him before. She was fastening her loose breeches at the waist which must have come undone in the fight. She pointed a finger accusingly at him.

'You of all people, a comyenti, have become more human than I, a halfling ever will!'

'By preventing our kind from further thinning out; mixing with humans? *We* are the future, Sula, clearly you see that!'

'No, I told you, not like this. And *this* is certainly not the way, not by force, sheer violence! Is that what you think is the comyenti way! What do you want to teach your children? That we have become like *them*?'

He bit his lip at that. 'How can I give you up now, after all these years of searching?' he asked with tears streaming down his face.

'If *you* had the decency to agree to my plan, you wouldn't have to give me up all together. You could have perhaps fathered my children and stayed around; at least I offered you *that and* my friendship!'

'I'm sorry, Sula,' he shook his head in regret. 'Our choice has been taken away from us, I *had* to act now to bind you to me. Your husband would never have respected our decision.' He touched his heart.

'He would have, if *you* had respected our relationship. You were trying to rape me, Shazar, for it was against my will and I will never *ever* forgive you for that!'

He lowered his head.

'I wanted to impregnate you, yes. However…not against your will. If you had only gone along with my plan I wouldn't have had to use pheromones on you. You're fertile now, Sula, we can't wait any longer. Don't be selfish. I thought you would never have let me try otherwise. I wouldn't have taken you by force. I am sorry if you think otherwise.'

'Well, that won't do!' She was near tears herself now, embarrassed and disappointed in her own species. 'I could tell how badly you *wanted* me for your own pleasure. You're the one who is selfish here, not me! Using pheromones on me was the lowest you could have gone! And I still call that attempted rape!'

'I have not touched another woman, Sula. I've waited for you; saved myself for you. There have been many women who wanted me but I refused all of them.'

'And should I be grateful for that?' she asked with one eyebrow raised, shaking her head in disbelief.

'I have been more disciplined than you,' he pointed out.

'Well, excuse me, at least *I* didn't hurt anyone in the process!' she raged and towered above him.

*Oh you did, you will. We always do…*Shazar thought grimly.

'I am beginning to hate my comyenti side, Shazar, and you have made it worse. I'm even questioning *why* we have to use the abilities of animals for our *own* survival. Are we useless without them?'

'We would be human and have gone back a million years in progress, Sula.'

'Then it is perhaps true that we descend from humans and we are what they will one day become?' Sula asked.

'I correct myself; what they *could* be if they, just like our ancestors, abandon their evil side and ways,' he explained.

'How'd you know if they ever did? Do you think if they do then; humans will *become* comyenti?' Sula asked him.

'Who knows? Perhaps gradually, mankind has the potential. Especially some sensitive children who are still very close to nature. But like I said; it will take a million years, like evolution always does. It must have taken the best part of thousands of years for our kind to evolve on our home planet. But this is just guesswork though. I personally don't think we are related,' He toyed with the pendant around his neck. 'I might know a bit more on that if you're interested?'

She sighed wearily, 'Now is not the time, Shazar. I've had it! I need to go back to see if Felix is ok and not missing me. Maybe it's for the best that he doesn't get to know what happened between us. It would worsen the matter.'

He stared with soft eyes at her.

'You must love this man greatly, to give me up and our shared history… and our future…'

'We can still have a comyenti future, just not together,' she looked at him calmly. 'It's up to you. It has to be completely on my terms now; you have left me no choice. You either go along with my suggestion to find yourself a human mate and once you have conceived with her, let me know. If you don't respect this and ever try anything like what you've done tonight, on me or my children, I will *never* want to see you again. I will know if you follow us and I warn you not to do so for your own good.'

Shazar stared at her, feeling her disappointment but also her determination. Guilt and regret were building up inside him. He had to make it up to her somehow.

'We will reach Rosinhill tomorrow afternoon,' Sula finished saying. 'And I suggest you tell me your decision first thing in the morning.' Sula walked away and left him scattered and beaten, both in mind and body.

I have failed, was all Shazar could think of. *Failed…Or have I?*

Chapter 25 Departure

To Sula's relief she found Felix still fast asleep when she returned to the tent, but on closer inspection, mind to mind, she realised that he too had been drugged. He had been unconscious and not sleeping after all. She found a tiny bloody spot on his lower back. A bite-mark!

Shazar has used the sting of a poisonous spider! Sula was most upset at that. Not just because he had used his skills to assail her husband but also because he had to be very skilled to be able to link with insects whose time scale was different from mammals and communication with them near impossible. She'd never been able to, nor had her mother, as far as she knew.

So he had to get rid of Felix last night and by using the spider's sting, Felix would have been sedated for over two hours, she reckoned. Time enough for him to…

She didn't want to think about that anymore and cursed herself for not being aware of the imminent danger and not shielding herself from him by closing her ears, nose and eyes to him. What was done was done, she thought to herself, sighing. At least he didn't get as far as to actually rape her.

Sula sat watch for the rest of the night until Fay woke up and then finally so did Felix. Unfortunately, though she had initially wanted to keep it from him, she couldn't. It wouldn't have been fair. Besides when Felix woke up he remembered that something had stung him on his back and he had instinctively known it had to have been big bug Shazar.

'That creepy crawly son of a…-' he started saying loudly but Sula placed her hand closely over his mouth, so that Fay wouldn't hear him swear. Their daughter giggled at seeing her father so angry, for she rarely witnessed scenes like this. He mumbled on behind her hand until she asked Fay to go and prepare breakfast. Felix started going purple in the face so Sula had to let go of his face and let him carry on his rant.

'How could he? I warned him! Are you alright?' he asked suddenly and held her closely, examining her face and noticed a big red mark in her neck.

'Of course I am, you know me!'

'Did you fight or,' and he looked closer. 'Is that a…hicky?'

Sula shrugged at that.

'He's got marks and bruises too, you can be sure of that!'

'But he is comyenti, like you! You told me…he wouldn't be a threat! If only I had listened to my own gut feeling then…then-' 'It's all over now. I told him it's either my plan or nothing.' Sula replied sternly.

'He will never go along with that! Never!' Felix shouted.

'We will see about that.' Sula spoke calmly and then got changed into different clothes, trying to get rid of Shazar's smell on her.

After a rather tense breakfast they saw a figure standing a short distance away. Felix had hardly eaten at all, too wrapped up in anger and wrath to eat. He had been constantly on the lookout. It was Felix who saw him first and he jumped up and started charging towards him.

'Felix, don't!' Sula shouted after him.

'For Fay's sake, don't!' she screamed desperately. She had to give him something to think about in his rage. It was a poor excuse but Fay witnessed it all. Felix did actually stop when he neared Shazar.

'You heard my wife; I will respect her wish but I assure you if you *ever* touch her again I will… I will make sure you wished you'd never met me!

'I have come in peace, Felix. I apologize to you and Sula. I was a fool,' Shazar said grimly without any emotion in either his voice or his expression. Shazar didn't know whether Sula had told him about the details of their encounter last night or his actions.

Felix narrowed his eyes and stared with distrust at him.

'I will never trust you again, nor will Sula. If you so desperately want a family create your own!'

'I understand.' He looked over Felix's shoulder and saw that Sula came closer.

She came to stand next to Felix and she laid her hand on his shoulder. Shazar followed the gesture with his eyes and instantly felt jealous.

'Please, don't look at me like I am your enemy. I have come to apologize, for I know I was wrong. I was desperate. You know how desperate one can be.'

Felix regarded him and said, 'Respect. You wondered what she sees in me. Now, *that's* what she sees in me! We respect and trust each other. You acted out of order!'

'Being the last and understanding a *lot*, I still would never have done what you did to me; not only using your abilities against me but also forcing yourself upon another comyenti,' Sula spoke to Shazar. 'It was an evil thing to do, Shazar.'

He closed his eyes and swallowed hard at that, knowing her to be right.

'I will leave,' he said opening his eyes slowly.

'Good!' Felix said. 'And never come back!'

Sula ignored him and asked Shazar, 'Where will you go?'

'To Southland, to a village called Randaria; near the Derubian Sea in the area known as Naru. I know a woman there I can trust. She loves me. I'd like to know how she fares.'

Sula's eyes softened and she nodded.

'Go then and may you find happiness and love and share that special bond which will ease and lighten your soul.'

'If I do…and produce offspring…I would like in return to know where *you* live, so that our children together–'

'Very well. If you promise to listen and to respect me,' Sula said with angry eyes, still not sure if he was being genuine.

'But I already have!'

'For now, but I strongly advise you to keep your promise. Leave my family and me alone. You have to give me your Comyenti Oath.'

He nodded with a fire in his eyes. 'I will. I will only visit you on your terms.' He touched his heart and said, 'I hereby promise I will leave you and your family alone and *only* visit when I have a family of my own. I swear.'

There was a stirring in the air and a soft breeze lifted Shazar's hair from his forehead and blew on past the trees. The Comyenti Oath, they both knew very well, was binding and could not be broken without risking losing all of ones traits, abilities and gained skills. They would be plain human. Both Sula's and Shazar's parents always stressed this.

Felix wanted to object, still not knowing anything about the powers of the Oath, warning her with his eyes, but she nodded for him to hush.

'Alright, you have promised. May you face your fate if you break the oath and with that our kind will be forever doomed,' Sula stated.

Sula told him where she lived and where Rosinhill was located. It was printed in his mind and he would not forget.

'My thanks to you… sister,' he said formally and bowed slightly. 'May we meet again.'

'When you have good news, brother. When you have a family I would love to meet your children one day and hope to see you changed into a loving father and person. Farewell until then.'

He smiled lightly, 'Farewell, sister.' He lowered his eyes.

'One last word of advice, brother,' Sula started.

'Yes?'

She looked at him intently and said, 'It might be too late for that but whatever you do…do not become what you hate.'

He narrowed his eyes at that, gazing at her with his jaw clenched in annoyance. 'And you…be careful to not become what you pretend to be.'

And with that Shazar turned around and walked off into the woods in a southerly direction.

~~~

'Do you trust him, Sula? Do you really think he will keep his promise after all he has said and done?'

Sula side glanced at Felix. 'I know he will, Felix. He will have to.' And she finally told him about the binding promise.

'Hmm, that seems a bit far-fetched. How can we know for sure that this is true?'

She glanced over to their little daughter and shrugged, 'It has to be true; it is very well known. It must be; my mother was never wrong. And if he does come back he will have to face three dangerous opponents. He did not defeat me nor will he ever overcome our little girl. I will start training her when we get back, so she will be strong and ready either way.'

Felix still looked worried.

'It's okay, honey. Comyentis don't fight each other.' But she remembered the previous night with a dull ache in her heart.

'Well, at least that is not the comyenti way *I* like to teach *our* children.'

Felix smiled at that and hugged her close.

'Agreed, and Fay could have sisters and brothers so she won't be alone. She shouldn't have to carry the burden alone if that guy fails. *We* could raise an army of children just to show him how it's done!'

Sula started to laugh out loud; she hadn't done since they started their holiday.

'I have you back.' Felix said with tear stung eyes.

She smiled at him and shook her head.

'You never lost me.'

PART IV Autumn Leaves

If we should touch, hand to heart
You would feel my soul within you.
Knowing not, from where we end
The start of melting flesh and sinew.

J. Ferguson

Chapter 26 Home

The sun set over the village of Rosinhill and the sky was bathed in orange and pink. Glancing down at the lush green and golden meadows with little white dots here and there, the grazing sheep and goats, Sula felt a pang of longing in her heart.

This is where I belong.

'Home,' she whispered, breathing in the familiar scents. Felix heard her. He came to a standstill next to Sula with Fay sitting on his shoulders pointing to the village below. He carried a rucksack too with another bedroll, their provisions and some clothes that didn't fit in the big pack that Sula carried.

'I can see our house!' Fay shrieked.

Sula smiled at her daughter and also looked into the distance; the village was still too far away to be seen.

'No, you can't, silly!'

'I can!' she answered back stubbornly.

Maybe she can…

I do, look, mummy! her daughter answered her briskly back in her mind.

Sula hadn't taught her to Mindmerge with an eagle yet so she was surprised.

She concentrated.

My mind, your mind, my heart, your heart. Your sight, mine.

Felix saw her eyes changing colour and rolled his own eyes at that, even though it was alluring, he could never get used to it.

Here we go again, he thought. 'Come on girls!' he said aloud and marched on impatiently.

The family's rucksack suddenly went extremely heavy on Sula's back as she lost contact with the elephant inside of her, now concentrating solely on the eagle. She dropped the bag onto the grass for a moment as she couldn't go into more than one animal's Mindmode at a time.

Now that would be something if we could combine the strengths of animals!

But sure enough now with the help of the eagle she could see their cosy little home on the hills from here. Fay's eyes were younger than Sula's eyes; or halfling eyes as Shazar would no doubt have said. So who would know whether Fay could see the house with or without the need of her abilities?

She shrugged her shoulders and knew she would have to talk to Fay to find out more later. Concentrating on the elephant again she picked up the heavy rucksack with most of their gear and followed her husband and daughter home at last.

~~~

Fay ran over to the family's goats and hugged them one by one. Sula and Felix laughed and smiled at each other at the sight. They had been away for more than two weeks. Their cats, Wave and Tiger, padded over to welcome them back home too, meowing and nudging their legs.

Felix's sister Feline had been looking after the animals while they were away and she had also kept the garden under control and tended to Sula's wide range of flowers. A bunch of fresh wild flowers (not from Sula's garden) awaited them on their kitchen table with a welcome back note.

'How sweet of her!' Sula exclaimed, smiling as she glanced around their cosy tidy home.

It was bigger than when she first came there; they had built an extension to house two extra rooms; one of which was Fay's bedroom filled with her toys and little treasures and another larger one which served as their bedroom. These days it was more of a family home and no longer a bachelor's pad. It had more storage and cupboards now and even had a big wooden table with chairs; all handmade by Felix of course. Nowadays it had little touches of Sula too with splashes of green and purple here and there, her favourite colours. However the garden was more her territory than the house would ever be for she was very much like her mother who had never lived in a house and who had been dubious about living in one.

Living in a house had been new to Sula for she, from the day she was born, had always been on the road with her mother. Until she met Felix she had never experienced a roof over her head or owned anything, but a rucksack and a couple of books, in her life. She could now finally appreciate having a home she could return to and find safety and familiarity there. Maybe it was her age and she had simply not been ready before. Thirty-nine years of having led a nomadic life had left its mark on her soul, in both positive and negative ways and she still sometimes had a hard time coming to terms with it all. Especially when coming home after being away, she thought she would miss the open road again. But when she went away she soon missed her home…

The garden she had created was a place in between, her little bit of wilderness and it was hers and hers alone. Here she could spend hours at a time; planting, sowing, deadheading, tending to her roses, watching birds, butterflies and frogs. She had made a mini garden for Fay too, with a little village; little trees and flowers, a stream which was the river and even with a working waterfall. Fay played here with her small wooden puppets for hours at a time while Sula worked in the main garden. Behind the house they had their vegetable plot and more flowers for the bees. They kept ducks who ate the slugs and snails and they had made little hedgehog hide-outs to welcome the little creatures too.

Sula walked into her precious garden as soon as she had dropped the rucksack in the kitchen. Inside the house Felix unpacked it, Fay ran to her bedroom to play with her toys. A chilly gust of wind blew straight past Sula and even lifted some strands of hair, brushing along her face like a caress.

Mother…

She was here! Sula could feel her and wondered what it meant; she hadn't felt her presence in a long time.

'Bedtime, young lady,' Felix spoke behind Sula and wrapped his arms around her waist, breathing in the scent of her hair. He startled her for she had not heard him approaching, very unlike her. In fact she nearly jumped out of her skin! It made Felix laugh.

'I thought you meant Fay!' she stated a little annoyed.

'Well as she is already well on her way to Dreamland I have another young lady left to send to bed. One also very dear to my heart, but in an entirely different way.' He smiled.

She looked over his shoulder. 'I didn't say goodnight to her or give her a kiss!'

'She got two; one from me and one from you. Now come. I've missed our bed!' And he pulled her arm softly. 'And you.' He looked at her with craving. 'It's never been that long before! Two weeks!'

'I'm tired, Felix.' She gave him a half smile and shook her head.

'I know. I'll give you a massage, come.'

She followed him in. He had made them both fresh redbush tea with honey, her favourite in the evenings. When they were both in bed and Felix had given her a massage she felt her eyelids getting heavy and she sighed contentedly. He kissed her gently on her left shoulder and again on her neck but she dozed off and mumbled to him, 'Thank you. Night, night, my love.'

'I've missed you,' he whispered back.

She opened her eyes, realising the impact of the last few days on him and rolled over on to her back to face him. 'Come here,' she opened her arms to him and he fell on top of her, nearly knocking the air out of her. He sometimes forgot her human side when she was tired or relaxed she wasn't using any of her abilities. It made her think about Shazar unwittingly…

Felix nestled his face, with golden stubble in Sula's dark hair. She smelt his pungent sweat and she could feel his need hardening against her thigh.

'There is plenty of time for that later, my love. It's been an exhausting couple of days for both of us,' she whispered with her soft voice in his ear which made him moan. She forgot how much he loved her speaking softly in his ear and what it did to him.

'You tease!' he grumbled and rolled off her.

'Think about something else. Think about…ice and snow and cold showers.'

'Not funny! You know that makes me think about you even more!'

'Oh, thanks for that,' she mumbled.

'I mean; wintertime, when we first met, darling.'

She didn't respond as she was already asleep.

Chapter 27 The Poet

'I cannot bear it!' Sula spoke with flare in her voice.

Felix's sister Feline stared at Sula patiently, letting her rant. Sula had run long and hard and had flown for hours to clear her mind in order to let off some steam. Anyone else would be exhausted but not Sula. It had calmed her down a bit and taken the edge off her anger as always.

'Felix has changed! He won't leave me alone anymore! When he is not out in the fields or the barn; it seems that everywhere I go he is there! In the house and even in my garden. If he's not hanging around me then he's half dragging me into the bedroom. He is driving me insane!'

Sula paced to and fro in Feline's kitchen. It was late at night and she had made her way up through the woods to her sister-in-law's little cabin, as she had done for the past few evenings. She felt drawn to Feline and relished in her easy company. Feline lived alone with her pale ginger cat and was usually up until the early hours writing poetry or painting. She too was an artist, like her brother, and in fact resembled him very much in looks but in many other ways she was his opposite.

'Perhaps,' Feline said handing her a steaming cup of redbush tea and honey 'it is *you* who has changed.' Her voice was mellow and she sat down at her table rubbing her eyes, which were strikingly blue. Wearing nothing more than a short nightgown and long socks, she looked gorgeous.

'What do you mean?' Sula shook her head trying not to stare at the other woman's open neck and bosom.

'Well, if I remember correctly, you were besotted with Felix. You guys were always so cuddly and intimate. Nothing can have changed that much, surely. I know it's been nearly five years but I remember my mum and dad when I was young and well they're still like that!' she tried to cheer Sula up. It hadn't worked; Sula stared in thought at the fireplace.

'That was when he still behaved normally.' Sula sat herself down at Feline's kitchen table, cupping the brew with both hands. She knew Feline had picked the redbush leaves herself from her own garden on her own island in the South. It was Feline who provided the family with the tea as well as the oranges and almonds.

She and Feline had much more in common than she had with Felix. Gardening, her love of travelling, but moreover the freedom and independency it brought. Felix nowadays only travelled with his family, never alone anymore. He hardly hung out with his buddies either and he didn't want to. Sula on the other hand needed to be alone from time to time but Felix found it hard when she was gone and she felt guilty. She craved to be either alone or here with Feline. She needed to regain her strength and sanity. Sometimes she took Fay on her travels into the wilderness, but more often she left her with her father or Feline.

'He loves you. I can't blame him for that. I mean…*you* can't blame him.'

Feline stared at Sula, pupils dilating until her eyes seemed like wells of shadow. She chewed her lip when their eyes locked. Then Feline shook herself and a little betraying colour stained her cheeks. She ran a hand through her hair. It looked adorable. Sula always felt Feline had a soft spot for her but only now did she realise the magnitude and depth of her feelings for her. In that moment it had been as clear as crystal.

'Anyway, you two are so strong together, nothing can change that. Surely it's just a phase,' Feline tried to steer back to their conversation.

Sula shrugged. 'I don't know, Feline, maybe you're right. Maybe I have changed.'

'Perhaps you've both changed since you've met Shazar?' Feline asked. Sula had told her about the meeting with the other comyenti and their struggles.

'Maybe I've come to realise how very much like animals men are! Driven by hormones and lust.'

'But don't you love animals?' Feline asked teasingly with a smile.

Sula narrowed her eyes at that and then with a smile, threw a scarf at her, which had been lying on the table. Feline caught it and laughed.

'Felix is like a dog in heat! It's as if he wants to…I don't know, make his mark on me. Possess me.'

Feline had just taken a sip of her tea and nearly choked at that. Laughing she said, 'Please spare me the details. As much as I love my brother that is a picture I'd rather refrain from seeing.'

Sula gave her a half smile, and couldn't get over the fact how alike brother and sister looked: the same bright eyes, perky nose, high cheekbones, a dimple in just one of their cheeks when they smiled. Only Feline's hair was longer, it was a fair bit wavier than Felix's and she wore it in a high messy ponytail with locks dangling in front of her face and her mouth was slightly fuller. Her physique was slimmer and round and all female, her bosom nice and soft.

Sula of course had never had a sister or even girlfriends before. Her mother had been her best and only female friend. Lately she had missed having same age female companions and she couldn't help but wonder what it would be like to touch her. Feline stared at Sula as if in thought, chewing her lip again.

Sula had told Feline she was different, a comyenti, soon after Fay had been born. She didn't want to have secrets from her best friend. Like Felix she had been impressed but was not fazed by it and they soon became friends. Their parents and the villagers still didn't know and Sula's wish was to keep it that way.

The bond between the two women had always been strong and Feline had been there for Sula many times when she had found living on the edge of the village hard, or with a partner, and even having a child. Fay could be very determined and stubborn at times, though their bond was strong; especially because mother and daughter could communicate easily with their minds. All that had improved over the years but Sula had no other mothers to talk to. She loved Feasgar, Felix's mother, but she still preferred to stay away from people all together and always wore her green hat to keep her ears covered.

Sula, who had been a nomad, free and wild, needed her solitude and nature. Feline could relate to that, since she travelled southbound twice a year on her horse. The travelling alone could take up about a month for that is how long it took on horseback and to cross the sea between Northland and Southland. During the autumn and winter months she would reside in the eastern part by the sea mainly, on her small island that she had named Irinia. Like the swallows she would only come back in the spring when she would help out on their parents' and her brother's farms and do her artwork. Feline resided in the woods during those summer months. The family always looked forward to her visits. She seemed very much at ease with herself and the world and appeared to have no problems at all. Perhaps that was what intrigued and draw Sula so much as she herself was sometimes tired of her complicated and domestic existence! She craved a simple life and a simple love…

~~~

'I don't like to be possessed nor to be owned. I need to be free!' Sula continued her angry outburst.

'Sure, I know you do, but well… that is hard, now that you have a family. I mean being totally free. It's not just you anymore. With family life come certain responsibilities. That's the choice you have made, Sula. That's why I've chosen a different life.' Feline had told her she never wanted a romantic relationship with anybody because she wanted to remain truly free. Although she had made it clear she had lovers during her travels, she had made no lasting bonds.

She would have made a better comyenti than me! Sula thought grimly.

'I'm sure Felix will change back to his old self soon,' Feline continued. 'I can imagine he is sometimes too eager, you're beautiful. But he loves and respects you and knows you are…what does he call you, oh yes: a unique bird that cannot be caged.'

'Hmm. He has been like this for the last two weeks now, ever since we got back. If he ever called me that, I'm sure he's forgotten, for he treats me like some pet animal to use and abuse whenever it pleases him.'

'Does he know you're coming by almost every day? Or did you have to use a sleeping spell on him tonight to knock him out?' Feline winked.

Sula raised an eyebrow, Feline always called it 'magic' and referred to her abilities as 'spells'.

She shook her head. 'No, after our argument earlier on he started drinking and you know what that does to him. He'll be out for hours. That's another thing that worries me. Since we've been back he's taken up drinking and is even developing a bit of a paunch.' And she pulled a face.

'Well, if you're not giving him what he wants, he needs to find his satisfaction in something. Better the bottle than other women for sure?'

Sula sighed, 'Well, I don't like it! It makes him more aggressive and that's not like him at all.'

Feline agreed with that.

'It seems you are very much wanted lately,' Feline said almost seductively after some silence and Sula looked up out of her thoughts. Of course she had told Feline about her meeting with Shazar and Feline had been very helpful and was totally on her side. She also knew that Feline was a lover of women, although she rarely spoke of it.

Sula stared long into Feline's eyes and both felt warm all over and it wasn't the tea that did that.

'I…er…best be going,' she spoke softly and stood before grabbing her coat. 'Thanks for the tea.'

Feline swallowed, then nodded and let her go.

~~~

Outside, walking back through the dark woods the cold autumn evening scent brought her back to her senses.

I can't have feelings for Feline! She is my sister-in-law!

When she opened the door to her house she took extra care to be quiet so she wouldn't disturb Fay or Felix. It was rather late. As expected Felix was snoring on her side of the bed. An empty bottle of cider still dangled in his limp hand. Sula took the bottle off him and placed it on the nightstand, sighing. When her head hit his pillow all she could think of was his sister. Even in her dreams she was there…

~~~

Over the next couple of days Felix took Fay with him to their orchard to help him with the apple and pear harvest and when Sula had finished her chores around the house she would visit her garden and attend to the last roses left blooming before heading over to Feline's. Every day she stayed at Feline's a little longer.

It was a wonderful crisp autumn day with a clear blue sky and the foliage the trees were about to shed, looked as if they were on fire. The sun shone down on Sula's hair making it look auburn in the light. She wore her special green hat with orange embroidery on it. Whenever she went out she wore a hat; in summer it would be a headband. The villagers only knew her like this.

Whilst she worked she swiftly cut a warm sunny yellow rose with bright peach at the corners, like summer blushes, and thought of Feline and smiled.

'For you,' she said when Feline opened her door to her.

'Aw, Sula! You're early,' she smiled at her friend, surprised, and at the rose she brought.

She took the stem between her fingers and smiled at the colours and when bringing the flower to her nose she inhaled deeply, opening her lungs to the scent, closing her eyes.

'It's got no thorns,' Sula said and she sighed, 'I couldn't stay away any longer, Feline. I *had* to see you.'

Feline frowned and chewed her lip, holding the rose close to her heart. 'I er… was just about to go out. Would you care to join me? I've heard that the geese are back in the lake. No doubt they're feasting on Bodi's corn at this time of day but there should be swans hopefully to gaze upon.'

'I'd love to.' Sula smiled warmly. Feline took the rose inside and quickly put it in some water first then shut her door. Together they headed to the lake deep in the woods.

'Any improvement on the home front?' Feline asked.

'Don't ask! Although to be fair we hardly see each other.'

'You're avoiding him?'

I feel so much more comfortable when I'm with you. But out loud she explained, 'It's harvest time.'

'But usually you're helping Felix. Is he alright with you spending your time… with me?'

'He hasn't said anything and anyway I'm my own boss! He can't make me do anything I don't want. He knows I need some time alone.'

Being with me is hardly time alone… Feline thought but shrugged, massaging her painful right shoulder. Even though the sun shone it was a cold day and the cold got to Feline's shoulder.

'Besides,' Sula concluded. 'he's got enough help from his friends. And I'm the one who does all the jam making.'

When they arrived at the lake they held their tongues so as not to disturb the wild birds.

They sat down at the lakeside on the soft yellow grass. No geese were to be seen but there were two beautiful swans grazing on the water plants of the lake, sticking their heads and their long necks deep into the water. Drops of water glittered in the sun on their pure white feathers.

'So graceful,' Feline remarked and Sula glanced at her.

'Did you know that the more similar the plumage of birds, where it's hard to tell the difference between a male and a female, the more likely it is that those birds are monogamous?' Sula asked.

'No, really?' Feline glanced from Sula to the water and chuckled. 'I knew about swans and of course your favourite snow geese and wolves. I suppose there is indeed no difference in their appearance in either gender from the outside.'

'Yes, in snow geese, turtle doves, storks, albatrosses, black vultures, bald eagles; both genders all look alike and often mate for life. And birds are not the only ones,' Sula added smiling conceited, looking back at the couple in the water. 'Wolves, prairie voles. All of these animals grieve when their partner dies.'

Sula didn't really want to think about Felix dying because ever since Shazar told her that she would outlive her husband she was worried. She would lose him.

I wanted to grow old with him…

'Just like that pair of storks who have a nest in one of those massive beech trees on the village plaza. They've been together for as long as I can remember,' Feline said with her jaw dropped, thinking quickly, her eyes darting from side to side. 'So the fact that male and female humans look differently from the outside would suggest they are…polygamous?' Feline wondered out loud.

Sula knotted her eyebrows and gave her a half smile. 'I think you might be right about that!' she laughed, 'Although Felix isn't as hairy or big as some men, I suppose an alien species looking at the two of you, not seeing the both of you naked, would be able to tell that he's male and you're female. In general women are more finely built and men the rough cavemen version and I suppose even uglier to an outsider, whilst in many other species it's the male who is finer looking and more colourful. Hmm, you're onto something there. Perhaps…,' and she looked intently at Feline. 'for people to be monogamous, humans should stick to their own gender?'

Feline laughed heartily but quickly tried to change the subject away from herself, 'Sula, it amazes me how much you know about animals! Have you learnt all this from your mother or did you actually encounter all of these creatures yourself and…merged with them?'

'Both. My mother taught me a great deal. She led me to all the creatures that could help me gain great survival skills and extra powers and I've explored a lot myself through various countries, asking native tribes at times. I understand so much more now and could give you weirder facts than I have just told you. Some insects and fish can change gender at will. Some can grow back lost limbs, some can even turn back time and become infants again.'

Feline's eyes grew big and she tried to read Sula's face to see if she was joking, but her face was as serious as ever and she knew Sula wouldn't lie to her.

'Sharks can detect a single drop of blood in the sea from miles away,' Sula smiled. 'A sea turtle can feel a twig moving on its shell and a catfish can detect an earthquake days in advance by its vibrations.'

'Are you trying to impress me?' Feline smiled.

'How can you tell?' Sula laughed.

'Well, it's working!'

They laughed and Feline suddenly flinched with pain. Sula was worried but the other woman just watched the swans and absentmindedly rubbed her shoulder. By taking in Feline with all her senses she recognised pain in her aura so much she felt slightly nauseous herself.

'Is it your shoulder, Feline?' The look in Sula's eyes was full of concern.

Feline massaged her right shoulder with her left hand and while looking away to the lake again avoiding Sula's loving warm jade eyes. Lately her irises showed more specks of orange than ever before. Her voice broke as she said through gritted teeth, 'I travel to Southland for a reason. Felix always says that if you can't cope with the winter you don't deserve the summer.' She shook her head rubbing her shoulder again with pursed her lips. 'He doesn't feel my pain! Even though we're twins he doesn't feel it. But you do! I've had this for a couple of years now. I've been to a couple of healers and they all say the same thing; I overdid it with this arm, worked too hard on the land. A 'frozen shoulder' they call it. Only warmth and light massage and gentle exercise soothes it, but it may never heal. The pain gets worse when the weather gets colder, you see. I might not deserve the summer in Felix's eyes but winters here are unbearable for me. To live in pain-'

'Oh, Feline, of course Felix mentioned it. He understands and has never said a bad word.' Sula laid a warm hand on Feline's bad shoulder.

'Not to you he wouldn't.' Feline smiled sadly relishing in Sula's touch.

I wonder if there is any animal ability that can help her ease her pain?

'Hmm, would you let me help you?'

'What do you mean?' Feline asked and she gestured at the swans.

'They will go south soon and so will I. I need to follow the warmth.'

'I can give you that. My name, after all, means 'Sun'.' Sula's voice was sensual and followed Feline's eyes looking from the swans back to her. Feline appeared as if in shock.

Their eyes locked and Feline felt warm alright.

'I…can try something. Birds are considerably warmer than mammals. If I go in, let's say swan-mode, my hands would feel warmer,' Sula spoke and laid a hand on Feline's shoulder again.

'What here? Isn't that risky?' Feline asked flustered.

'To give you a massage?'

'Yes, no, I…meant er…going into what did you call it, swan-mode?'

Sula smiled at that, suddenly confident.

'Let's go to your place then.'

~~~

The heat from Sula's hands was intense and seemed to burn through Feline's skin right through her nerves into her bones. It was just about bearable but it still felt great. Sula's hands moved in circular movements around Feline's shoulder, focusing on the centre of her pain. Feline could not resist an occasional moan. That made Sula's stomach flutter pleasantly, like a butterfly.

They were sitting on Feline's floor on some cushions in front of the smouldering fireplace. The blond woman had stripped to her bra. Usually the fire helped her a little but this; Sula's hands, her touch, so warm and loving exceeded any fire and even the sun.

'So, what's it like?' Sula asked, her eyes dark, coming to sit next to Feline when finished.

'It was excellent,' and Feline tried to move her bare shoulder, rolling it. 'It's completely gone…at least for now. Thank you.'

Sula smiled. 'That's good to hear but what I meant was… what's it *like* to make love to a woman?' Sula asked softly.

Feline took a sharp breath and looked away, shy all of a sudden, her face crimson, covering her shoulders by pulling up her cardigan.

'I'm sorry, I didn't mean to.' Sula rubbed her forehead, hiding her eyes in her hands, embarrassed.

Feline shook her head. 'It's alright. You haven't,' and looked at Sula again very bravely, tilting her head with a pensive look. 'I don't know if there is much difference but I wouldn't know as I've never lain with a man and wouldn't want to. I suppose a woman's body is softer, warmer, it feels familiar, safe. There is never a threat. Everything is equal and falls into place. I can just be myself,' she spoke softly as if to herself but Sula heard it as if she had spoken directly to *her*. Feline concluded, 'Well, that's how I feel personally.'

Sula swallowed, looking at Feline's moist lips, slightly parted.

I wonder…

She kept looking at Feline's moist mouth and licked her own while bending ever closer.

Feline shook her head, understanding what was going on but breathing heavily. Sula didn't have to speak because Feline knew her so well and could usually tell by looking at her expression what she was thinking or feeling. However this look was new to Feline; her eyes darker than ever, the orange specks shooting like stars. This was a look of want, of lust. Although they had shared some intimate moments whereby the two had locked eyes or held hands and both had felt warmed by it, Feline especially could have easily let herself get carried away. But she had always respected Sula, her brother and their marriage. Feline had never wanted to think more of it; thinking Sula's touches to be innocent.

Maybe they weren't, Feline thought and felt confused.

'No…Sula. Don't.' Her voice merely a whisper she had to look away to break contact. She stood and grabbed the empty tea cups from the table and turned her back on her and walked over to her kitchen sink.

'I suggest you go back home now, my friend,' Feline said whilst still having her back turned.

Feline stood like this for some time, shaking but frozen, trying to regain her composure. Trying not to think of stunning, lovely and good-hearted Sula and how it would be so easy to give in to the urge. An urge she had always felt from the moment she had first met her when her brother first introduced her. She thought of no one else but her initially. But Felix was so in love and the couple so happy. Feline had to accept this, although it was difficult at times because Sula's presence did not make things easier. And although Sula had indeed shown signs of needing her, especially the last few days, and given her hugs and kisses and told her almost everything, Feline had always taken those signs for close friendship or as sisterhood and nothing more than that.

Now it was clear something else was going on, something more and deeper. Perhaps it was just mere curiosity from Sula, but it both aroused and confused Feline.

It's not fair of her! Feline thought upset. *It wouldn't be right. Sula is vulnerable and doesn't know what she wants,* 'If you don't go now… I don't know if I'll be able… to resist you,' Feline, breathing heavily concluded.

But when she turned round she found Sula had already gone, the door still left ajar.

Chapter 28 The Training

Over the next few days Sula tried to occupy her mind by training Fay before school would start and the girl's mind would be clouded, taken over by learning to read and write.

Mother and daughter were walking through the mountains heading to a nearby lake where they hoped to find a flock of geese. A different lake to where she had been with Feline.

'The skill of flying is one of the most important skills to have as a comyenti,' Sula explained to Fay. 'Not only can you cover great distances in less time if speed is needed, but if you travel by land you may encounter many obstacles along the way such as dense woods, mountains, lakes and…human villages,' Sula glanced at her daughter whilst walking hand in hand with her. 'But up there you can pretty much travel in a straight line up, unbothered, using the stars, the sun and landmarks to navigate,' and she pointed skywards. Fay listened intently.

'Or down in the water by swimming and breathing under water as the sailfish; the fastest fish on Bhan.' Sula smiled at her daughter.

'But speed isn't always the answer so merging with a trout can prove to be just as effective. Those fish can stay motionless against the current and also stay warm and… anyway,' she saw the look of confusion on her daughter's face and knew she was rambling on the way she always did when talking about animals, and she stroked Fay's back lovingly. 'let's stick with the goose for now shall we? The goose has many other wonderful aspects. What do you think they are? For example how do you think she keeps herself warm?' Sula asked Fay.

'Her feathers!' Fay answered enthusiastically.

'That's right. She has multiple layers of feathers to keep her warm. It's called insulation. Instead of hair she has feathers everywhere apart from on her feet and bill. Because of her feathers she can stay warm and active up there in the coldest of winters and fly for hours on end without tiring. And there is another thing many birds in the sky have.'

'She can smell when spring arrives?'

Sula laughed at that. 'That too! Although there are other birds with a better sense of smell such as the giant albatross or even a pigeon, the goose is indeed a migrant bird and not that bad at smelling overall but I meant something else.'

Fay looked as though in deep thought and said whilst counting on her fingers, 'There is smell, touch, seeing, hearing, tasting…er seeing?'

'Right again, honey. Up in the sky you can imagine everything looks a lot smaller, her eyesight is not as good as an eagle or hawk but it's still a lot better than ours and she has a broader range. The goose has another great skill: she has an inbuilt compass! She has a way of knowing the right direction she needs to head in, even if the sun is behind the clouds or the stars, she can always tell north from south, even in the dark!'

'Really?'

Sula nodded. 'And when geese sleep they always keep one eye open and half their brain will stay alert to predators. This might come in handy one day, Fay, if you ever find yourself in a dangerous situation and you're not sure if you can fully trust where you lay your head down but you desperately need to rest.'

'A bit like Wave and Tiger?'

'Hm, a bit like that,' Sula said.

As they approached the shore of the lake, they soon spotted the geese. Trying hard not to disturb them, Sula walked with Fay by the hand to the edge of the water and concentrated on calling one of the snow geese over.

This was the first step. Sula could of course have chosen the eagle instead, as their eyesight, next to the ability of flight, was superb. However eagles were harder to approach and not suitable for a child that is just about to turn five. By merging with a goose, Fay would gain, if successful, five abilities over her own; better smell, flight, compass direction, insulation and broader better vision. A sixth ability would follow, not instantly but only after using it at least once: an inbuilt map.

The snow goose that responded would be the one who was willing to make the Mindmerge. It was a harmless procedure and did not involve any pain or loss on either side. If anything it was a gain for both parties, for the comyenti she would gain the animal's abilities and for the goose they not only received her respect and gratitude but the comyenti would also be indebted to them for life and promise safety for not only the individual but the entire species as much as they could. It wasn't the Comyenti Oath, but if they ever called out in need, Sula would hear it and she would have to submit to that call and aid the animal in need. That was the agreement. Such was the bond and respect, for without its abilities she would not be comyenti.

'Now, look, see here she comes,' Sula whispered to Fay who was kneeling down so that she would be at eye level with the goose that swam closer to them, leaving the rest of its flock.

Fay was exited and held on to her mother's knee, her eyes wide and full of anticipation.

'Remember it's the same as before, no different,' she reminded her daughter.

Fay nodded and crossed her heart with her tiny hands and concentrated trying to remember the right words but most of all the meaning behind the words, *'Greetings gentle soul. I am comyenti. You are goose. We are sisters. I give you my trust. I pledge you protection and life long safety should you ever be in need or your life in danger. I ask of you your skills: flight; the use of your wings, your sight, smell and sense of direction and the warmth of your feathers. That which makes you a goose. Do you agree?'*

The goose closed its eyes once and Fay heard the goose's approval. It almost sounded like a sigh.

Fay smiled and Sula knew she'd passed the first step.

Now came the hardest part: the unique Mindmerge. Not easy for a four year old quarterling.

My mind, your mind, my heart, your heart, my heartbeat, your heartbeat. Your mind, my mind, your heart, my heart, your heartbeat, my heartbeat. The chant went on for a couple of minutes until the link, the merge was established.

Both the goose and Fay had their eyes locked, the little girl's dark blue eyes shifted colour constantly but the goose looked like it was in a trance, and was completely composed.

Now came the third and most important step, and if they were disturbed it could be fatal for both of them as they could remain stuck in each other's head; thinking they were the other.

Sula protected them both with an invisible shield which she cast over them and held guard; a luxury Sula hadn't had during her training. In fact it nearly cost her her life once.

Your mind, my mind, your heart, my heart, your flight, mine. Your flight, mine, mine.

And it was done.

Fay thanked the goose as she felt the tingle of wings on her back and bowed slightly.

'Forever in your debt…'

The goose's eyes blinked and she also bowed, her head nearly touching the water, before turning and swimming back to join the flock.

Sula hugged her daughter proudly and shed a tear.

'That was amazing!' Fay exclaimed.

'You did great and remembered it all. A goose is a creature that links the sky with the earth beneath it and is much more than what most people think, it's an incredible, intelligent and versatile being. You'll discover that the more intelligent an animal is, the more impressive the experience,' and Sula stood. 'Come, we have to prepare you for the next and final step. To be able to use what you've just gained so that it all becomes a Mindskill. The one that will take some time to master will be one of the best abilities you'll ever possess, the power of flight.'

Fay smiled at her mother, her eyes shining with the excitement. From now on she would have the power to be the goose on command, her own goose would be inside of her.

~~~

'So how did it go?' Felix asked his daughter that evening over dinner.

'It was amazing, daddy.'

'She fell a couple of times but no broken bones. She did really well,' Sula added.

'Uhuh, I did. The start was the hardest,' Fay said facing her father. 'You sort of imagine your wings to open and start flapping them really hard, then you have to run faster and faster until you feel the air underneath your wings, which are not really there but I could feel them! And then you just take off! You should have seen me, daddy!'

Felix smiled at the stream of words coming from his precious daughter's mouth. So grown up.

'I'd like to, tomorrow. Just be careful young lady. I would like to see you grow old without killing yourself!'

'I am. As long as I stay con...cen...trated,' she said slowly, emphasizing the words. 'Don't worry, daddy, nothing can happen.'

Felix looked at his wife and clearly remembered her falling out of the sky that day they met. Sula had told him what had happened; she had lost the bond with the goose inside her for only a fleeting moment. She had been tired and the weather had been extremely bad.

Sula smiled at him, knowing what he thought, seeing the pictures he saw. He looked sad these days. She still wouldn't let him near her. For some reason she couldn't and the longer they waited the more difficult it got. Their bond was weakening significantly.

'We'll practise every day until flight becomes second nature,' Sula said.

'You like the goose, don't you mummy? I can see why now.'

'Yes, she is one of my favourite animals, as is the albatross, they are truly magnificent as they can even sleep in the air and don't have to come down to rest at all. One day you might need this ability, who knows, but for now the snow goose will do. Finish your dinner otherwise you won't have any strength for tomorrow.'

236

When Felix had cleared the table and he had put Fay to bed like he always did they were finally alone, for the first time that day. Sula felt awkward and ill at ease.

Felix came to sit opposite her by the big table getting a piece of wood out, along with a knife and his trusty chisel. Sula stared out of the window in thought. She seemed sad and miles away. Felix's eyes shifted from her to his new piece of wood, sighing deeply to himself and then began to work. She had her collection of dried flowers out but they were untouched so far. She loved to press them between thin layers of parchment so that their beauty would still be preserved over time, even though summer was long gone.

Felix stared at her while her gaze drifted from the window to the flowers and then finally to him. She had felt him staring at her and her hands moved with ease whilst she concentrated on her flowers again. They usually kept her mind occupied just as woodwork did for him.

Here we go again, Sula thought when he stopped his work and leaned in closer licking his lips as if to say something.

Why can't he just leave me alone for one evening?

'Isn't that somehow cruel?'

'What?' For a moment she thought he had heard her thoughts. *Impossible!*

He pointed at her work.

'Those dead flowers. That's somehow not like you.'

She shrugged her shoulders.

'Well, I always make sure I pick one or two and leave the rest.' She touched her flowers ever so gently with her fingertips. Felix was jealous of those flowers. They seemed to receive more love than he did.

'Yes, but they *die.*' It sounded more like a question or accusation than a statement.

'I only take a couple and leave the rest for the bees. The flowers would have withered away anyway,' she retorted idly without looking at him. 'They only last a couple of days, weeks at the most. And don't forget I leave the roots so that the plant survives. I know it might seem somewhat strange; me doing this, but the way I see it, by pressing them between parchment, the flower continues to live on. Their beauty remains.' And she picked up one of the parchments and showed it to Felix.

'Hmm, they sure are pretty like this; delicate and forever young. But their colour has faded, their scent and most important; their soul is gone. What you see here is only a reflection of what they once were.'

Silence.

She looked up from her dried flowers and stared into his eyes, reading his thoughts, but he had deliberately closed his mind from her, which he sometimes did when he didn't want her to know what he thought.

'What are you trying to say, Felix? That I'm like those flowers; my beauty faded and my being soulless?' She had raised her voice, becoming more irritated by him.

Felix grinned foolishly at that. 'No my love, never! You are as beautiful as ever and grow in beauty with every day, within and externally too.' He had spoken the truth for now he'd opened his mind to her to let her see he was being genuine. A picture of Feline flashed in his mind before he said, 'I... saw my sis today.'

Sula looked away quickly, avoiding his eyes, afraid to show him her feelings, swallowing hard.

'What did she say?' They hadn't seen each other since that day, now more than a week ago.

'Huh! She more or less gave me a lecture. How my eager behaviour and drinking is driving you away from me. I need to let you be yourself more. Give you more space and freedom,' he glanced at her flowers. 'Flowers can only be admired when they're still alive. As soon as you pick them, you become selfish, for you can never *own* their beauty; their love. Love is not about possession.'

Sula's eyes grew bigger.

'She told you *that*?'

Felix gave her a weak smile. 'More or less. She reminded me. She was always wiser than me. Even as a child she was more thoughtful. But it's true. *You* are a wild bird...or flower huh, it's all the same!' *Bottom line is...you're special...to me and I love you. I feel like I'm losing you.*

Sula sighed and smiled at him. She reached out over her flowers for his hands and held them in hers. They sat like this for a long time staring into each other's eyes. Felix looked almost tearful at her touch.

'I do love you, Felix.'

He had a pained look on his face.

'Then why do I feel that it somehow isn't enough?' he said with a broken voice.

'Because...' she chose her words carefully. 'I have this need to remain free...I can't explain it.' She looked down at her flowers.

I don't want to be like this! Cut off from my roots, picked and pressed to be admired. Dead. In a house...near a village; away from the untamed wild spaces.

'I will try my best, my love. Just tell me what I can do to help you.'

'Just let me be me for starters. Don't always try to make contact when all I need is some quiet time. Don't try to change me or catch me all the time. It chases me away,' Sula said carefully.

'Alright, I can do that. But...but I miss you. You're my wife...'

You just told me love is not about possession! Sula thought confused.

'Maybe comyentis are not supposed to be bound like this. Maybe we are not even...monogamous?'

Felix raised his eyebrows. 'Is *that* what Shazar told you?' He squeezed his eyes now into slits, ice cold in sudden anger and released his hands slowly out of hers. His knuckles were white.

'No, no! In fact he said comyentis mated for life through the Heartmerge.'

'Heartmerge!' he said it disdainfully.

'What?' She tried to find out what he meant but understood soon enough.

'What's it worth if not sustained?' Felix said with pain showing in his eyes.

She sighed. *Of course...* 'I'm just a bit tired lately!' she said upset.

'Why have I never been able to hear your thoughts, you can hear mine?'

'You know why, because you're human, Felix. Now, don't be such a martyr.'

'Shazar had no idea what marriage meant. He thought that I'm keeping you in chains or something, even though I told him I respected you. And I told and showed you the same!' he said upset.

'Well, you haven't been behaving like it lately!'

'How so?'

'You're always there!'

'I desire you! I love you! You can't blame me for that? I'm like a bee, Sula, I need to be close to you. I need your... honey, to survive on, to live... Without you... I will wither away and will be the one that dies.'

She smiled warmly at that and said, 'My heart as ever belongs to you,' taking his hands back into hers. 'Just as the birds in our garden are sometimes quiet, or even absent, and sometimes wild and fluttering, my heart is the same.'

'Will you stop comparing yourself to a bloody bird! You are not, you are human too!'

So that's it?

With an open mouth she withdrew her hands and feeling hurt she replied, 'You just compared yourself to a bee! Why do I have the feeling you can say and do anything you want but I can't! You do restrict me, Felix, by not understanding me properly!'

'I never knew you could be so dramatic, Great Bhan!' Felix said moodily.

She stood and paced up and down the room, just like she had done in Feline's kitchen. Like an animal trapped.

Feline.

'I've never felt like this for any woman before!' Felix said trough gritted teeth.

I have... Sula thought, thinking about Feline again. What was wrong with her? Here was her husband in front of her opening up his heart and soul to her, and all she could think of was his sister...

'You've not even asked what I'm making,' Felix said hurt. 'Before you were always interested in me and my art!'

She glanced at him and sighed guiltily, 'Sorry, what are you making?'

'Hmm, I wish I could read your mind at this very moment because that didn't sound very sincere!'

'It was! Never mind me. I just have a lot on my mind lately. Please, what will you make?'

Felix touched the piece of wood with his slender fingers. 'A goose.'

Sula bit her lip at that. 'For me?'

'No, for Fay.'

'Oh.' She was a bit hurt but then again she felt pleased for Fay, knowing the girl would love it.

'I was thinking of making a figurine every time she masters a new animal ability,' he said.

Sula was touched and a tear came to her eye. Felix saw.

'What's wrong now?'

'Nothing,' she looked away. 'I think it's a lovely gesture, Felix.'

'I'm glad you agree,' he said grumpily and he started working on his art. He used to do that in the farmhouse, instead he made a mess in their house. He knew how she hated that! Sula stood up suddenly and walked to the door.

'You're going out? To see Feline?'

She shook her head.

'Gosh, you've not seen her in a couple of days. Have you fallen out with her?' She noticed the hint or irony in his voice.

So he is jealous, 'No, no. I'm just going for a walk.'

Felix sighed, sad to be left alone again, feeling the urge to stand up and grab her, but he resisted, knowing he should leave her be. That advice from his sister didn't seem to be working much though…

She stepped outside and she was alone, finally but it didn't feel good like it usually did. Sula knew she should feel privileged to be loved by him. He was a kind and loving soul. He respected and honoured her most of the time, although lately, after they had returned from their holiday and having met Shazar, he hadn't given her much of that needed time alone. She had started to wonder if it was always like this for people who shared the Heartmerge but didn't maintain the physical intimate side of it. Perhaps it had side effects for humans she wasn't aware of?

Perhaps it needed to be kept warm; 'sustained' as Felix had called it, in order for it to work? If not, the two lovers would start to grow apart and even dislike each other?

What do I know?

She wished she did, but her mother didn't know for she left her lover before she could find out and Shazar…he might have known more about it, although he told her he himself had never experienced a Heartmerge before?

In her heart Sula knew she loved Felix still, even before they shared the intimate bond she had had feelings for him she could not explain.

But what if the Heartmerge actually worked as a certain *curse*? For both her and Felix?

But then I have no other choice than leave…

She had no one to ask and didn't particularly want to go and find Shazar to ask what he knew. He had told her where he was going, so that wouldn't be a problem, however… she was reluctant to go to him. She didn't dare to go see Feline, she was too afraid of the consequences.

Perhaps it was for the best to leave everything just for a while; to go and sort out her thoughts and give their relationship a well needed rest.

Yes, that's it. Fay's training will have to wait.

She decided to leave the next day.

Chapter 29 Spellbound

Feline's heart felt heavy as she made her way down to the village on her brown steed. It had been raining for the past three days and the forest floor was muddy.

She didn't feel like venturing to their house but she hadn't seen Sula or Fay for three weeks and her heart ached.

Moreover she was worried. She had spoken to Felix more than a week ago and he promised he would be better and give Sula more space.

But now she wanted to find out for herself if anything had changed. She owed it to Sula. They were her only family and her parents didn't want to interfere in their business. Apparently they too hadn't seen or heard from any of them, but her mother had told Feline that Sula was giving Fay some kind of training and not to worry.

Passing by her parents' orchard, she glanced at the pear trees where she and Felix used to play when they were Fay's age. They used to be best friends.

Carrying on down the road she soon reached their cosy home. Feline felt her heartache worsen upon smelling the scent of Sula's last roses. The yellow/peachy rose that had been a gift from Sula was still going strong in its vase on her kitchen table where they both spent so many nights talking and laughing.

Feline did and didn't want to be there.

She slid off her horse easily and looked around Sula's colourful garden with its many birds twittering and fluttering around eating the seeds Sula had left for them. She would normally have been here at this time of day, but she could be out with Fay or doing chores. She looked back and wondered whether to look for Felix to ask him.

After tethering her horse to a tree, she went around the house and saw the washing out on the line and the whiff of lavender greeted her but no sign of Sula.

She heard a sound coming from inside the house. On opening the gate to the garden and closing it behind her, she made her way to the door and just when she was about to open it, it flung open and there was Sula. Her normally olive coloured face seemed sallow and she was wide-eyed. Feline was shocked by the sight of her.

'Fel-' but before Sula could finish saying Feline's name she stumbled forward towards Feline who luckily opened her arms, catching her just in time.

She picked Sula up, all heavy and limp; Sula weighed more than she looked but Feline managed to carry her into the garden to get some much needed fresh air. Feline laid her down on the small patch of grass amongst the fresh roses. She patted Sula's cheeks but when that didn't bring her to she quickly rushed to their water pump to haul some cool fresh water and splashed it onto her face.

That did it and Sula roused slowly.

'Easy now girl,' Feline said with concern.

Sula opened her eyes and blinked a couple of times, unbelieving, but relieved. Feline stared into Sula's forest green eyes, thinking, *I wish I could stay here with you in your garden forever…to love you amongst the sweet scenting rose petals. Or just become two butterflies dancing around your flowers without a care. What I wouldn't do for that…*

'Feline…'

Feline on hearing her name said so tenderly awoke from her thoughts, 'I didn't know you were *that* startled to see me, Sula!'

Sula didn't smile but rubbed her eyes and lower back, making an attempt to get up.

'No, don't get up. Sit upright, but stay sat down, breathe in slowly and then tell me what's wrong with you.'

'Nothing. I just felt a bit queasy.' Sula avoided her examining eyes, taking a couple of slow breaths through her nose and out though her mouth. Sula noticed Feline wore her sleeves rolled up and she glanced at her bare tanned arms with the fair fine hairs and was fascinated by them. She wore a white linen shirt and brown tights.

'You? You're the strongest woman I've ever met! You're never queasy!'

Sula locked on to Feline's eyes then and took a deep breath before speaking in a frail voice, 'I think I need to tell you something.'

Feline had never seen Sula so feeble before, so fragile.

'Go on. Has something happened between you and Felix?'

Sula shook her head. 'No, he is busy doing his chores on the farm most of the time but at least he is giving me some space. We had another argument but I decided to go away for some days to clear my head, to rediscover myself. I had my bag packed ready to go, but then…then I realised I had missed my cycle by more than two weeks and I never miss my cycle and now…I feel about to explode both physically and emotionally. I'm so bloated, my breasts and tummy, I'm tired and agitated most of the time…'

'You're…with child?' Now it was Feline who looked pale-faced and startled.

Sula nodded, avoiding her eyes.

'I feel the same way as I did when I carried Fay. It was horrible in the beginning, same as now; feeling faint at times, exhausted, hungry, not wanting intimacy, but then again I do. Oh, I'm such a mess!'

'Where is Fay?' Feline asked wide eyed.

'Oh, she is with your mum and dad for the day.'

Feline's heart sank; she didn't know whether to be happy or sad. It was hard to tell what Sula thought, although she didn't look too pleased.

'Are you… alright about it?' Feline asked her when she composed herself.

'Well yes of course…and no. It couldn't have come at a worse time.'

'Have you told him yet?'

'No.' Sula shook her head.

'Why not?'

'Because it cannot be his!'

'What?' Feline's eyes grew bigger, but then it suddenly dawned on her and she remembered what Sula had told her.

'Shazar?'

'Who else?!' Sula shot Feline a hot headed look which almost made her fall back on the grass. Sula had shouted at her, something that she had never done before.

'But, but, you told me it never came to that?'

'I know I did! I can't remember it properly!' Sula shouted out again.

Feline looked upset and near tears and Sula felt sorry for being so angry towards her.

'I'm…I'm sorry for shouting at you, I'm not myself lately. Maybe it's best if you stay away from me. I don't like myself very much right now. All my senses are enhanced and I feel grumpy and overwhelmed most of the time.'

'No,' and Feline shook her head. 'I have been doing that for too long. I've tried, but I've missed you and it looks like you need me. If… it's alright.'

'How come I have no memories of what exactly happened that night?' Sula asked her confused, tears in her eyes, avoiding Feline's stare, plucking at the grass.

'With Shazar? I don't know; he must have used a spell on you.'

'He used pheromones on me; that's what he did. There's your spell!'

'But surely *that* wouldn't have caused you to completely black-out would it?'

Sula looked at her with a frightened look in her eyes. For the first time in her life she felt fear; raw and uncontrollable fear. Moreover she felt utterly powerless and out of control, just like she always had in frightening situations during her travels, when her emotions overwhelmed her so much that she couldn't use her skills. Also, Shazar had broken all the rules and had shattered her trust and admiration for comyentis and not only that, Sula realised once more, she knew so little about comyentis and their ways. *And their magic…*It was almost as if she heard Feline think.

Perhaps we were not the good guys after all…What if comyentis were not all that perfect? Sula pondered. 'I don't think so, no,' Sula said aloud.

'Selfish asshole! He used you. Raped you!' Feline coiled her fists in anger and stood up. 'Where does he live? Tell me!'

Sula grabbed one of Feline's hands and pulled her down to her. This was exactly what she feared if Felix ever found out; his reaction would be the same, or worse…

'Please no, I need you now, here with me. Your calming self. I've missed you.'

Feline was taken aback at that so she nodded. Sula embraced her and Feline felt warm all over and held her tight, their hearts beating closely.

'I'll get you through this somehow,' Feline whispered in her ear and inhaled Sula's familiar scent.

~~~

'I'm starting to wonder about this whole Heartmerge thing,' Sula said after a couple of minutes cuddled in Feline's arms regaining her strength, drinking her favourite tea with honey, gradually feeling better. 'Whether it does indeed weaken if not sustained.'

'You have a Heartmerge with Shazar now, Sula. That is why,' Feline said with insight while stroking Sula's hair gently.

Sula looked up at her with big eyes and fresh tears started to well.

'You think?'

Feline nodded.

'It explains a lot. How else can you explain your aversion of Felix all of a sudden?'

'But I don't dream of Shazar or even feel anything remotely for him, *especially* after what he has done to me!' She shook her head confused and she glanced at Feline for help and comfort.

And it doesn't explain why I'm feeling like I do for you, 'I don't understand anything anymore! It's like I'm losing myself completely!'

She started crying helplessly and Feline held her and rocked her.

Such a strong woman, what happened to her? If I ever meet this Shazar I'll show him what I think of him! But...what if it has nothing to do with him? What if this is just her hormones or this mysterious Heartmerge with Felix breaking down slowly; losing its effect on her, but why not on Felix as well?

'You've got a little one growing inside of you; that's why you feel different.' Feline laid a hand on Sula's tummy, but felt a bit embarrassed by the intimacy of that so she stroked her hair instead. Feline felt Sula's heartbeat close to hers, her breath warm in her neck, her soft lips...Lips?

Sula's lips were kissing Feline's neck, soft and warm. Feline let Sula cover her with kisses, motionless but moaning uncontrollably. Sula's mouth had made her way down to Feline's collarbone and she now kissed her between her breasts where her shirt had opened. Feline felt for her moist warm mouth and using her hands cupped her face pulling it towards hers and kissed her tenderly. Sula closed her eyes as they found each other's lips and tongue.

No, how right this feels but how wrong! Feline thought and shook her head, withdrawing. She held Sula's face close and whispered with closed eyes, 'How much I wanted you to do this to me when I first met you, when Felix introduced you. When you hugged me warmly that winter's day and I welcomed you into our family. How envious I was of Felix and his luck.' She opened her eyes to look into that of the comyenti.

Sula sat up straight with her mouth slightly parted. *She is so beautiful, out of this world...* Feline thought. *And she is so very dear to me but...*

'I sometimes wish,' Feline started to say softly, her voice breaking, her clear blue eyes welling up. 'that it was me on the ice that day and not *him*. As much as I care for my brother, I have always loved you dearly, from the moment I first laid my eyes on you.'

Feline's eyes were big, tears now streaming down her face, wiping them away with the back of her hand.

'But...as much as this excites me; to have you finally within reach, it pains me also, for it's too late now,' she held Sula's hand with the wedding band and they both looked at it. 'You're married, you have chosen *him* and you have Fay to consider.'

'But I love *you*, Feline. It *should* have been you that day when I fell down on the frozen river.'

Feline closed her eyes and sucked her lips in at that and more tears flowed.

'Oh, Sula. The tragedy of it all,' she held Sula's hand to her mouth, and kissed it. 'But in all honesty, if that was the case you wouldn't have had Fay. And my brother is not a bad man.'

'I know, I do love him but I'm also attracted to *you*. How is that possible? I always thought I could only give my heart to one person.'

'Perhaps it's because I remind you of him?'

'Yes and no,' and a small smile flickered on her face. 'You're the female version but you're calmer, patient. You listen and never judge. You're wild and free, like me and moreover,' and she rolled her eyes alluringly, 'You're not overpowering.'

'How can we know this is not some... phase you're in at the moment?' Feline almost whispered.

'I've always admired and loved you and over the years grown fonder of you. But there is only one way to find out,' and Sula grabbed Feline by her shoulders and made her look at her. 'Lie with me.'

Feline's heart skipped a beat and then started to beat faster. She bit her lip at that and took a moment to gather her thoughts.

'Oh, Sula, please don't tempt me any further!' She pulled back a bit. 'The last thing you need right now, is another Heartmerge, however much we both want it. This is not the answer. And no Heartmerge is needed as I'm already spellbound by you.'

Sula smiled sadly at that and shook her head slowly.

'A Heartmerge with you *is* the only answer. There is no need to be afraid,' *To get rid of the memories of both men...*

'You're beginning to sound like Shazar...' *My God, what if he's inside of her, somehow?*

And Feline backed away, even more in shock, distrusting Sula all of a sudden.

Sula looked in horror at her, noticing her reaction.

'What is it?' Sula asked.

Feline stood and rubbed her chin, surprisingly similar to the way that Felix did, avoiding Sula's eyes, staring at her roses instead, thinking.

'There is only one way to find out more about this Heartmerge; if Shazar did something more to you than just impregnate you. And that's not by having sex with me. That won't solving anything. You have to tell Felix you're pregnant.' She hung her head low.

'No, I can't do that! You know what he's like! If he learns it's not his he won't understand. He can never know!'

'You're right,' Their eyes met; Feline's cold now. 'Then I see one last option; sleep with your husband.'

Sula's mouth opened slightly to protest and swallowed away new tears, feeling rejected. For that was an entirely new feeling to her. Although knowing Feline wanted her, she was indeed the wisest here. For she didn't want to see her brother get hurt.

I don't either, but why can't I love both? She didn't say I couldn't...

But in the end Sula conceded.

Chapter 30 The Choice

The leaves on the trees in the woods were turning golden and the days were shortening. Wind and rain came more frequently now. Sula's scented roses had all but wilted now and she had collected enough rosehips to make lots of jam with. They had so many berries from the garden and the woods, that the only way to preserve them was to make jam to last them the coming winter, spring and if they were lucky even the summer. Of course there were also all the apples and pears to store in the farmhouse. This was Felix's task.

Fay helped Sula by the table in the kitchen. She was quiet and not her usual chatty self and now and then she looked up from arranging all the glass pots for her mother, ready to be filled with the thick jam and gazed at her intensely, only to look away again pensively.

Of course Sula noticed. Things didn't stay unnoticed for long between them and she felt sorry for the girl. They were so close and before it had been so easy to share each other's thoughts without the need to speak as the thought was already on its way to the other. Not so anymore; Sula had deliberately shielded most of her thoughts from her daughter. She felt she had to as the adult things that were on her mind were not for her child's ears or heart...

She stirred the sweet contents of the big pan, trying to avoid her daughter's eyes, whilst feeling guilty. The sweet hot steam rising up from the pan left Sula feeling a bit sick.

'Ah, rosehip jam, mmm, my favourite!' Felix said stepping through the doorway, closing the door behind him with help from a gust of wind. He rubbed his hands together to warm them and quickly stepped out of his boots and embraced the two of them from behind, cupping Sula's belly with both hands now, nestling his face in her neck. Sula had her hair up in a high ponytail. She laughed and patted his hand. Fay's face lit up.

I'm so happy, Felix thought and Sula heard it clearly.

She felt the same way; everything seemed to be back to normal since she'd slept with her husband again. She had waited another three weeks to tell him she was pregnant, hiding her symptoms very carefully and Felix as predicted was over the moon.

But, as much as she tried; her old feelings had not completely returned. The Heartmerge was still there; she could feel her love and affection for Felix, in her heart and her body certainly responded, however not as strongly as before. Every time Felix touched her, she thought of Feline's mouth and hands. Her mind was clouded; her heart belonged to Feline too, was that why the Heartmerge had not fully re-established itself? Because her heart wasn't completely open to him?

She felt like she played a role, putting on an act. Felix had returned to his old self and was content and drank less.

If it worked for him then why not for me? His heart is only calling out for mine...and mine alone. She clearly remembered his thoughts when they had made love again after many weeks on Feline's suggestion, *Mine, you're all mine....*

Now that she knew the answer to that question she felt she had to let Feline know. But they had avoided one another and had not seen or spoken to each other since Sula fainted, since their kiss, since that day, three or more weeks ago...

Felix had not thought it strange as Feline often went away on her travels; sometimes without saying farewell and as she had no farm of her own she had no responsibilities.

Has she left for the sun, the South without saying goodbye?

Sula's eyes met her daughter's examining eyes.

You're thinking about aunty... she had heard her daughter speak in her head; for a moment she'd forgotten Fay was there and had left her mind open...

Sula crimsoned slightly. *Yes.*
You miss her terribly.

I do, Fay. I do.
Me too.

Fay looked away from her mother, understanding. She stared out of the window before she said, 'But you love her,' Fay said out loud.

Felix, still holding his wife heard it but misinterpreted it.
'Yes, I love your mother very much.'

Sula touched Fay's hair, feeling weak.

Please, don't tell your dad. Please.

Fay met her mother's eyes again and saw her fear; something she'd never seen before in her and it scared the little girl.

Slowly Fay nodded.

A single tear ran across Sula's cheek.

'And I love your father, Fay,' *Never forget that, darling. I love them both…*

I understand mummy.

Fay hugged her parents and together the three of them stood like that for a while.

~~~

The trees were bare now with the air crisp, the sky blue and white clouds racing overhead. Most birds had left for the warmer countries south and it wouldn't be long before the whole landscape was covered in snow again. Like the birds, Feline followed their migration pattern. She knew Sula was intrigued by this; Feline leaving with Sula's favourite snow geese and returning with the swallows in spring time.

Feline glanced up from her mare, Ula, at the trees as they slowly trotted homewards. Usually the blond girl left for her island when the first leaves started falling. Feline and Ula had spent a couple of days in Westland instead near the sea that Feline loved so much. The clouds were moving fast and she thought, again, of Sula.

She had given Sula and Felix some time and space for them to make up and she chose to travel west as it wasn't too far away yet still very beautiful.

What a sight it would be to see her fly! Feline thought, but no one apart from Felix and Fay ever had. Feline had never dared to ask Sula knowing she was a little private about her skills. Feline respected that and knew how important it was to keep it a secret as well.

Her sky blue eyes stared at the hills ahead of her and met the pine forest which held her cosy home safe within its clutches; such a familiar heart warming sight. As much as she loved travelling, nothing compared to coming home. At least, that was how she had always felt before. Now for the first time her heart felt heavy and she was reluctant to urge her horse on.

She was however driven by the need to see her parents again; her brother, Fay and...Sula. But her sister-in-law had made it hard for her. Feline wanted to be close to her. Now that she had had some time to think about things, having spent time by the sea, which helped her clear her thoughts, she was sure about one thing; they could never be.

For the first time ever during her time away, she had felt lonely, empty, and her life meaningless. She had missed Sula's company so much that she could not bear to stay away any longer. Though Feline's frozen shoulder ached more and more and she desperately needed the sun to stop the constant pain, the thought had crossed her mind that Sula might need her, especially now during her pregnancy. And in the meantime, she could give her shoulder some of Sula's bird-mode warmth?

This will only complicate things more! She can't possibly give me treatment every day! Her touch...but it's not just that. How I long for her eyes, her voice... Feline thought with a sting in her heart and she urgently nudged her mare on.

~~~

She decided to go and see her parents first of all in an attempt to distract her thoughts and lighten up her mood. Her parents were very good at that and she loved their easy warm company.

That evening in the dark she walked into the village of Rosinhill and approached her parents' house. Feline saw and smelt the smoke of the hearths in the people's homes and memories came flooding back to her. She smiled when she saw the familiar house and the figure of her mother moving in front of one of the windows. It looked like she was clearing up the table. When Feline came closer she heard a distant clatter of plates and muted voices and when she opened the door she was greeted with laughter.

'-No way could you have moved that tree on your own, son!' she heard her father say. He was blocked from her sight by her brother. 'You must have had some help.'

'Well, I'm telling you the truth, dad,' Felix who stood with his back to her said. Sula who sat next to his father was finishing her desert of what looked like apple pie. At that moment Sula eyes met with Feline's and her hand with the spoon still in her mouth froze.

'That tree nearly crushed your house yesterday and now all of a sudden it's gone!'

Feline could hear her mother in the kitchen, mumbling presumably to Fay.

'It was only a big side branch that came down in the storm *in front* of our house. The tree is still standing. Besides we had…help.' Feline could hear by the tone in her brother's voice and by the look on Sula's flushed face that they felt trapped. It must have been Sula's strength that had removed the branch easily. Her parents of course didn't know anything about Sula's strengths or her being a comyenti and Felix and Sula had insisted in keeping it that way.

'Who from?' her father Jolaz asked.

'From me!' Feline interrupted loudly, sensing the tricky situation.

All faces were moving her way now and the startled looks made her smile.

'Feline?' she heard her mother Feasgar ask.

Felix turned round and raised an eyebrow at her.

'Ula helped remove that branch earlier on.'

'You're back!' Jolaz smiled and stood but Felix was faster and embraced his sister casually, whispering, 'Thanks, sis.'

Jolaz embraced her next and kissed her on the cheek. Her mother, Feasgar, came running over. 'Feline, we thought you might have left for the season altogether?' she asked before embracing her daughter too.

'No, very soon I will though but I had…some business to attend to in the west country.'

'Auntie!' Fay hugged Feline from behind.

'Hello Fay, I…missed you earlier on when Ula and I removed that branch. How did your first day at school go?' she asked, remembering.

Fay giggled, knowing somehow that Feline had lied about the branch, but didn't give it away.

'It was okay.'

The only one who hadn't greeted her was Sula. She still sat in the same position as before, looking dumbstruck at Feline.

'We're all complete now,' Feasgar said smiling with a sigh. 'Did you have your supper, sweetheart? I might still have some left?'

Feline avoided Sula's stare and nodded. 'I have, thanks. I brought some mushrooms for you but I'll let Sula inspect them first since she is the expert.' She slowly walked over to her.

'Alright, who wants tea and who wants acorn coffee?' Jolaz asked cheerfully and went to the kitchen whilst Feasgar took Sula's empty bowl from her.

Fay jumped on her chair next to Sula whilst Feline took off her coat and hung it over a chair before emptying the content of her bag on the table.

'Hmm good mushrooms eh, mummy?' Fay said.

'Er yes.' Sula looked flustered eying the mushrooms, biting her lip.

'Hello Sula. It's…good to see… everybody again.' Feline said.

'Yes, it's good to see you too,' Sula said warmly and briefly met her eyes before disengaging again.

The awkwardness between them soon disappeared when they all sat down around the table, chattering away in small talk, drinking their warm beverages with the cosy fire popping and hissing. Feline hadn't felt more at home than this in a long time.

~~~

'But I'm a nomad,' Sula said to Feline the next morning whilst strolling through the woods together around Rosinhill. Fay was ahead of them, running and bouncing up and down, chasing the colourful leaves that blew on the wind. Having Fay with them was a safeguard really, for both of them; so they wouldn't be able to get too close to each other.

'The vastness of freedom…it's a lure I cannot deny. I wasn't born to spend my life in a house and neither was any comyenti. How can I do that to my children? How can I deprive them of a free life in the wild?'

Feline's shoulder brushed hers and she had to raise her voice to be heard above the sweeping wind through the pine trees. A wind that reminded her of the sea and her time away from Sula.

'You are part human, hence the struggle. You will always be caught between both worlds. But who is to say if comyentis are truly nomads or whether it is *you* personally who craves freedom and the wilderness? You've only ever met two; your mother and… Shazar. And don't forget they both travelled out of need. Sula, your search is over, there is no need to travel anymore; save for pleasure and showing and teaching your children about all the animals you love in the world. It's up to you to find a balance and inner peace with your choice,' she looked from Sula to Fay who was now climbing a tree. 'Fay seems pretty happy with

257

where she is; it's as close to a life in the wild as any child can get, growing up in a friendly village in the mountains and woods, travelling to different parts of the globe every summer. I'd say she is pretty lucky.' Feline glanced at Sula. 'Your children will make their own choice one day. They might decide to live a life of travel or build their own house. Until then you can only give them the best start in life; a safe home, a loving environment. You're doing fine.'

'I'm not human and not comyenti.'

Feline stood still, as did Sula.

'You're both, which is better.' Feline smiled warmly at her.

Sula smiled back and they started walking again but her smile soon faded. She said, 'And I love both you and Felix, a man *and* a woman. Does that make me better too?' she said with a hint of sarcasm.

Feline's eyes flashed to Fay.

'Oh, don't worry, she knows. She read my mind when I was thinking about you...again.'

Her hand reached out for Feline's, taking her hand in hers, rubbing her palm gently.

Walking hand in hand they heard a familiar sound; the honking of geese above the treetops on their way south. Sula normally would have smiled at the melancholic sound with love and warmth in her heart, but not now for it meant something else...

'I wish I could come with you. I miss the freedom, the adventure. When you are going next, please take me with you?'

Feline halted and looked at Sula's hand on her shoulder, taking it gently into her own hand, avoiding Sula's tear stung eyes, she looked down instead. Sula's normally flat belly was now round and showing ever so slightly as were her breasts.

Feline tore her eyes away and shook her head looking ahead still walking hand in hand. She had sincerely hoped her time away from Sula would have helped both their feelings to cool down and the Heartmerge to have re-established between Sula and Felix. It clearly hadn't worked out the way Feline had hoped.

'And then what? You travel with me for part of the year with the children or without? And live in Rosinhill reunited with Felix when we come back? How is that going to work?'

'I don't know.' Sula's voice sounded quiet.

'Are you thinking about leaving him all together, to pick up you travels again?'

Sula looked at Feline with wide open eyes and Feline read the answer in them. Feline halted.

'Sula! You have found a home here and a family. You can't give it up for an uncertain rough life on the road. Yes, you loved it whilst growing up, but you've also told me how you always craved a steady home and a garden. Now that you have one, you can't give it up again. And what about Fay and your new baby; surely they deserve a home, their friends *and* their father. What about Felix? You can't have both.'

'Ha, it's not all domestic bliss! I've told you!'

But when Feline didn't respond Sula sighed, 'You're right. I can't give it up all together. I do love him. I...love cheese *and* jam...but why should I have to choose? Sometimes I crave cheese and sometimes jam, why can't I have both in my cupboard?'

'Oh, you don't know that. What if this is just a phase and I'm just an experiment?'

Sula suddenly tightened her grip on Feline's hand and pulled her close so that Feline had to look Sula in the eyes which were changing colour rapidly. She was furious.

'Don't ever say that! I've always loved you! I would never use you and cast you away like an old shoe!'

Feline stayed calm, her breathing quickened but it was from desire, not fear. Sula was even more stunning when angry.

Oh, if only I gave in! Feline thought. *It would be so easy.*

'Sula, I love you too; more than anything, but you can't compare me and Felix with *food*. We are living beings with feelings. Felix won't want to share you and neither would I...Neither Felix or I will have you *completely*...I never thought I'd say this as I never wanted a lasting relationship before but since I met you...But it won't work, so whatever you choose; one if us is going to get hurt. And that will have to be me! I cannot be responsible for Felix's pain nor that of your children. We won't act upon our feelings and he can never know.'

Sula let go of Feline's hand slowly and sighed, 'Why do you always have to be so rational and…and so self-sacrificing?'

'Don't you think it's strange that ever since you met Shazar and he…he impregnated you, you are feeling this way?'

Sula was quiet.

'It's the Heartmerge, I'm sure of it. He has done something to you!' *I need to know for sure!* Feline thought and the seed for an idea was planted inside her head.

'No, not where my feelings for you are concerned, how could he have?'

Feline shook her head trying to avert her eyes from Sula's hurt eyes.

'I leave in two days time, Sula. I'm sorry.' Feline's face was pale and she reluctantly put space between herself and Sula, walking backwards, with tears in her eyes.

'Feline?'

'I'm sorry.' And Feline turned round tearing her eyes away from Sula's and started running.

'Feline?!' Sula called after her. Fay looked up and came skipping towards her mother.

'Where did aunty go to, mummy?'

'Home, Fay,' she answered, staring absently with longing into the distance, thinking about different woods and mountains with new skies, new horizons and felt envy. Her heavy heart would leave with Feline.

'Home'.

Chapter 31 Questions

Feline was inside her cosy home, standing by her window looking out. Sula could see her clearly from where she hid outside, knelt down on the forest floor, looking in. It was dark in the woods and Sula breathed in the damp spicy smell of decaying leaves. From the glow inside of the house, she could tell Feline had just had a bath as her hair was still wet and she wore her light blue night gown; matching her eyes perfectly.

In fact the whole room had a bluish glow to it; Feline was lighting three white candles on her window sill. Sula felt a little guilty for watching her, it was like she was spying on her. She didn't mean to but she had to see her before she would leave…

The flames from the candles flickered pale blue; the first one she lit blew out so that she had to light it again.

She must have the window open a bit, but I can't tell, Sula thought.

Then the second candle also blew out and the third, and again and again she had to re-light them. Feline tried so hard and Sula felt sorry for her. Until finally the first two remained lit but the last one, a smaller candle, wouldn't stay lit.

It flickered in vain but then died out. Feline eventually stopped trying and seemed to accept it and went back to staring absent-mindedly through her window into the night sky. Sula was about to get up, to go to her, but then she heard someone coming towards her, rustling through the leaves…

'Sula?' she heard the familiar voice of her sister-in-law call out.

Sula stood and made a small startled sound, luckily it was too dark for Feline to see she blushed with embarrassment.

'What are you doing here?' Feline asked excitedly.
'How did you know I was here?' Sula whispered, why she was

261

whispering she had no idea.

'I…saw your eyes. They *glow* emerald in the dark, really *glow!*'

No! 'I'm sorry, Feline. I didn't mean to spy on you, I was going to knock on, but then…then-' Sula felt Feline's lips press on hers, hard and wanting, her way of stopping her from talking. She pulled Sula gently towards her and then down to the forest floor and they lay down upon the crisp autumn leaves…

Passionately Feline brushed Sula's hair out of her face before covering her with kisses, caressing her body and skilfully unbuttoned Sula's shirt in the dark with one hand, the other moved slowly between her legs…

Before Feline knew it, Sula was on top of her, like a predator; biting her neck and burying her face between her breasts, cupping them with her hands, finding her nipples which were already hard. Panting and moaning their bodies entwined and their hands locked together, their lovemaking was desperate but deep and they both climaxed at the same time with the other's name on each of their lips…

~~~

In a sudden state of a shock Sula opened her eyes, calling out Feline's name, her face flushed and with a throbbing wet feeling between her legs. She looked around; she was in her own bedroom.

A dream, it was just a dream…

She felt her round belly, she could feel a twinge and glanced over at a still sleeping, soft snoring Felix. It was not yet morning, and still dark outside, just like in the dream…

I'll go and see her this morning, Sula decided. *Before she leaves.*

~~~

Feline had said she would leave in two days' time, but she had actually gone the morning after. Feline hated saying goodbye.

It had now been a month since she'd left Rosinhill and she missed Sula with every heartbeat, but hopefully in the spring she would return with the answers to their questions.

She had followed the sun south, and headed for the West now. Usually she would head south and then east, camping out in the wild, but this time she stayed overnight in inns as the cold weather had already set in and the damp bothered her shoulder. But soon it would start to get warmer; she could feel the rise in temperature already, ever so slightly, the further south she was, as she was closer to the sun. Her island, Irinia, would have to wait. She remembered Sula saying that it was here; Randaria, in the dunes of Naru that Shazar had gone to live. Hidden away no doubt, like a rabbit in a hole, so more than likely it would be very hard to find him.

It was cloudy today, so Feline needed to take her compass out of her saddlebag and with one hand holding the map she stared from one to the other. The friendly innkeeper from the night before had very kindly marked the map for her and was relieved to discover when looking at the landscape ahead of her, that she was getting closer. The steppes and plains had gradually changed to undulating fields with friendly birch and small patches of spruce and she could see the first dunes in the distance through the trees. She could almost smell the sea. This trip had so far cost her quite a few pennies along the way and she had had to sell several items to fund the journey. But deep down she knew the sacrifice would be well worth it. A few blonde strands blew in her face from out of her ponytail and while lost in her thoughts she brushed them behind her ear and mounted her horse, Ula, once again.

~~~

"There is no one by that description or name living here, sorry," was the response Feline got time after time when asking the few people she came across living scattered in the dunes. She then entered the small cosy village of Randaria, named after a mermaid Randa, who, after she was rescued by a fisherman from his nets, is said to have appeared every so often to say thank you to the fisherman, for years after.

The land behind the dunes near the village was fertile and there were many fruit trees. The houses appeared to be well maintained and it did indeed look prosperous. But there was no sign of Shazar. Even when giving his description to them, it did not seem to ring any bells, so either he had never showed his face there, which most likely he wouldn't have from what Sula had told her; comyentis stayed away from people and their settlements; or he never made it there in the first place. Which meant that she had no idea where else to look.

Feline packed up her mare, whilst staring at the sky, and upon seeing a flock of geese above her thoughts went immediately to Sula and Felix, *With Felix your heart is caged with ribs for bars, Sula. With me your heart would not be entrapped and the cage would always be open; you would be soaring free...*

She grabbed the pommel of the saddle and hauled herself onto the horse's back; she stared around at the trees and suddenly felt very tired. She pushed herself and her horse westward.

Then just when she was about to give up after several days of combing the dunes for holes and caves or signs of dens in the surrounding woods, a tall dark figure appeared before her, blocking her path...

He stood between the small spruce trees with his hands by his sides, legs spread wide and his eyes, dark green with a hint of ruby; looking menacing.

She was startled and felt a bit scared too. Ula nearly stumbled at the sight of Shazar but the mare seemed to calm down when he looked at her with soothing eyes. The horse's head hung low as if she submitted. It was not the same look from him for Feline though.

'What do you want from me?'

Swallowing away her fear, she tried to focus on the good things Sula had told her about him; his compassionate side and love for animals.

'Shazar…My name is Feline,' she took her hood off, so that he could see her features. 'Felix's sister.'

His eyes changed and grew lighter when he saw the resemblance to her brother and golden flecks seemed to sparkle upon hearing his name. His posture changed visibly too as he relaxed his arms and legs and stepped closer. He was dressed in tight fitting black clothes and wore a matching headband.

'Have you come to bring news of them; of… Sula?' he asked gingerly.

'Yes and no. I have come to find you. Where can we talk? Where do you live?'

Confused he bit his lip. 'I'm staying with a friend and her son,' he answered hesitantly.

'How come I didn't find you, I've looked all over?' she asked him.

An arrogant smile flickered across his face now. 'I am well hidden. Besides you should know I have no intention of wanting to be found. But for Sula's…acquaintances I make an exception.'

'Family,' she corrected him. 'I'm her family.' And she gave him a fake smile back. He was certainly very handsome with his smooth almost feminine dark looks and Feline was amazed that Sula had not been attracted to him.

Perhaps she prefers blonds, she thought, but she reminded herself of his act towards Sula. Knowing *that* and his arrogance and his dogmatism, besides being married to Felix had been the greatest hindrance for any kind of relationship between the two of them.

Shazar studied her face and she had to remind herself that he couldn't read her mind.

'We can talk *here*. Now tell me, how is Sula faring?' He came a bit closer with a concerned expression on his face.

'She's doing reasonably well all things considered,' she retorted.

'What'd you mean, all things considered?'

'She told me what you did to her,' Feline who normally was so calm had to try her best to keep her anger and frustration under control, but still she felt her blood boiling and her heart raging. 'How could you?

What right did you have? She is your only living link to your ancestors! You took advantage of her, you…you raped her!' and she coiled her fists and stepped closer to him even though he was about a foot taller. Shazar paled visibly, not because of her accusations, but because of Sula's feelings towards him. Sula had told this…human…this girl?

'She told you? She…remembers?'

'Ha, so you admit it!'

'Pah, I never meant her harm! I told her so!' But he relented a bit and added softer, 'Does she hate me for it?'

Now Feline felt pride and strong and she spat at him, 'She *despises* you!'

Shazar felt incredibly hurt and looked away, rubbing his neck nervously.

'Please sit down,' he said gesturing towards a fallen tree. 'Let's talk.'

She gave in but sat down opposite him on the forest floor whilst he sat on the tree, looking like a king.

'What do you know?' he asked her.

'Everything.'

'So why are you here? To tell me this or to accuse me?'

'Both, but I have questions that need answering.'

He rubbed his forehead; touching the black headband and opened his hands.

'Why isn't Sula here herself?'

'She doesn't know I'm here.'

'Hmm, interesting,' *Are they spying on me?* 'Speak then.'

'Tell me more about the Heartmerge,' she said very suddenly.

Surprised he frowned and then narrowed his eyes at her, cocking his head slightly and she tried very hard to compose herself so as not to be affected by his arrogance.

'The Heartmerge with Felix has weakened, has it not? I'm guessing that's why you're here. I'm surprised your brother is not here instead of you,' he said in a cocky manner, almost mocking. 'Does he always let his sister do the work for him?'

'He doesn't know you raped her,' she said bluntly with fire in her belly. 'and he won't! It will kill him and,' she looked him right in the eyes furiously, 'it will be the end of you as well, if he ever does! So answer me this if you want to keep it a secret between us: I know Sula can still hear Felix's thoughts and she does love him but he on the other hand worships the very ground she walks upon, but...you-' and she asked pointing at him. 'Do *you* exclusively have a Heartmerge with Sula now; did you break *theirs* somehow by raping her?'

He stared at her blankly.

'Interesting,' he said after a while. 'Very interesting.'
'I asked you a question,' she retorted annoyed.
'Would you say she is thinking of me?' he asked frowning.

He is so arrogant! I can't stand him and now I can see why Sula couldn't!

'No she doesn't think or dream about you at all! She loves Felix and...another but it's not you!'

Those words hurt him immensely as was Feline's purpose.

She loves another?

Confused he rubbed his neck and he raised one eyebrow.
She has a human heart after all so she can *love more than one. There is still hope for me...* He thought oddly.
Shazar, being a full comyenti however, who according to his family, could only bond with *one* alone, knew now that the Heartmerge with Sula hadn't worked for either of them. For even though he loved Sula with all his heart and she would always be 'the one' for him and maybe one day she would be his, he already had feelings for Ashanna. Sula clearly didn't think about him or miss him but already had moved on to someone else *and* she still loved Felix. *How very human.*

His plan hadn't worked; it had been so quick that Sula could never have enjoyed it; one of the key elements for a Heartmerge to work in the first place it seemed. But then again he had had a second motive; a child. But Feline was here. Surely she would know by now...

He cleared his throat, composing himself.

'You have come all this way from your friendly little village up north, all through the wilderness, faced the elements and dangers of the road, especially dangerous for a pretty girl travelling on her own, just to have *that* question answered? I admire you for that,' he stood. 'But…I'm afraid I'll have to disappoint you, for that information will not be shared with the human race.'

Feline frowned at that and shook her head incomprehensively.

'Sula is half human and I am her family after all.'

'So she's told everyone what she is then, including this other person?' he said with a raised voice, accusingly.

'No, not everyone; only Felix and I know and *that* I can assure you. You needn't worry. Now,' and she also stood. 'I would like my question answered please for I'm not leaving without an answer.'

'I don't deal very well with threats,' he said through pursed lips.

'It is not a threat. Look,' she said sighing, opening her hands. 'This might be hard for you to understand, not having a family and all, but I care about Sula and she knows so little about the comyentis and their ways and she has so many questions. *You* are privileged to have lived with your people who undoubtedly knew a lot more. Why not share it with me so I can tell her?'

'And why should I tell you, when I could tell her myself?!' his voice rose and she stepped back in shock.

'You can't!' Feline said with sudden alarm in her voice.

Shazar painfully remembered the promise he made to Sula; the binding Comyenti Oath, to stay away from her until he had children of his own. Did Feline know about that too?

He lowered his head in defeat but then looked at her with his eyes dark and narrow, like a wolf.

'I've searched high and low for her. You really think I will let go of her *that* easily?'

Feline's heart raced in her chest, afraid for Sula, not herself. What if it was just a trick; the Comyenti Oath to ease Sula's mind; but what did she know? But then again he wouldn't harm Sula, would he, or Felix?

He was comyenti who apparently wouldn't hurt a fly. No, Sula had been pretty adamant about it; the Comyenti Oath was something her mother had lectured her about. It was mainly used to thank the animals that had shared the Mindmerge with the comyentis. No, he couldn't return to Rosinhill. He had made his promise and if he broke it, his abilities would be taken away as a punishment. Sula and Felix were safe until…Shazar had produced his own children. It sounded like a curse, what if the Heartmerge worked in a similar way? Feline found herself thinking. What if her brother was in danger?

'I can understand what Sula did,' Shazar said standing, 'but I *cannot* fathom *why* she had to *marry* the father of her child!' he mumbled throwing his hands about.

'That's love,' Feline reflected, shaking her head. '*You* would have married her if you could have, why not Felix? Oh, I know, because he is *human?*'

He bared his teeth at that. 'Precisely!' And Shazar suddenly saw Felix in her; the same furious eyes, the same grin.

Feline sighed and suddenly she blinked a couple of times remembering.

'Hold on, are you not staying with a human at the moment?'

He didn't answer but he didn't need to as his face showed the answer.

'So, why is that any different?'

He turned round so he didn't have to hear her anymore; trying to block her out.

'Please leave!' His voice thundered.

'I would like to meet the woman who can put up with you!'

His shoulders shook, as if he laughed at that, but she couldn't tell.

'It would only be polite to invite me to your home,' she said daringly.

'You're not welcome. They have enough on their plates already,' he mumbled.

'Your girlfriend doesn't know about Sula? Surely she needs to know, if this is the woman you mentioned to Sula. Doesn't she deserve the truth; that you…*raped* a woman?'

The word 'rape' resonated in his mind, over and over…

*Ashanna, no- she would never understand…*He turned round angrily and hissed. 'Do not mention her! I've told you to leave! Now!' he shouted at her. Her horse whinnied in alarm, but Feline wasn't fazed. She wouldn't leave until she got what she came for.

'I can't,' she stood rigid, trying to be strong although she felt fear rising up and her heart hammering against her chest. But she wouldn't leave without an answer. For Sula, for Felix…and for herself too. 'For Sula's sake, answer me! Or I will tell your girlfriend all about Sula and what you did to her!'

Shazar felt a sudden weight in his boots as if his heart had sunken. Ashanna was never to know. The once priestess who was kidnapped and raped on a daily basis. And as perspicacious and compassionate and different from any human being he'd ever met as she was; she wouldn't understand. Even if Shazar explained the reason behind his actions, that it was to continue the comyenti line and could not be compared with any other situation. Empathetic as she was, she was still a woman with terrible memories of abuse. And she would never forgive him…

The knowledge would kill her! Shazar thought.

Rage, blind rage, old and familiar rose within him, with himself and with humans. With a strength he forgot he had, without using any abilities, he stormed into her; knocking the air out of her, grabbing her by the throat. He threw her against a tree, still holding her, squeezing the life out of her...

'Never!!! he roared.

Feline gagged and turned white, her eyes growing big, begging him, pleading with him with her expression to stop. He didn't see her anymore though; only the people that had killed his family; humans, always humans ruining every little bit of hope and love the comyentis had. And seeing the resemblance of Felix in her; the man that had occupied and taken Sula away from *him*; the only comyenti man left alive, only angered him more!

Sula and Shazar should have been partners for life by now, ensuring the comyenti line with many children.

He heard her choke in the distance of his darkened mind, but very far away.

After a while it just… stopped.

He felt a limp weight in his hands; he let go, horrified. The woman dropped to the floor, dead.

Looking down on the body, Shazar blinked a couple of times and shook his head, unable to believe what he had just done, but too late to change it.

The story continues in Book Two, Children Of The Sun

If you've enjoyed this book, please consider leaving a positive review on Amazon or Goodreads, or ideally both. Many thanks.

Glossary

Mindmerge: This is the special merging or linking of minds. Technically speaking a merge between comyenti and anything with a soul. It happens through eye-contact, no touch is necessary. Up until now only with animals; usually mammals, birds, reptiles and fish. Only very advanced comyentis can merge with insects in order to gain their super abilities. The more animals they encounter and merge with, the more powerful a comyenti becomes. This requires a life of study and meditation.

It's a mutual agreement, no one loses anything but both gain: the comyenti gains an ability and the other animal, a life long commitment of safety and protection if that individual is ever in danger. Of course the older a comyenti gets, the more creatures it has met and the more powerful and more understanding he/she could become. It's not just the power but a sympathy for everything alive; a sense of oneness.

Mindskill: The gained ability of an animal after doing a Mindmerge. The comyenti now has a useful skill to be called upon when needed. They can only call upon the skills of <u>one</u> animal at a time. The skill is used by 'deceiving' ones mind and body to believe it to 'be' that animal. A comyenti using a Mindskill whilst in a specific animal-mode, will not loose their identity. They can still think and act humanoid whilst going into a chant to call upon the requited Mindskill.

e.g. Whilst flying using the eagle's skills they can do everything an eagle can do so fly plus have a superb eyesight and insulation of imagined feathers, however if an arrow is flying towards a comyenti whilst in eagle-mode they cannot call upon the thick skin of a turtle to protect themselves! Only one animal at a time.

Mindmode: Eagle-mode/ bat-mode/ goose-mode etc. Term used to describe what animal called upon. What Mindskill called upon.

Heartmerge: The very powerful spiritual merging of one mature comyenti with another. This merge between two lovers is done through sexual contact only. The first merging between new lovers is originally a lengthy ritual and both have to climax in order for their hearts and souls to make the lasting Heartlink. By merging both adults will experience a powerful telepathic union.

Heartlink: Is a strong bond achieved after the Heartmerge between two comyentis and is a life long lasting spiritual bond between two mature lovers. They are able to hear each others thoughts and sense one another's feelings and presence effortlessly. Communication runs smoothly.

It can only be broken if <u>one or both</u> partners fall(s) out of love with each other or if they, or one of them, have lost their heart to someone else. In which case the Heartlink has to be severed before a new one can be created, because having two Heartlinks at the same time is <u>not</u> possible.

Comyenti Oath: Is a powerful promise and not lightly given because it is binding: breaking or forsaken it would cost the comyenti to loose their unique abilities and they will be nothing but human…They have to cross their heart whilst speaking out loud.

Comyenti Weakness: Their own over-sensitivity. Too much sensory input causes their mind to get over-stimulated to the point that they are so overwhelmed they cannot go into a Mindmode at all or it causes them to loose contact with the Mindskill called upon.

References

Life On Earth-David Attenborough

The Living Planet-David Attenborough

Supersense-John Downer

Wikipedia

Also by Natasja Hellenthal:

The Queen's Curse

Chained Freedom

Children Of The Sun, Comyenti Series #2
City of Dreams

Keep up on Natasja's latest news and projects:

http://natasjahellenthal.wordpress.com
https://www.facebook.com/pages/Natasja-Hellenthal

Follow Natasja on Twitter:
@natasjahellenth